Designed *for* MURDER

Susan Toalson

TREATY OAK PUBLISHERS

Publisher's Note

This is a work of fiction, based entirely on the author's imagination. Any resemblance to actual persons, living or dead, is unintentional and coincidental.

Published and printed in the United States of America

Treaty Oak Publishers

ISBN-978-1-943658-62-6

Available in print and digital from Amazon

For Carolyn and Suzy

CHAPTER 1

Marilyn Quinn could have been drunk.

It was late. Dark. She stood near the top of a marble staircase, naked except for a silk dressing gown that hugged the prominent bones of her shoulders and hips. Both of her hands, the skin slacked and blue-veined with age, clenched the handrail.

She glared at the shadows behind her, beyond the top of the stairs. Holding her breath, she listened until she was satisfied no one followed. Then she continued her descent, struggling to control her quick, shallow breathing as she moved.

At the bottom of the staircase, the icy-white glow of outdoor Christmas lights shone through narrow windows by the front door and through an entire wall of windows at the back of the mansion. Marilyn abandoned the handrail, pulled the dressing gown tight across her chest, and staggered across the entryway toward the kitchen. Facing a closet door in the mudroom, she groped inside the pocket of her gown and pulled out a cell phone. After blinking at its face, she stabbed it with her finger, waited a moment before she mumbled a few words, and then stabbed it again. She opened the closet door, losing and then recovering her balance when the catch gave way. She clutched a coat, yanked it toward her, and wrestled her arms into the sleeves as she lurched back to the entry hall. A glance up the staircase assured her she was still alone.

She stumbled forward until she reached the front door. Her fingers trembled on the metal handle as she turned it, and she was vaguely aware that it gave way too easily at her touch; the door had been left ajar. With a final glance behind her, she pulled the door open and stepped toward the veranda.

A gun discharged. The thousands of Christmas lights covering the vast façade of the mansion winked out.

Silence.

A cloud slipped away from the face of the moon, revealing shadows of thin, bare tree branches that reached across the veranda like claws. Inside the threshold of the open door, Marilyn Quinn lay motionless, a dark hole in what only seconds ago had been her left eye.

CHAPTER 2

The next morning in south Austin, several miles and millions of dollars of real estate away from Marilyn Quinn's mansion at the lake, Alice Abbott plucked crusty cat turds from a line of tall, spiky blades of monkey grass and dropped them into a bag.

Alice was a small, roundish woman in her mid-seventies with smooth, even features and a fair complexion. She wore frameless glasses and no makeup. Loose curls of thick white hair emphasized the pink in her cheeks, flushed with the exertion of bending and stretching. She sat open-legged on a stool, in tennis shoes and a faded cotton dress. Out of modesty, she'd wrapped its skirt around her thighs.

Finished with the cat droppings, she turned her attention to the last of the tulip bulbs she'd been planting in a trench that bordered the monkey grass. Her formerly lush, colorful garden had almost gone to seed in the last year, but Alice hadn't found the interest or the will to care for the garden or to do any other maintenance around the house. None of it brought her joy anymore.

She pressed the bulbs into the trench, root-side down, and pushed soil over them, relieved the chore was almost over. She had intended to leave the damned things in the back of the refrigerator and pretend she'd forgotten them, but her neighbor Connie had given them to her for Christmas and insisted Alice plant them today, while the weather was mild. A Texas blue norther was on its way with cold and lots of rain, a frequent follow-up to a warm, early-January day in Austin.

More cold weather. Great. She could expect another high electric bill next month. Her 75-year-old house had no insulation, so she spent most winters in the living room in front of a fire. Still, she had to use the central heating from time to time.

She flinched at a sharp pain in her left knee as she covered the last of the bulbs, promising herself a reward in the shape of two frosted cupcakes she'd left on the kitchen counter when Connie knocked on the back door this morning. To remind her to plant the bulbs.

Jeez. Connie, only forty-three, had been like a mother hen lately, a constant reminder to Alice of her advancing years. Sometimes Alice wanted to scream at her, *I'm not old! I'm poor and I'm bored!*

Not that Alice would do that. She never screamed at anyone. And, of all the people she knew, Connie would have least deserved such an outburst. Dr. Connie Morris loved Alice for some reason that Alice couldn't understand. In fact, since the deaths of two of her dearest friends, and the loss of another who had moved to North Carolina to be near her grandchildren, Connie was the oldest, closest friend Alice had.

In the garden beside her, Arthur, the generous feline donor of all the fertilizer in the monkey grass, lay on his side, his mountainous belly rising and falling in even rhythm. Alice pushed a handful of mulch onto the bulbs and watched the big cat lift his head. She followed his gaze across the yard to a woman standing at the open gate. The woman's hand rested on the fork latch where a padlock dangled by an open shank. Alice had been looking for the key to the lock for days.

"Are you Alice Ann Abbott?" the woman called. "I rang the bell, but I don't think it's working."

Alice paused. Another thing she needed to do: Replace the front doorbell. "Yes, I am." Alice stood, bending forward and pushing herself off the stool while the woman introduced herself as Detective Olivia Cabrera.

Alice's eyebrows shot up. A detective?

"Can I come in?"

Feeling a trace of hesitation, Alice nodded, and the woman approached her. She was about Alice's height, five-foot-four or so, but a good deal younger and thinner. On an otherwise pretty face with dark eyes and full lips, a ragged white scar sliced across Cabrera's cheek almost to her lip.

Alice spoke first, focusing on Cabrera's eyes to avoid the scar. "What can I do for you, Detective?"

With the back of her hand, she pushed her glasses up the bridge of her nose and smiled at the detective to get on with it. Her knee hurt, and the cupcakes called to her.

"I'm here about your employer." Cabrera paused a moment. The sun slid from behind a cloud. She squinted against the brightness but kept her eyes riveted on Alice's face. "She was found dead at her home this morning. She was shot."

Alice's eyebrows shot up again. "Dead?" She shook her head. "I'm sorry, but you have the wrong person. I work for Marilyn Quinn."

"Yes, ma'am. I have the right person. You're Ms. Quinn's personal assistant, right?"

Alice stared at Cabrera. She turned and hobbled across the stone patio to the wooden steps that led to the back door of the house. Both hands on the rail, she bent her knees and sat on one of the steps. "Shot? Murdered?"

Cabrera's face was expressionless.

The sun disappeared again, bathing the yard in an eerie shade of pewter. The rain would start soon.

"But the family was there!" Alice looked away from the detective and watched Arthur lunge at a small bird, trapping it in his huge paws. She knew he would toy with it, let it limp away a few times before he sank his teeth into the soft feathers at its neck. Her lips trembled.

"Ms. Abbott," Cabrera said, after a moment. "Why didn't you go in to work today?"

"It's my…" Alice swallowed. "It's my day off," she said, her voice toneless, her eyes still focused on Arthur. "The first Friday of the month. My extra day off." She wiped her dirty hands on the hem of her dress and ran her fingers through her hair.

"I see. Your employer's cell phone records indicate she called your home phone number last night. Did you talk to her?"

Alice turned to Cabrera. "Marilyn called me?" She rolled onto her right hip and reached deep into the left pocket of her dress, but came up empty-handed. She tensed when the detective stepped away from her and grabbed for the gun on her hip. "Oh, my God," she said. "I don't have my cell phone. I missed her call."

"Ms. Quinn called your home phone, not your cell phone, Ms. Abbott. Why would she do that?"

"Oh. My, uh, my cell phone is…" Alice's neck flashed with heat, an annoying physical reaction to emotional stress that she'd endured since childhood. Her cell phone was missing. A lot of things had gone missing lately.

"Do you have an answering machine, Ms. Abbott? Maybe there's a message."

"The answering machine, of course. In here." Alice pulled herself up, and Cabrera followed her limping gait past the kitchen and the dining room and into the living room, the wooden floors creaking beneath their feet. Alice found the answering machine on the coffee table under several days' worth of unopened mail and an empty Hershey's Kisses bag. "I never listen to this thing," she muttered, half to herself.

The light on the machine indicated recorded messages. Alice poked at the "Play" button.

You have two messages, the machine announced. The first message, recorded on Tuesday morning, was a woman's voice, saying she had left her husband. The woman was leaving Buenos Aires and expected to be in New York by the end of the week.

Alice glanced at Cabrera. "That's Twyla, my sister."

Message Two, Friday 1:03 a.m., the machine continued. It was Marilyn's voice, speaking in a slurred whisper: *It's Marilyn. I'm coming over. I'll call you again from the car.* A deep breath and then, *Dear God, she—. Why would she—?*

Another click and then the long, flat beep. *End of messages.*

Alice stared at the machine and lowered herself to the sofa.

CHAPTER 3

Alice agreed to meet Detective Cabrera at Marilyn's home later in the day. Still in shock, she showered and then stood for a moment staring into her closet. She sighed, closed the closet door, and pulled her coziest sweater and pants from a bureau drawer.

Her employer had loathed comfortable clothing, but Alice didn't think she could face the day in belted slacks, trussed up like a tamale. Besides, Marilyn wouldn't be there, would she?

Dead! She gasped and fumbled behind her for the bed. She lay back and pressed her fingers tight against her eyelids. The detective's words pounded in her ears. *She was found dead at her home this morning. She was shot.*

How? Who? Women like Marilyn weren't shot to death.

Alice pushed herself up from the bed. In the bathroom, she splashed cold water on her face. She rested her elbows on the sink and held her head in her hands.

A few minutes later, she perched on the arm of a shabby green recliner in the living room. With a a cup of coffee in one hand and one of the cupcakes in the other, she stared at the telephone. A local news anchor on the television screen hammered viewers with what little information he had about Marilyn's death.

Alice bit into the cupcake, fending Arthur off with her elbow, and sipped the coffee.

Haydn. She could call her friend Haydn. He wouldn't know what to do, but he would listen. She crammed the rest of the cupcake into her mouth, licked her fingers clean, and dialed Haydn's number. He answered on the first ring.

"Alice, did you get my message on your cell phone? Where have you been?"

"Are you watching the news?" she said, struggling to swallow all of the cake. She gulped coffee and then blurted what she knew about Marilyn.

He didn't reply right away. When he did, his voice was a whisper. "Are you okay?"

She imagined him listening to her shocking news. He would still be in his bathrobe, his sweet face unshaven, his thick gray hair tousled into a mess.

"Of course," she said. "I wasn't even there. Please don't worry about me, Haydn."

"Is the daughter okay? You mentioned last week that the daughter was there."

"I think it was only Marilyn. I don't know any details. I'm on my way there now to talk to the police."

"What? You can't be serious. Someone dangerous is there! I'll come and get you. I'll be over in fifteen minutes."

He was overreacting, she assured him. With the police all over the mansion and its grounds, it would be the safest place in Austin. "We'll talk later." She hung up.

His response sobered her. She understood his concern about her safety. Could he be right, about Marilyn's home being a dangerous place? She assumed some stranger had surprised Marilyn, an intruder looking for valuables in the ritziest part of town.

But Cabrera had not said that. Was the murderer someone Marilyn knew? Someone Alice knew?

Haydn had said something about a message he left on her cell phone. She hadn't asked what the message was.

THE STORM ARRIVED IN FAST MOTION. Heavy, dark clouds tumbled across the sky and temperatures plunged. When rain fell in dense, opaque curtains like this, Austin traffic stalled, so the ten-mile drive to Marilyn's would take a while.

In front of Alice, tourists darted across South Congress in tight, wet knots of twos and threes. She studied their movements, surprised that the shattering event in her own world hadn't disturbed the lives of others. Watching them lifted her spirits. Things would be okay.

On the sidewalk, the tourists huddled under awnings as they pressed up against storefronts.

Were they preparing for a weekend of fun and frolic in SOCO, the funkiest part of Austin? Or were they leftovers from the recent New Year's noisy, drunken celebrations? Not that it mattered. Tourists had become a feature of the city, like the bats under the Congress Avenue Bridge.

She understood the attraction to Austin. A glance in her rain-streaked rearview mirror revealed the easy slope northward to the state capitol. In front of her, various icons remained of the quirky culture that created the neighborhood in the 1960s through the 1980s: the Continental Club, Hotel San José, Ego's. To her right, one of her favorite buildings caught her eye. The Austin Motel, with its iconic penis-shaped sign, a twenty-five-foot, bright-red neon shaft, its vertical heft supported by a ship's mast. A smile tugged at her lips: Austin locals referred to the motel as The Phallus Palace.

Marilyn. The smile vanished.

She squeezed her eyes shut and took a deep breath, letting it out bit by bit through pursed lips. Someone behind her honked, and she flinched. The traffic ahead of her had inched forward.

Concentrate! All you need now is to have a wreck!

She glanced again at the hotel and forced herself to focus on the first thought that elbowed Marilyn from her mind.

Austin was changing, and she worried about places like the hotel. Would they be safe from destruction as the city changed from the laid-back, hippie-lovin' music mecca she loved to a sophisticated, urban community? Most of the grimy bars she had haunted as a student at the University of Texas were gone now: the bars that reeked of stale beer and commercial cleanser, the bars where she and friends could get a couple of cold Lone Star longnecks and a seat near the band for a few dollars, the bars that had helped create Austin's charm. Razing them had made way for stylish wine taverns and chic restaurants.

She shivered. The heater in her little Corolla hadn't worked all winter. And she'd lost her gloves.

The car in front of her moved, and she bent forward. The Toyota pitched onward in the face of a strong wind, and bolts of lightning tore the sky in rags.

Marilyn had been shot dead.

How? The woman had been a talented interior designer, creating sumptuous living spaces for wealthy clients all over the world. Alice knew Marilyn's Austin residence well, but it was only one of three homes she owned. The second was in Paris, the third in London. Marilyn was one of the rich and famous. People in her circle weren't murdered.

Marilyn was popular among her clients. Her staff had loved her, too, until she survived a heart attack last summer. As soon as she returned home from the hospital, the once charming, generous woman had turned irritable and insensitive. Alice had read that such personality changes were common among heart attack survivors, but it was out of character for

Marilyn to a shocking degree.

Last November, Marilyn had come home from a conference in New York with a fifty-five-year-old, outrageously handsome man she had married after knowing him for only a few weeks. Marilyn glowed. Alice had never seen her happier.

Then, after a brief honeymoon in Paris, the couple returned to Austin, and Marilyn fell ill again. But it wasn't her heart this time. She complained of horrible stomach cramps, and the worse the pain got, the more impossible Marilyn had become to live with and to work for.

Alice shifted her butt on the torn fabric of the car seat and reminded herself to brush the frayed ravelings off her coat when she arrived at the estate.

All of Marilyn's staff had remained on high alert, waiting for the next tantrum she would throw. Alice wilted in the palpable tension that permeated the glorious mansion, and she'd thought several times about finding another job. Right. Find another job at her age. No problem.

Shit!

The driver in front of her slammed on his brakes. Alice's reaction was well timed, but her large, overstuffed shoulder bag slid to the floor, and something under the car creaked.

She let go of the steering wheel long enough to scoop the tissues, pens, loose change, an address book, a chunk of a Christmas candy cane, a box of cookies, and a flashlight back into the bag and set it upright on the passenger seat floor. She tried to press the bag closed; then, in frustration, she snatched one of the tissues and dabbed her eyes. Cedar fever season was at its peak, and Alice's time spent outdoors in the garden that morning was enough to cause her allergies to flare.

Focus!

A thin finger of electricity touched earth and struck the dark highway with light. Alice' skin tingled, the hair on her arms and neck stood on end. She stared wide-eyed at the road in front of her. Thunder boomed and shook the little Toyota as if it were a Tonka toy. "Oh, my God," she gasped. "I've just lost my job!"

You can lose your way in a Texas thunderstorm, Alice remembered one of her professors telling her English class at the University of Texas. The professor's wife and child had drowned in the October 1960 flood, and every time it rained like this, Alice recalled his sad eyes and heard his warning.

By the time she arrived at Marilyn's, the rain fell sideways in sheets, pushed hard by a strong north wind. As Alice's car inched its way up the circular drive, a police officer wearing a yellow slicker ran to the driver's side window and asked Alice for identification.

"I'm Alice Ann Abbott, Marilyn Quinn's assistant," Alice shouted through her open window, rain pounding in on her face. "Detective Cabrera asked me to come."

"One moment, ma'am. Wait here." He sprinted away, the slicker spanking his legs, toward a group of uniformed officers standing under the roof of the veranda, out of the rain.

She squirmed at the idea of parking here in the grand driveway. Her usual spot was tucked away by shrubs at the back of the house.

Just beyond the flat nose of Alice's Toyota, Marilyn's silver Jaguar waited outside the front entrance. Alice squinted through the rain to find the most recent dent in the flawless metal of the expensive car. Marilyn was not a careful driver. The dent and several uneven gashes across the side of the car were new. She turned off the ignition, the wipers stopped, and the sleek lines of the Jaguar blurred in the downpour.

Holding a large umbrella, Detective Cabrera appeared at the window. Alice scooted forward and pulled herself out of the car and onto the driveway, her left knee throbbing. She had taken aspirin earlier in the day, but now she couldn't remember exactly how long ago. It had either worn off or hadn't yet had any effect.

"Thank you for coming, Ms. Abbott," the detective shouted. Under the umbrella, with Alice leaning on Cabrera for support, they half-ran toward the front entry, toward the yellow police tape that whipped in the wind.

Alice stopped on the veranda. Her shallow breaths created puffs of smoke in the cold air.

Cabrera opened the door, but they stood on the veranda while they shrugged off their raincoats. When they stepped over the threshold into the warm entryway, Alice's glasses fogged, blurring the dramatic view of the lake through the glass panels at the back of the house. She removed her glasses and blinked. On the floor in front of her, strips of bright yellow tape outlined a cookie-cutter pattern.

She staggered a half step backward. The yellow tape marked where Marilyn's body had fallen.

Until this moment, Alice had not considered the sheer weight of what happened. The murder was a shock, but also unreal. Now the horror of it engulfed her. She stood riveted to the marble floor, her eyes locked on the yellow tape.

Cabrera took Alice's elbow and guided her into the sitting room in the west wing of the home.

Alice hugged her belly, wishing she had said no to the cupcakes earlier. A thick, metallic taste burned in her throat. She lowered herself into an imposing chair near the fireplace, rested her head on its high back, and concentrated on slowing her breathing.

On the opposite side of the fireplace, Cabrera stood behind a chair identical to Alice's. A few moments passed in silence.

"Where is the family?" Alice said.

"Upstairs."

Alice nodded. "This is one of my favorite rooms in

the house," she murmured, trying her best to erase from her mind the yellow outline in the foyer. "Marilyn was known for an 'effortless ability to...' " She tried to quote a line from an article in *Architectural Digest* that recently featured Marilyn's work, but the words weren't there.

Two or three logs burned in the fireplace. Brass andirons caught the firelight and made it dance on twin antique gold mirrors on the back wall. An elegant Japy Freres clock on the wall facing Alice counted seconds. Japy Freres, a brand unknown to Alice until she processed the order and the payment of the expensive timepiece.

Over the mantel, a large oil portrait done several years earlier of Marilyn and her daughter, Georgia, showed the women in a tender, contemplative moment. Marilyn was stunning, healthy, not the emaciated shell she'd become in the last few months. Subtle makeup accentuated her eyes and cheek-bones, and her lovely champagne-colored hair hung in loose strands over her shoulders.

Seated, she gazed at a slight angle into the eyes of the viewer in a way that caught the brilliance of a pair of three-tiered diamond earrings that almost touched her shoulder. A black, knee-length sheath with a deep V neckline and long sleeves completed her ensemble.

Georgia, in a sleeveless, high-necked black cock-tail dress, stood by her mother's side, her head tilted downward, revealing her face in three-quarter view, a shadow darkening her right cheek. Georgia's hand rested on the chairback.

Heavy draperies on the French doors flanking the fireplace muffled the din of the storm outside. A bouquet of blush-colored winter roses spilled from the neck of a glass-and-bronze vase on a table in front of the sofa. Alice's gaze lingered on the flowers. One of them shrank beside the others, its stem too short to reach the water. Marilyn would—

A tear pushed its way down Alice's cheek, and she hunched her shoulder to catch it on her sweater. She ran her fingers over the brocade edging of the chair and realized she hadn't scrubbed the garden dirt from beneath her nails. She smoothed her pants. Her hand found the pain in her knee and lingered there.

"Looks like you're feeling better." Cabrera moved to the sofa and sat facing Alice.

Alice shifted her position, now aware that the detective had been watching her. The heat rose in her neck. "Yes. Thank you. I am." She straightened her left leg and stroked the knee. "Please tell me what happened, Detective. Was the house robbed?"

"It's too early to know anything certain. You can help us by sharing what you remember about last night."

"Oh. Well, the family was here, in this room," she said, still rubbing the knee. "They're newlyweds, you know, Marilyn and David. Marilyn's sister, Ava, came a few days ago from Santa Fe, and Marilyn's daughter, Georgia, was here from New York for the holidays." Alice paused for a few moments and considered her nervous chatter. Talking calmed her. She went on.

"Georgia broke her ankle in New York a week or so ago, and her doctor put her in a heavy cast almost up to her knee. She made quite an entrance when David carried her into the house from the taxi. Such a beautiful, beautiful family." She pulled a tissue from her sleeve and swiped it under her nose.

"Were you here in the room with them, Ms. Abbott?"

"No, no. I was in my office finishing some editing on a bid Marilyn wanted sent to Barcelona next week. Because of the placement of my desk, I see a lot of up-and-down staircase activity." Alice's face reddened. She felt like an old woman with nothing better to do than to wheedle her way into other people's private lives. Is that why the detective wanted to talk to her? Because she thought Alice was a gossip?

She swallowed and continued, her eyes focused on the pattern in an Oriental rug that covered the floor. "The Johnsons from next door had come for dinner. They left early, at nine o'clock or so." She turned to Cabrera. "Funny," she said. "Marilyn rarely entertains at home. I was surprised when she invited the Johnsons."

"This is Javier Johnson from next door?"

"Yes. He owns Top-of-the-Line Used Cars. I bought my car from there." Again she glanced at

Cabrera, surprised she'd added such a trivial detail.

She went on. "Marilyn's chef left without notice yesterday morning. I offered to find someone to fill in, but Marilyn insisted she'd take care of it." She shook her head. "Dinner was a disaster. I don't know where Marilyn found the chef, but she should have saved her money and served cold cereal."

Why was she rambling on in such a casual way, as though she'd forgotten the horror of the tape silhouette just down the hall? Didn't she remember she was talking to a police officer about a murder?

A rumble of thunder echoed through the room.

A strand of Cabrera's hair kissed the scar that marred her pretty face. She held a small notepad and a yellow pencil, one of those cheap mechanical ones that Alice liked to use. The detective chewed her bottom lip and watched Alice.

Alice straightened herself in the chair and wiped her glasses on the sleeve of her sweater. "I'm so sorry, Detective. I haven't even asked you why you wanted to see me today." She put her glasses on and pushed them into place.

"Only to ask you about last night," Cabrera said. "You're doing fine. Please go on. You mentioned a bad meal?"

Alice looked at the floor. "Yes, it was bad. I got a plate from the kitchen and took it to my office. It's there." She pointed. "My office. Just under the west staircase."

Cabrera glanced in that direction. "Right," she

said as she made a note in her book.

"Marilyn's standards are quite high, and that meal—well, I passed on dessert, decided I'd do better to save myself for ice cream when I got home."

She sat back in the chair. "I don't think anyone noticed the bad meal. I could hear them. After a few cocktails, they were all pretty... Well..." She peeked at Cabrera. "They were drunk. There was a lively discussion going on between Marilyn and Javier—that's Mr. Johnson—at about the time Trish served coffee."

"This would be Trish Askelson, the maid?" Cabrera said.

"Yes. On my way back to my office from the kitchen, I passed the dining room. Javier was pushing his chair away from the table, insisting he was right about something or other. He stumbled a little as he got up. He and Mrs. Johnson left soon after that."

Pellets of hail peppered the windows, the sound peaking with intermittent gusts of wind. Cabrera leaned close to Alice. "Please go on."

"Just after nine o'clock—I remember the clock chiming—Ava tried to help Marilyn up the stairs to bed, but Marilyn slapped her away."

Alice paused for a moment. "She was so sick, so weak." Her eyes darted to Cabrera. "Her stomach, you know. David finally took her in his arms and carried her up. She slapped at him, too, and cried, but he wouldn't put her down."

"Did everyone else go to bed after that?"

"Soon after, Ava prepared tea for Marilyn and

then David came down to carry Georgia upstairs."

"Because of her ankle."

"Yes. Georgia can't use the stairs at all."

A speck of dust settled on the brass base of a marble lamp next to her. She reached out to wipe it away.

Cabrera cleared her throat, then said, "Did they speak? Georgia and David?"

Alice curled her fingers into her palm and drew her hand back from the lamp. She straightened her posture and looked at Cabrera. "Nothing I heard."

"Okay," Cabrera said. "You're doing fine. Please go on."

"That's pretty much it. I finished the edit at about ten o'clock, and I locked up and went home." Alice wiped her eyes, pushed her glasses upward toward her brow, and then re-settled them on her nose.

"When you left, the chef and the maid had already gone—is that right?"

"The chef had left, but I think Trish stayed in the maid's quarters, next to the pool house. Sometimes she does that if she expects to start work early the next morning."

"The next morning—that would be today? Was anything planned for today?"

"No." Alice shrugged. "Maybe Trish was just extra tired."

Cabrera asked something, but another rumble of thunder buried her words.

"Did you speak to the chef?" she repeated.

"No. When I went to the kitchen to get my dinner, Trish told me he'd gone outside with David. I never saw the chef. I only tasted the fruit of his labors."

Cabrera locked eyes with Alice until Alice looked away. Another inappropriate, lighthearted comment. What was wrong with her?

"Why did David go outside with the chef?"

"I don't know. Trish said David knew the chef. She said the chef made David nervous."

Cabrera made a note. "You mentioned stomach problems?"

An ear-splitting crack of lightning sent a shiver of electricity through the room. Both women shuddered at the sudden explosion. Cabrera braced herself and sat up straighter.

Alice ran her fingers through her hair. "That was close."

Cabrera raised her brows. "You were going to tell me about Ms. Quinn's stomach problems."

Alice scooted to the edge of the chair and locked her hands between her knees. The sound of the hail was deafening now.

She was ready for this interview to be over. She spoke in rapid-fire tones. "Some kind of virus, I think. It started just before Christmas." She swallowed and stared into Cabrera's eyes. "Marilyn's health had been so good after her heart attack, and then soon after her honeymoon she was tired all the time, weak, complained about stomach cramps. Some days she couldn't get out of bed, and when she did she stayed downstairs for only short periods."

"When was the last time she left the house?"

"Yesterday. For a hair appointment. She and David had an argument about her driving the car in her condition."

"Did David drive her?"

"No. When Marilyn wanted to do something, she did it."

Cabrera made a few notes in her book. She shifted her weight on the sofa. "You spent a good deal of time here with Ms. Quinn, is that correct?"

"I'm here every day from nine o'clock in the morning until I go home."

"You knew Ms. Quinn very well."

"No, I...well, I was her assistant. I wouldn't say I knew her personally. I worked for her for five years."

Cabrera pursed her lips. "Do you know anyone who could have been particularly angry at her? Anyone she'd had problems with recently?"

Alice hesitated. Was it her place to tell Cabrera that, except for her clients, almost everyone was angry with her and had been since her heart attack last summer?

"No," she said at last.

Cabrera waited.

"Um," Alice said. "She fired the gardener yesterday. Marilyn was proud of her roses, and she and Owen had issues in the past. But I don't think he would—"

Another boom of thunder, and Alice jumped to

her feet. Cabrera stood, too. She moved close to Alice and locked eyes with her.

"Ms. Abbott, are you aware that Marilyn Quinn was having an affair with the gardener?"

CHAPTER 4

A lice got home late. The press had shown up at Marilyn's, and news of her death went viral, not only in Austin and in Texas, but—it seemed to Alice, who took all of the telephone calls— throughout the world. She hadn't seen the family, and no one mentioned not needing her. So far, she supposed she still had a job.

She threw her coat over a kitchen chair, reached under her sweater to unclasp her bra, and then pulled it off through one of the sweater sleeves. She tossed the bra on top of the coat and poured herself a glass of wine. Arthur followed her, rubbing himself against her ankles.

The house was cold. She turned up the thermostat before she flipped through a stack of mail she'd left on the counter yesterday.

Yesterday, forever ago.

Bills, ads, invitations to open credit accounts. She tore into a yellow envelope stamped "Past Due" in large red letters to see what the late fees were on her electric bill. After a brief glance, she shoved the bill back into the envelope and chucked it onto the counter.

She stood for a moment and looked around the kitchen. What a difference to be here after spending the day in Marilyn's home. The walls needed paint, the linoleum floor in the kitchen was peeling in one corner, and the sink and counter were outdated and stained.

She had to have a job. Her financial situation continued the downward spiral that started with paying her aunt's medical bills. Alice found herself struggling to live on a teacher's pension and an even smaller Social Security payment. That income barely covered her expenses. For anything else, she drew on her dwindling savings.

Her small Craftsman home remained one of the few original buildings in her neighborhood, which was being gentrified at a head-spinning pace. To her benefit, her age provided an exemption from skyrocketing property taxes, but maintenance expenses took their toll. The year Aunt Zola died, the seventy-year-old clay plumbing had to be replaced. After that, she needed a new roof, and then the twenty-year-old air conditioner breathed its last, weary breath. This year, wood rot chewed at the door and window frames.

When her savings ran out, she would have to sell. She'd toured several apartment complexes in cheaper parts of the city, cringing at the lack of privacy they offered. And then what? When she could no longer care for herself? Nursing homes terrified her.

She switched on the back porch light and peered outside. The heavy rain had morphed into a dense, wet fog. She took an old sweater from a hook by the door and walked out to inspect the damage the recent storm had brought.

An entire line of shrubs sagged along the fence line. Water puddled between broken bits of patio stones and in sunken areas of the garden. The monkey grass lay flattened against the mulch she'd used to bury the tulip bulbs just... was it earlier this same day? Was that possible?

Who would buy her little house if she had to give it up? She was told that, as one of the original Sears Roebuck and Company kit homes scattered throughout town, it would bring a pretty penny, but would it be enough? She remembered reading somewhere that the kits—each containing thousands of construction pieces, detailed assembly manuals, and 750 pounds of nails—were sold through catalogs and shipped by boxcar to their destinations.

She pushed her glasses up to the top of her head and picked up a chipped ceramic pot from a stack of others, each nestled awkwardly into another. What had she planted in it last? Herbs, maybe? Thyme, that was it. A beautiful, thick bunch of thyme that she'd—

"Alice," someone called from inside the house.

Startled, she dropped the pot, and it shattered on the patio. Arthur shot under the porch just as Haydn appeared at the back door.

"Oh, Haydn, you startled me. What are you doing here so late?"

"Sorry. I was next door at Connie's, and I saw your light. You were expected, you know. For dinner. We missed you."

"I forgot about dinner."

"Come inside," he said, pushing the toe of his boot against the bottom of the screen door. The old wood swelled in the rain and often stuck to the frame.

He pulled her close to him, wrapped his long, thin arms around her shoulders, and held her in a tight embrace. It wasn't like him to touch her like this, but it felt good. As she'd aged, she was surprised how few opportunities for physical contact she had with other people beyond an occasional handshake. She buried her face in his coat, inhaling the comfortable smell of him.

"It's late," he said after a few moments. "Have you eaten?" He studied her face, his dark brows pinched. In his late seventies, he was still a handsome man who had maintained his tall, erect figure due not to any discipline on his part, but to good genes. Often careless about his appearance, tonight he had tried to tame his wiry hair for dinner at Connie's.

"No," she said. "I haven't eaten. I don't think I've ever been so tired."

"A good meal will help. Let's see what we can find."

He settled her into a chair at the kitchen table before he turned his attention to the refrigerator, where he found eggs and Swiss cheese, all he needed to whip up her favorite omelet.

As soon as his back was turned, Alice reached for her discarded bra and slid it off the coat and onto the seat of the chair, out of sight. "Haydn," she said, "when we talked earlier, you mentioned a message you left on my cell phone. What was it?"

"Suppose this Chardonnay will pair well with eggs?" he said, as though he hadn't heard her question. He smiled while he pretended to study the label on the bottle she left on the table. He refilled her glass and poured a glass for himself. Watching a pat of butter melting in a pan, he grated cheese.

Arthur slipped back inside while the door was open. He caressed Alice's ankles, crying for her touch. She ran her hand along his back to the tip of his tail, freeing a tuft of white hair that settled airily on the kitchen floor.

"Looks like someone missed you," Haydn said, smiling at the cat.

Alice scooped the cat into her lap.

Haydn continued with his work, dropping slices of bread into the toaster. Alice watched him, thinking how attached they had become over the years they had known each other.

He had been raised in Boston by two professors of classical music who were surprised rather late in their lives to learn they would be parents. When their son arrived, they had no idea what to do with a baby, so they hired a succession of nannies to get him through the diaper-and-teeth-cutting stages and then took over themselves, treating him forever after as an adult. He responded well, earned his PhD in music at age twenty-five, and did exceptional research in his field, most of it centered on compositions for the harpsichord by Jacques somebody-or-other, a seventeenth-century Parisian musical genius.

Unfortunately, he also possessed about as much practical sense as his parents. Some of the situations he put himself in surprised Alice, although she realized his blunders were a part of what made him so dear to her. She remembered having to pick him up at a coffee shop on Great Hills Trail late one afternoon soon after they met. He'd loaned his Mercedes to a total stranger who said she only wanted to borrow it to pick up a friend. Weeks later, the police found the car—totally wrecked—in a back alley in San Antonio.

She smelled the butter melting and realized she was famished. She shoved Arthur to the floor and pulled her chair closer to the table. Haydn turned to look at her and held up one finger. "Almost done," he said.

Ten years ago, he took an early retirement from his university career and moved to Austin to help an old friend through a painful illness. The friend didn't live long after his arrival, but Haydn liked the city, so he stayed. He met Connie and Alice at an art show on Sixth Street that featured Ellsworth Kelly prints. The three of them had bonded over the *Color Squares* sequence and left together for drinks at a bar close to the gallery.

"Let's go see a movie tomorrow," he said as he

grated the last of the cheese. "Have a few margaritas and enchiladas at Guero's. You can get a good night's sleep, and we'll go early."

"Haydn, I'm going back to Marilyn's tomorrow. I have a job there. I need the money. I can't just stop working."

"*Ah!*" Haydn cried. He dropped the grater and covered his thumb with a dishtowel, which right away soaked through with blood. Before Alice could speak, Haydn turned to her, red-faced, jaws clenched. "*No!* You cannot go back there!"

Arthur shot out of the room, leaving Alice staring at a man she had never heard raise his voice.

He shook his head, calming himself. "Please," he begged, softer now. "Please. You can't go back there."

He sat beside her at the table, still holding the towel around his thumb. "It's not safe until they find who... who did that horrible thing to Ms. Quinn."

Alice looked at him, still shocked by his reaction. And then she noticed several scratches on his face, one that was particularly deep. She reached out to touch it, to soothe him, but he pulled away.

She pushed herself up from her chair and shuffled to the hall, pausing at the doorway. "I'm going back until someone tells me I'm not needed anymore," she said over her shoulder. "I have to have a job. Policemen are all over the house and grounds. I'll be perfectly safe there." She returned to the table with a box of Band-Aids and placed one over the cut on Haydn's thumb. Despite all the blood on the towel, the wound was small.

"Will you reconsider my offers to move in with me?" he said. "I have more space than I can use." He tucked his chin and gave her a small smile. "Besides, it worries me a little that Geoffrey will decide he needs to take care of me in my old age."

"It should worry you," she scoffed. Geoffrey James was the adult son of the dying woman who had brought Haydn to Austin years before. Haydn never heard from Geoffrey except when Geoffrey wanted money. Haydn thought of the man as a joke; Alice saw him as a user and an opportunist. God forbid, Alice often thought, if Geoffrey were ever to be responsible for Haydn's care.

Haydn insisted on finishing the omelet, and she ate like a person starved, following each huge bite with a generous swig of wine. After only a few moments, she sat back in her chair and set her empty plate on the floor for Arthur.

She looked at Haydn's face, wanting to ask him how he had scratched himself, but she was too tired to hear the answer. She rubbed her eyes with her fingertips. She would need an antihistamine tonight. "Please tell Connie I'm sorry I missed dinner."

"How early will you have to leave tomorrow? You really need some sleep. Besides, tomorrow's Saturday and there won't be any traffic. That should give you at least another hour."

She stood. They often joked about being family. She had never had a better, more devoted friend.

She once thought they would marry, but he never initiated any intimacy between them, and she refused to take the lead herself. Somewhere along the way, she abandoned any hope of a relationship beyond friendship. Even if she considered moving into his home, he had clearly indicated she would have a bedroom at the opposite end of the house from his own. On occasion, Alice wondered if he was gay.

She made her way to the bathroom. Arthur, licking melted cheese from his face, followed close behind her.

As she stood under the pounding of hot water in the shower, Haydn cleaned the kitchen. She turned her head toward the half-shut bathroom door when he let himself out.

CHAPTER 5

The next morning, Alice's alarm shattered what little sleep she had gotten. She turned on her side and drew her legs close to her chest. Arthur squeezed himself into a ball at her stomach and they listened to the news on the radio, catching only the end of a frantic report of the horrifying event at Marilyn's. Today would be a hard day, and, according to the weather report, another strong storm was racing southward toward Austin.

She put water on for her coffee and lit the gas heater in the bathroom. Then she stepped into the shower, determined to resurrect her lifeless body.

Funny, she thought, as she massaged shampoo into her hair. *The world as I knew it crumbled yesterday, but this morning all I can think about is a minor item of yesterday's news.*

The revelation about Marilyn and the gardener fired her imagination like kerosene on dry grass. Maybe her mind was protecting her from the over-whelming dread of what had happened, or maybe it was her lonely, seventy-three-year-old, sex-starved lifestyle, but images of Marilyn and Owen in bed crowded her brain. Owen's thick lips on Marilyn's tiny porcelain breasts; his dark, rough hands on her thin, white butt.

Most of her staff knew that Marilyn had had a good deal of plastic surgery, enough to make her look fabulous in her tiny size 2 couture clothing. But surely Owen could tell he was with a woman more than twice his age. Did he not care?

Had Marilyn always been promiscuous, or was Owen a kind of gift Marilyn gave herself after surviving the heart attack?

She stepped out of the shower and glanced at a blurred image of her naked body in a steamy mirror on the opposite wall. She wrapped herself in a towel, wiped away some of the steam with the flat of her hand, and stepped closer to stare into her eyes.

Would anyone ever want her again, a woman who had grown old without the benefit of surgery, expensive creams, and magic elixirs? She had no money and owned a home she'd probably have to sell before it collapsed from neglect.

Marilyn had had it all—a fabulous career, magnificent homes, plenty of money to travel and play, and she had stayed as young as modern medicine would allow. Best of all, her beautiful, successful daughter loved her, and her attractive new husband would help her start a new beginning in her glamorous life.

Now Marilyn's life was over, and Alice's job would end. What would she do?

I shouldn't need to work at all. I've been thrifty all my life and saved a good deal during my career. I retired in good shape financially.

But then her Aunt Zola had broken her hip on a visit to Austin, and Alice insisted on helping her cousin care for her because she wasn't eligible for Medicare. And then a few days a week turned into full-time duty when the cousin disappeared, and by the end—when her aunt died and Alice walked outside dazed and blinking against the sunshine— she realized she had lost two precious years of her life. And most of her savings.

Alice wanted a family, but she was always suspicious of men's attentions and their promises. Her mother had fallen for that and—although the woman never said a negative word about her husband, about what a coward he was to walk out of the house and never return—Alice grew up hating the emptiness he left behind. She was eleven, the only girl in her class without a father, the only one of her friends who brought her lunch to school in a paper bag, the only one whose shoes and clothing became shabbier as the years went by. She despised him, despised the poor circumstances he'd left for her. Without the prodding of her sister, Twyla, who had insisted Alice get a student loan and put herself through college, Alice admitted she would probably have waited tables all her life.

She touched her face, tracing the crease from the side of her lip to her chin. Was that new? She wiped more steam from the mirror and leaned in close. Oddly, her smooth skin tended to droop rather than wrinkle. This latest ravage of age made her mouth look like a marionette.

Fuck.

She hadn't always been alone. While she was in school, she married a math major whose quiet personality was a match for her own. And then soon after the wedding, she returned from an English class to their tiny apartment on the edge of campus and found him gone. He decided, he told her in a note, he no longer wanted to be married.

Long after that shattering surprise, when she began to date again, she was even more emotionally shut off. She got only so close and then pulled away, deciding it was easier to leave someone than to be left.

As she grew older, men's interest in her declined, and her childbearing years tapered to an end. Then one day it was too late for babies, too late for a family. She remembered thinking of that time as the beginning of the second chapter of her life.

Have I now begun Chapter Three?

When did she become old? It hadn't happened quickly, although there were sudden, obvious changes—like this new crease on her face—but in retrospect, the years had stretched smoothly and subtly until her body eventually, quietly, gave into the strain.

Wiping more steam from the mirror, she stepped back and dropped the towel. Her breasts—never large—flattened against the papery skin of her chest.

Her stomach had dissolved into a thick roll of skin that tumbled over the skin below it. Her body had melted, like a candle.

She sighed. Her interest in sex had vanished years ago, a fortunate feature of the aging process. You don't miss what you've forgotten to love.

WHEN ALICE ARRIVED AT MARILYN'S later that morning, she found Trish carrying lunch up to Marilyn's sister, Ava. Alice and Trish had grown close in the last few months, partly out of a need to commiserate about their situation with Marilyn, but foremost because they genuinely liked each other.

"You were here Thursday night, Trish? How awful for you," Alice said, drying her hair with a kitchen towel. The short walk from her car to the house had left her drenched.

"I heard the shot."

Trish always looked tired, but today she appeared exhausted. The bags under her ice-blue eyes were heavier; limp strands of her gray hair hung at the sides of her face. Under her dark dress uniform, her strong shoulders drooped.

Alice watched as her friend continued up the stairs. The woman was not the maid one would expect to find in an elegant mansion like Marilyn's. Her large frame was made for hard work, her big feet designed to anchor her to the earth. Trish was a chunk of fudge dropped into a box of bonbons.

Alice returned to the sitting room, where she had spent most of the previous day returning calls to customers and business associates concerned about Marilyn's death. Trish had started a fire, so the room felt cozy as the temperature outside fell. She felt comfortable here, but she longed for the familiar surroundings of her office. The police were still combing through her files and correspondence.

Before her first call of the day, Detective Cabrera appeared in the doorway. Her hair was pulled back in a tight ponytail, the white scar fully exposed.

"I brought two coffees from Starbucks," the detective said. "Would you like one of them?"

Coffee. Alice looked at her watch. Already nine o'clock and she hadn't eaten anything. She followed the detective into the kitchen and spooned sugar into one of the steaming cups Cabrera had left on the counter. Before she sat, she opened the pantry door to look for a small snack, knowing she wouldn't find much. Marilyn wasn't exactly the peanut-butter-and-crackers or cracked-pepper-potato-chip type. God forbid a hapless chocolate doughnut found its way into the house.

Cabrera popped the plastic lid off her cup. After a few minutes of poking through the pantry, Alice sat across from her, holding a small cellophane packet of oyster crackers.

A bright flash of lightning shot through the windows, startling both of them.

"I hope we don't lose the electricity," Alice said,

tearing into the packet of crackers. She held them toward Cabrera.

"Thanks, but no," Cabrera said with a dismissive wave of her hand.

"Detective, who killed Marilyn? How did it happen?"

"We still don't know much, I'm afraid."

Alice nibbled on a handful of crackers and washed them down with a swallow of hot coffee. She shook her head. "It's still so hard to—"

"You seem to be more comfortable here today, Ms. Abbott."

"Yes. I do feel better today. Thank you. I'm still a bit wobbly—I didn't sleep much last night—but I'm okay."

"I have some good news. We should be finished here in a few hours so you can go back to your office." She sipped her coffee.

"That *is* good news." Alice watched the rain pummel the windows and chewed on another few crackers.

"I had some ideas last night, Ms. Abbott. May I ask you a few questions?"

Alice's jaw locked, mid-bite. She swallowed, brushed crumbs from her hands, and straightened her posture. "Okay." She cleared her throat.

"Please don't be nervous. This is just routine." Cabrera opened the same notebook she had written in yesterday and clicked the yellow mechanical pencil. "You worked for Ms. Quinn for five years. Surely over that length of time, you got to know something of her personal life."

Alice shrugged. "Well, as you know, I was a member of her staff. From time to time, I overheard conversations. I handled her correspondence, drafted project specs, managed her files and her calendar, so most of what I did was work-related."

"Did you know she was getting married?"

"Oh, heavens no. That was a total shock to everyone. She left one Thursday for a conference in New York and came back a week later married to a man she'd met there."

"Well, if she didn't tell you, who would have known about it? Would she have told her sister?"

"I don't think they were close. Ava never married, you know, so she and Marilyn kind of raised Marilyn's daughter, Georgia, together. That is, Marilyn often left Georgia with Ava when she traveled. From what I've heard, the sisters never had a warm relationship."

Alice picked up a couple more crackers and furrowed her brow as she chewed them. "In all likelihood she told her daughter," she said. "Yes, she probably told Georgia. They're very close." She looked at Cabrera and dusted the crumbs from her fingertips. "As for personal friends, Marilyn had a large social circle that gave parties, lunches, fancy dinners, but no one seemed especially close to her. She worked long hours every day, and she was away from home a lot." Alice gave a crooked smile.

"But you got along with her?"

Alice felt a hangnail on her thumb and picked at it. "She was a lovely person until her heart attack, Detective."

"And then?"

"She became resentful. Hateful. I understand it's a common reaction after a heart attack."

"Tell me about the day Marilyn was killed. That would be the day you discussed a Christmas bonus with her?"

Alice's mouth dropped open. "How did you know about that?"

Cabrera said nothing.

Maybe Trish had mentioned Marilyn's tirade. Heat crawled up Alice's neck.

"Uh, yeah. Marilyn came home from her hair appointment in a horrible mood," she said. "And she did get loud when I asked her about the bonus she usually gives me at the end of the year." By now her neck and face were scarlet.

"I guess we've all had difficult bosses. Did you see her at all the rest of the day?"

"Not until that evening. I closed my office door and worked there until the front doorbell rang. The Johnsons arrived for dinner, and I welcomed them and escorted them into the sitting room. I left my door open when I returned to my office, since I felt a little caged in."

"And then later you heard the argument between Javier Johnson and Ms. Quinn in the dining room?"

Alice looked up, pleased that the conversation had

veered away from Marilyn's angry outburst at her. "I didn't hear anything clearly, just raised voices. Then, when I passed the dining room to get a plate for myself, Mr. Johnson stood up and stumbled. He was tipsy. They were all tipsy, except maybe Georgia. I can't imagine her drunk."

"What do you mean?"

"She's so… poised. In control." She shrugged.

"Were their voices raised in anger? Could Mr. Johnson have been telling a story, or a joke?"

"No." Alice shook her head. "He was pointing at Marilyn, and he sounded mad."

"How did Marilyn react?"

"I didn't see that. I was just passing by the door from my office to the kitchen."

Cabrera wrote a few notes. She traced the scar with the eraser end of the pencil. "The Johnsons left, then the family went up to bed, and soon after you went home. Is that right?"

Alice nodded.

"Were the outside Christmas lights on or off when you left, Ms. Abbott?"

"Oh, they were on. They're programmed to go off at 6 a.m."

Cabrera chewed her bottom lip. "I notice there are no decorations *inside* the house. Why are the *outside* lights still up?"

"The décor service was here earlier in the week to put everything away. The lights are still up because it was Owen's job to take them down. And he was fired before he could do that."

"Did the lights ever flicker, or short out?" the detective said. "Someone down the hill saw outside lights go out on Thursday night at about midnight."

"No," Alice said. "Marilyn was a perfectionist. She would never have allowed a defect like that. It would have been repaired right away."

"Ms. Abbott, was anyone with you at your home on Thursday night?"

Alice was about to mention Arthur, and then she realized what the detective was insinuating.

"You—you want to know if I have an alibi for the night Marilyn was murdered?"

Cabrera looked straight into Alice's eyes. "Yes, I do."

"No, Detective," Alice said in a flat tone. "I was alone. I live alone."

Alice slid off the stool and crumpled the cracker packet into her empty coffee cup. She dropped the cup into the trash and turned to face the detective. "What does this mean, Detective? Am I a suspect in Marilyn's murder?"

"Yes, ma'am. At this point, everyone who knew Ms. Quinn is a suspect," Cabrera said, closing her notebook. "I'll need your cell phone as soon as you find it. And please don't leave town without letting me know."

Alice turned, wide-eyed in shock, and walked toward the sitting room.

"Oh, one more thing," the detective said.

Alice stopped at the door but didn't turn.
"An officer will be taking your fingerprints."

A FEW HOURS LATER, Cabrera gave Alice permission to move from the sitting room into her office. The police had plundered the room. Her computer was gone. Every visible surface on each piece of furniture was blanketed in fine white powder. Fingerprint powder, she supposed.

Cabrera's questions rattled her. It had never occurred to her that anyone might think she killed Marilyn.

She collapsed into her desk chair. The desk had been ransacked, its drawers emptied and upturned on the floor, pens and stamps scattered among the paperwork. She sat, resting her heavy bag in her lap, and swiveled the chair to face the glass doors that opened onto a small garden that cowed under a dark blanket of rain.

Alice watched snapdragons, purple stock, and creamy-white winter honeysuckle give in to the incessant downpour, flattening themselves against dark mulch like wet confetti. Beyond the garden wall, the lake was barely visible through the rain. Alice wondered how her favorite part of the grounds—the rose garden outside the downstairs guest bedroom, the yellow room—was faring in this deluge.

Her life was a disaster. She needed money, she would be out of a job, and now, as if reminded that things can always get worse, she was a suspect in a murder investigation, and she had no alibi.

And Cabrera implied Alice also had a motive. As she watched the storm pummel the garden, she remembered the awful exchange between Marilyn and her that last morning of Marilyn's life. Alice waited as long as she could before she brought up the Christmas bonus. Why hadn't she waited one more day? Surely Cabrera already knew Alice needed money. Would they assume she was desperate enough to kill Marilyn in a fit of anger? No wonder Cabrera considered her a suspect.

Well, if she was a suspect, everybody who knew Marilyn should be suspects, too. Cabrera had said as much.

It was in September or October—only a few weeks after Marilyn returned from the hospital—when Alice had first felt the sting of Marilyn's temper. Alice forgot to brush Arthur's white hair off the cuffs of her trousers before she left the house. The cat was a prodigious shedder, and Marilyn insisted her house and all her staff be kept in flawless order. Marilyn looked at the hair on Alice's cuffs with horror and shrieked, "Come in here clean, or don't come in here at all!" After that, Alice joined the rest of the staff as another of Marilyn's punching bags.

And then, after her marriage, Marilyn's stomach problems began, and her temper shot off the charts. How many chefs, some of them excellent, were humiliated by her tirades? At least five left, either fired or, mortified by Marilyn's fault-finding, vanishing on their own. It became impossible for the service agency to find help who would agree to work for her. Undaunted, Marilyn fired the agency and hired someone on her own, refusing Alice's offer to find a chef. That had been the chef who prepared the fiasco for the dinner party the night of her death.

A heavy blast of rain caught a trellis that supported a Lady Banksia rose in the garden, ripped a corner of the trellis from the fence, and left it wobbling in the wind. Alice watched, unfazed.

Owen, the gardener—the *lover*, she reminded herself—was hired a few weeks after Marilyn's heart attack to replace a delightful older man who had cared for Marilyn's grounds for years. Despite Owen's place in her bed, if not her heart, he was also the target of Marilyn's rage, mainly due to his neglect of her precious roses. Once or twice he didn't water them thoroughly enough before a freeze; other times he hadn't managed the deadheading according to her specifications.

Owen never seemed bothered by Marilyn's rages. Maybe he felt a certain job security based on their intimate relationship.

The only times Marilyn softened were around her handsome new husband. Recently though, even he— poor, startled thing—had tiptoed in her presence.

Alice managed to stay out of Marilyn's aim by making herself invisible, something she found easy to do at her age. What Marilyn wanted was silent obedience and immediate response to her every need, which included ushering clients into and out of Marilyn's office and having any information she needed at a moment's notice, twenty-four hours a day, seven days a week. Alice did her best to satisfy those requirements.

In fact, the more invisible Alice became, the more she seemed to please Marilyn. Alice fit the physical profile of someone who could serve as a constant reminder to Marilyn of her good looks, her power, her self-assurance, all of those attributes that Marilyn seemed unaware of before her heart attack. Every time Marilyn floated into her office in smart heels and a designer dress that clung to her slender shape like cellophane, Alice crab-scuttled out in a shapeless, off-the-rack, no-name frock, no one having spoken to her or even having met her eye.

But that was before Marilyn's last illness, which left her shrunken and feeble. In fact, Marilyn hadn't *floated* anywhere—much less got fully dressed—in days. She even wore her cotton houseshoes to drive herself to the hairdresser's.

Alice plowed through her bag until she found a box of sugar cookies at the bottom. She lowered herself to the floor with the cookies and reinstalled the drawers in the desk. After the cookies were gone and she had wrestled the last of the drawers back in its place, someone knocked on the door. She peered over the top of the desk.

"May I have a moment, Alice?" Ava said.

"Of cour... of course," Alice said, eyebrows raised. "Please, come in." She pulled herself up, her knee screaming from her awkward position on the floor. *Where did the police put my aspirin?*

Alice directed Ava to a chair that faced the desk, but then held up her hand, palm forward. She grabbed a wad of tissue from a box tossed on the floor and wiped white dust off the chair's wooden armrests.

"Such a mess," Ava said, looking around the room. She was Alice's age, a few years older than Marilyn. Ava was attractive, but not at all the great beauty her sister had been. In fact, the women looked nothing alike. While they both had the angular jawline, smoothed forehead, and plumped cheeks of older women who'd had expensive facial surgery over the years, Marilyn's face had a softness about it that complimented her large, intelligent eyes and bright, passionate mouth. Ava's features were less generous. Shadows and highlights applied with artistry helped to make her small eyes appear rounder, but she made no effort to diminish the harsh effect of her thin lips that stretched into a horizontal slash when she smiled.

She wore a short, taupe jacket over black, wide-legged silk pants. Her long, slender fingers were unadorned except for a magnificent black opal dinner ring on the middle finger of her left hand. Her long, still-dark hair was pulled away from her face in a tight chignon.

Alice sat behind the desk. She straightened her

leg, rubbing the angry knee.

"How are you holding up, Alice?"

"I'm okay. It's such a shock. I'm so sorry for your loss."

"Thank you," said Ava. "I wanted you to know that funeral arrangements are being made, so you won't be bothered by any of that."

Alice nodded.

"What will you do now?" Ava went on. "Have you had time to think about what's next?"

Here it comes, the I'm-sorry-but-we-don't-need-your-services-anymore speech.

"I have to find another job, but I haven't a clue about where I should look, or how long I'll be needed here." She frowned at the thought of past pathetic attempts to make herself look younger for job interviews.

"Well," Ava went on, "of course you'll get your paycheck at the end of the month."

Ava opened her checkbook and asked for a pen. "And I'd like to give you something extra for your loyalty during this frightful time." She balanced the book on the armrest of the chair, scribbled for a moment, and tore the check out of the book. She reached over the desk and handed the check to Alice.

Alice's eyes grew wide when she saw the amount, which was more than her Christmas bonus would have been. She would be able to pay the electric bill and take a bite out of her credit card debt.

"Thank you. You have definitely made my New

Year brighter." Alice smiled and tucked the check into a pocket on the inside of her bag, careful to keep it separate from the clutter straining the seams of the faux-leather tote.

Ava sat back in her chair and smoothed her pants. "Marilyn never paid you what you were worth to her. Everyone knew that."

Oh, really?

"Would you like coffee, Ava?"

"No, thanks," Ava said. "But I'd like to help you with your job search. How about working for me?"

Alice looked at her in surprise. "For you? But you live in Santa Fe—"

"Well, not exactly for me, but for Marilyn's estate. I'm helping Georgia in her role as executrix of Marilyn's will, which will reimburse me when the will is settled. You would stay here, move in until the house sells. Part of your job would be to oversee the sale of the house, all of the furniture, close out all of Marilyn's accounts, do all of the things that have to be done at a time like this. You would confer with me, of course, on all the big decisions."

"Oh, Ava, I can't." Alice felt the flush spread upward from her neck. That kind of responsibility was way beyond her capabilities. She'd been a teacher, for Pete's sake!

"We'll keep Trish and a cook, of course. You would manage the daily affairs and upkeep of the house, basically become lady of the house until it sells."

Lady of this house. Impossible.

The flush was in full bloom now. The heat in her face, her neck, heightened.

"I would love to help—"

"I have my work in Santa Fe," Ava said. "Georgia needs to get back to New York right after the funeral to see her doctor. I told her I'd talk to you about the business end of things."

"Well, of course I want to do whatever I can, but I can't do what you ask. I'll be happy to help someone else with all of that."

"I expected you to say that, but let me finish. There is a second part of the job I'm offering you, something no one but you can do. And I don't want Georgia to know about this."

Alice swallowed, anxious but interested.

"I want you to keep a close eye on David. He has no money, so I expect he'll stay here in the house until it's sold. I don't trust the man, don't trust what he'll take or try to sell on his own. He will not be included in Marilyn's will."

But they were married, Marilyn and David. Wouldn't he inherit something even if the will didn't name him?

"David has a job in Houston, doesn't he?" Alice said. "Surely he'll go there."

Ava's face hardened. She stopped Alice with a piercing glare.

"He has *no job*," she said. "He'll be *penniless*, just as he was before he married Marilyn. I expect him to lurk around here, acting so desperate we'll toss him a bone to get rid of him."

Alice looked at her hands. David had traveled several times to Houston for overnight stays and Alice assumed he was doing business there. Maybe Ava didn't know about his work. Alice was suddenly ashamed for him. If what Ava had said was true, he would be leaving Marilyn's lavish lifestyle and returning to the same poor, banal existence as Alice.

Still staring at her hands, she said, "I couldn't begin to do what you ask. I'm happy to stay until after the funeral to make sure Marilyn's desk is cleared, but I don't have the experience to manage a house like this."

"Just promise me you'll think about it. No one knows the house and the business as well as you do. You'll be perfectly safe if that's a concern—I've hired a full-time guard service to be on the watch of this house and its property."

Alice nodded.

Ava stood and walked to the door. She turned and looked at Alice. "Oh," she said. "And think about the kind of salary you rightfully deserve for your responsibilities. How about double what Marilyn paid you?"

CHAPTER 6

Alice left Marilyn's house early and picked up some wine at HEB Grocery, expecting Haydn to stop by. At the beverages aisle, she realized she hadn't grabbed a cart, so she stuck a bottle under each arm and grabbed two more, one in each hand.

She passed a woman her age on her way to the cashier who held her gaze, each of them struggling to remember how they knew each other. An old book group? Bridge? A teaching colleague?

And then a strident voice over her shoulder broke the moment. "How are we doing this evening, honey?" said a short, mousey-blonde woman in an HEB uniform.

Alice took her time turning to face the woman, who was familiar only through casual, patronizing exchanges like this. The woman was probably on her way out for a smoke. She had the puckered lips and yellowed teeth of a smoker.

"I think we need a cart, don't we?" the woman called out, no doubt to compensate for Alice's difficulty hearing.

"No. I'm fine. Thank you."

"Okay. Looks like we're having a party, huh?"

Alice brushed past her, muttering under her breath. "No, no party, you cheeky bitch. I'm breaking these to use as weapons." She didn't need another reminder of her age. She needed to find another grocery store.

She waited for Haydn until eight o'clock, sipping wine and munching on crackers and peanut butter and a shriveled apple she'd found in the crisper drawer in the fridge. At last, she took a sleeping pill and went to bed.

THE NEXT MORNING, the Sunday *Austin American-Statesman* had been delivered by the time Alice got up. Saturday's edition had run a front-page story with Marilyn's photo, but offered only a few facts.

She pushed her slippers through the wet grass in the front yard and pulled the plastic sleeve off the paper before she got back to the house.

There they were—Marilyn, Georgia, David—in separate photos under a headline that read,

WEALTHY AUSTIN INTERIOR DESIGNER MURDERED IN HER HOME

She snapped the paper to its full size. A photo of Marilyn's mansion spread across three columns below the fold. Alice touched her lips.

A major architectural firm had used the same photo on a national magazine cover several years earlier.

It was shot at twilight, with all the inside lights on to show the horizontal expanse of the estate through the heavily wooded landscape. Cream-colored Texas limestone walls climbed up three stories of the main house and spread across identical wings to the east and west sides. Dark French mansard roofs added elegance to the impressive size of the residence, and in the grand circular drive crouched Marilyn's silver Jaguar, contributing a bit of lived-in hominess.

Alice spread the paper on the kitchen table, made coffee, and fed Arthur. Then she sat down and read the article, searching without success for any details that would help her understand what had happened.

She dialed Haydn's number. No answer.

An hour later, she was showered, dressed, and back at the kitchen table with her checkbook. She snatched the electric bill from its envelope. An open box of granola with chocolate chips waited close at hand.

"Here you go, you money-grubbing bastards," she whispered as she wrote the check and signed it with a flourish. She inserted the overdue bill and the check into the return envelope.

She endorsed the check Ava had written, filled in a deposit slip, and tucked them into a stamped envelope as well. She would drop one envelope at the post office and one at her bank on the way to Marilyn's.

It was a bright, beautiful day, entirely welcome after the last storm. She hoped Connie would be home, but she never knew, with the crazy hours emergency room doctors kept. Her car sat parked in the driveway, so Alice took a chance and walked next door for a visit. Maybe Connie had heard from Haydn.

Connie met her at the door, wearing a long, turquoise silk caftan and silver slippers. Her eyes were lined and shadowed, and she wore bright scarlet lipstick. When Connie was off-duty, she sometimes went overboard in compensating for the boring scrubs she wore at the hospital. Not that she didn't attract attention in her scrubs. Her voluptuous figure, red hair, and sleepy eyes—bedroom eyes, Alice remembered thinking when they first met—made her a classic Rita Hayworth standout. She caught Alice in a long, warm embrace and then stepped away and held her at arm's length.

"You've had me worried sick! Haydn told me what happened. I've been calling you all day."

Alice apologized and explained that she'd lost her cell phone. "On a lighter note," she said, "I got the bulbs planted."

Connie shook her head. "You and that cell phone," she said. "Not a marriage made in heaven."

Alice shrugged, and Connie invited her in.

"Hey, Alice," Connie's partner, Patsy, called from the sofa, where she was bent over a laptop computer. She wore huge black-framed glasses that covered most of her tiny, heart-shaped face.

Connie led Alice into the kitchen and closed the door so they wouldn't disturb Patsy. Over fresh coffee, they sat at the kitchen counter, as they had done many times in the years of their friendship.

Connie played with a long feather earring that hung almost to her shoulder. "Did you hear the sirens last night?"

Alice shook her head. "Another break-in? When will the police catch those kids and teach them a lesson? Better yet, when will their parents wake up and whip their butts?"

"They were close this time—just a block down from us."

They sat in silence for a moment. Connie covered Alice's hand with her own and looked into her eyes. "Is Marilyn's daughter still at the mansion?" she said. "This must be awful for her."

Alice sipped her coffee. "Poor girl also has a broken ankle. She can barely get around the house without help."

"She's hardly a girl, Alice. She must be in her 50s at least."

Alice frowned.

"I'm sorry," Connie said. "It's a bad break?"

"Trish overheard her tell Marilyn that she had surgery to realign the bones. It must have been quite serious."

"Well, if she had surgery, she'll be in that plaster cast for weeks. It'll be difficult for her to take a shower, much less prance down a fashion show catwalk. What'll she do about her job?"

"I have no idea. Surely models have insurance for

that kind of thing, don't you think?"

Connie held the flat of her palms out to Alice. "My specialty is medicine, remember? My world is about as far away from modeling as it can get."

Alice nodded. "Well, we know Georgia won't starve. Not with the inheritance she's got coming to her."

They sat in silence again for a few moments.

"Alice," Connie said in a gentle tone, leaning close to her friend, "you know how worried Haydn is that you're staying on at Marilyn's."

Alice sighed and inhaled, the better to answer.

"No. Let me tell you this," Connie said. "You haven't asked me for advice, but I agree with Haydn. It's not wise for you to be in that house. Please stay away from there until the police make an arrest."

Alice smiled at Connie and thanked her. "I'm truly not worried about being there." Connie listened as Alice told her about the full-time security-guard service that Ava hired.

"Georgia wants to sell the estate right away," Alice said. "Marilyn's sister asked me to oversee the sale, but I don't know the first thing about managing a project like that."

Alice shared the details of Ava's offer, leaving out the part about having to keep her eye on David.

"Double your current salary. Sounds a little fishy, don't you think? That's a lot of money for something Ava could get a professional to do much cheaper. You need to turn her down." Connie leaned forward on the counter. "You're seventy-three years old, for heaven's sake."

Alice straightened. What had Ava seen in her that Connie refused to see? "I promised I'd stay until after the funeral, so I can't leave yet. In fact," she said, glancing at her watch, "I need to go now, or I'll be late. Thanks, Connie."

Alice got up and carried her cup to the sink. On her way out, she stopped to say goodbye to Patsy.

"By the way," she said, glancing from one of the women to the other. "Have either of you heard from Haydn recently? I thought he'd come by last night, but he didn't and he's not answering his phone."

Patsy shook her head.

Connie said, "I haven't talked to him since he was here for dinner. "

ALICE DROVE TO THE POST OFFICE, to the bank, and then to Marilyn's. The sun was out, and the air smelled clean.

As soon as she pulled into the driveway, she paused. Marilyn's car had been moved. So she could step from the veranda and into the driver's seat, Marilyn always parked in front of the main entrance with the driver's side closest to the door.

Today, the car was parked several feet from the door, facing the wrong direction. Maybe someone in the family—David or Georgia or Ava—had used the car?

From this angle, Alice couldn't see the deep gashes in the silver paint of the car that she noticed in the rain on the morning of Marilyn's death. Marilyn must have scraped something when she went to the hairdresser's. She really shouldn't have been driving, as ill as she was.

Alice pulled around to the back of the house.

She was accustomed to greeting the cook *du jour*, asking what was for lunch, and pouring a cup of coffee on her way to her office, but today no one was in the kitchen. Alice had called the placement service the day before and asked them to send a chef as soon as possible.

A luscious four-layer chocolate cake beckoned to Alice from under a domed glass cake server on the counter. *I see the service has followed through.*

Of the chefs who cooked for Marilyn through the years, Alice's favorite baked cakes like that. Before Marilyn had made him mad enough to leave.

She spoke to the cake: "Later."

As she crossed the entry hall on her way to her office, she listened, trying to pick up sounds that would indicate where the family might be. Nothing. Morning sunshine flashed on the lake, and she paused a moment to admire the view. She bent at the waist and rubbed her knee before she moved on.

When she opened the door to her office, David was sitting at her desk, looking through mail and phone notes. "Damn! What are you doing here?" he shouted. He jumped up from her chair and stared hard at her, demanding an answer.

"I—I'm doing my job. She asked me to—"

"Well, I live here, at least until I get dropped out on the curb, and I don't want you here. So get out."

He scrambled around the desk toward her, and she ran for the back door. She sprang into her car, jammed the key into the ignition, and turned it. Nothing. The poor old car had taken this opportunity to refuse to move. She stretched across the seat and slammed the door locks closed. David rushed out of the house toward her. She froze, terrified.

"Alice, wait." He dashed around the car to the driver's door and stopped, his hands spread on the window glass next to her face. He smiled, lifting the corner of his upper lip, like Paul Newman in *Hud*.

After a long exhale, she unlocked the driver's door. He opened it and held her elbow as he helped her from the car. "I guess the stress has finally got the best of me. You didn't deserve that outburst. Please forgive me and come back in the house."

He remembers my name? Despite the fear she felt only moments ago, Alice couldn't help but detect genuine apology in his face. His beautiful face, covered in early-morning stubble. He looked at her, and a tight-lipped smile pulled the skin at the corners of his eyes. Gray eyes, she would remember later. The color of slate.

The muscles in his cheeks flexed as he set his jaw. "I...well, I..." Alice let him help her out of the car.

He shook his head and escorted her into the kitchen. He pulled out a barstool for her at the counter and then flipped a switch on the wall. Twin chandeliers over the counter lit the room. Within seconds, more subtle lighting came to life in and under cabinets. Alice loved the kitchen.

"Would you like some coffee?" He turned to the machine and pressed a button. "I haven't had any yet, and I'd love for you to join me."

"Georgia? Ava? Are they here?" She shifted sideways to look through the doorway.

"Gone. And gone. Meeting someone for brunch someplace. I was cordially not invited to join them. It's just you and me, kid."

She placed her bag on the counter, but then grimaced at how cheap and dumpy it looked against the gleaming granite surface. She dropped it to the floor by her feet.

David returned to the counter with two mugs of coffee and sat on the stool next to hers. He smiled at her and added three generous spoons of sugar to his mug. He shrugged. "Sweet tooth," he said. "Sweets will kill me one day."

"Bad habit," Alice said as she added an equal amount of sugar to her mug. "Love the stuff."

He took a sip from his mug and turned to face her. "I've been totally shattered by all of this, Alice."

Alice could manage only a shy glance in his direction. He hadn't shaved, and his shirtsleeves were rolled up, exposing fine, blond hair on his toned, honey-colored arms. She'd seen men like this in movies, but this was the first time in her life she'd been this close to a man like David.

"Well, we're all...shocked," she managed to say.

"I loved her, you know, loved every crazy, beautiful, rich, bitchy bone in her body." He bent his head and pressed his fingers to his eyes. "She was so sick," he whispered.

"Yes. I'm sorry." She risked another glance at him. "If there's anything I can do, please tell me."

He took a deep breath and swiped at his eyes with the palms of his hands.

Without the faintest idea how to comfort the man, she said, "What were you looking for in my office? Maybe I can help you find something."

He shrugged. "Nothing in particular. The police have taken every shred of Marilyn from here. I only wanted to feel close to her. I'm sorry I scared you."

"Not to worry. I'm not accustomed to announcing my presence, but I'll try not to surprise you again." She explained that she would continue to work in her office every day until after the funeral. "Will you stay, David, until the house is sold?"

"Until there's an arrest, the police won't let me leave Austin. I gave up my apartment in Las Vegas when I came here with Marilyn." He sipped from his mug. "I need to give some serious thought to where I go from here."

Las Vegas? Alice assumed David had lived in Houston, or maybe in New York where he met Marilyn. "What about your work in Houston? Will you have to give that up?"

"Work?" David said.

"The business you do in Houston?"

"Oh, that," David said, placing his coffee mug carefully on the counter. "It's an informal situation I can handle from here."

But Ava said David had no job. What took him to Houston, if not work? She didn't ask. It wasn't her place to ask. Not her place to push.

"Well, if it's any consolation," she said, "I can't leave town either. And I'll have to rethink my life, too. All her staff will."

A knock at the back door interrupted them. Alice slid off her stool and went to answer it.

"Lillo!" she squealed, pronouncing the name as he had taught her: LEEloh. "You're back?"

She flung open the door and threw her arms around a mountain of a man dressed in chef's whites. She turned to David and introduced the man as Benedetto Cambria, better known as Lillo, who had cooked for Marilyn after her heart attack.

Alice sensed a slight pause before David greeted the man. She suspected that David, like many others, was put off by Lillo's startling appearance. Long black hair pulled back in a bun, pockmarked, dark Italian skin, and a horseshoe mustache that grew unevenly under a large, slightly off-center nose added menace to his presence. At six feet, three inches, well over three hundred pounds, and with a habitual expression that made him look as if he smelled something foul, Lillo looked more like a burned-out prizefighter than a first-class chef.

"I saw the cake this morning." Alice gestured to the tall chocolate creation. "You made it last night, didn't you?"

"*Certo!*" His stern features melted into a smile, an expression Alice hadn't seen often. "I was here but didn't find you. I was afraid you had quit your job. So many chefs have worked here since I left. It's *meraviglioso* to know you're still here."

David stood. "I'll let you two get reacquainted." He glanced up at Lillo's bulging biceps and raised his eyebrows. "I need to get to the gym." He walked to the door and turned back to Lillo. "By the way, Lillo, the chops you prepared last night were exceptional. Thank you."

"I need to get to work, too," Alice added, "so the kitchen is all yours."

ALICE HUMMED AS SHE WALKED to her office, light-hearted for the first time in days. So David had been living in Las Vegas, not Houston or New York. *What kind of work did he have in Las Vegas? How could Ava suspect him of taking anything from the house?* The man was obviously devastated with grief.

On her desk lay two notes from Ava, handwritten on Marilyn's heavy, cream-colored stationery. Other than the notes, everything she had left the afternoon before was unchanged. David had either just begun looking through her desk or was very careful not to disturb anything. *What did he expect to find?*

One of the notes from Ava said she and Georgia would be out for lunch but return home for dinner. It asked Alice to tell the chef they wanted to be served light meals in their rooms at seven o'clock. The note also reminded her that Ava was eager to hear Alice's decision on her offer.

The second note advised Alice about Marilyn's funeral service, which was to be on Tuesday morning at 10 a.m. It would be a private affair, only family. She apologized, but said she knew Alice would understand not being included.

Relieved she wouldn't have to find something appropriate to wear to such a posh event, Alice went back to returning calls of condolence. As she dialed, David crossed the entry hall and drove away in Marilyn's car. And then, as though he'd been waiting for David to leave, Lillo appeared in Alice's doorway with a tray that he placed on her desk.

"I don't want to disturb your work, Alice. *Buon appetito.*" He turned and left.

He had rescued a few of the scarlet snapdragons from the devastation of last night's storm, arranged them in a crystal bud vase, and put it on the tray with a generous slice of the cake and a cup of coffee. How she had missed the big, tender-hearted soul.

Feeling only a tinge of guilt about indulging in so much chocolate this early in the morning, she dug in and washed down a huge chunk of the cake with the coffee.

As she reminded herself to look for her cell phone again at home, she picked up her office landline and dialed Haydn's number. Still no answer. She frowned, anger simmering at him for ignoring her for so long.

IT WASN'T UNTIL THE END of the day that Alice remembered the car hadn't started earlier. She shook her head as she recalled her fear and running from David, believing he would harm her.

How will I get home? She couldn't help but think of Javier Johnson sitting down to cocktails in his mansion next door. How much profit did he make on the money she borrowed to buy a car that was probably a piece of junk? Maybe she should walk over and ask Javier for a lift home. Dark clouds were building north of the city. The rain would start again soon.

She took a deep breath and opened the door. On the driver's seat, two small Richart gourmet chocolate squares—Salted Butter Caramel and Venezuela Ganache. Taped to the steering wheel, a note:

So sorry I scared you this morning, Alice. Javier from next door (he's a great mechanic!) found the tools he needed to fix your car in the garage. It's good to go now, but he suggested you take it to a shop soon. Enjoy the sweets! David

What irony. The guy she bought the car from says she needs to take it to a shop. But Javier is also a mechanic? He looked as much like a mechanic as

Lillo did a chef. She settled her bag on the passenger seat beside her when her shoulders tightened. *What is a murderer supposed to look like?*

She turned the ignition, and the little Toyota started right up. She peeled back the wrapper on the Salted Butter Caramel and popped it into her mouth. She murmured a quiet thanks to David, a kindred sweets lover, and drove home.

THE NEXT MORNING STARTED gray and windy again. The temperature had dropped, and rain loomed in the forecast for the afternoon. News stations and the daily paper issued warnings about possible flooding.

Alice lurched along the Mo-Pac expressway with all the other Monday morning drivers. She looked forward to seeing Lillo, to having some normalcy back in her life

When her little Toyota pulled into the driveway at Marilyn's, Owen Murphy's white pickup truck blocked her way to her regular parking place at the back of the house. Marilyn had fired the gardener. Why was he here?

Her spirits flagged, and her breath came in short gasps. Did he know his relationship with Marilyn was common knowledge? A hot flash ran up her neck.

"Good morning, Ms. Alice," Owen called to her as he walked toward her from the garage. He seemed unfazed, his handsome face open and friendly. He was short for a man, but well-built, with a broad chest and narrow hips.

Alice opened the window.

"Want me to move my truck out of your way?" He leaned on her door, his strong arms crossed to brace himself, and without warning, as if something broke inside her, Alice's embarrassment for Owen turned to fear. Could Owen have killed Marilyn? He was a jilted lover, spurned, banished. What was he doing here? She swallowed hard and refused to meet his eyes.

"Some bad business here, huh?" he said, shaking his head.

She swallowed again.

Silence. The heat in her neck throbbed.

"Have you spoken to the police?" she said in a low voice, still not meeting his eyes. And then, because the question sounded accusatory, she looked at him and added, "We all had to talk to them, all of us who knew her."

"Yeah. They came for me at my brother's house in San Marcos and asked lots of questions. I was with my brother when she was killed. Detective Cabrera told me I could come today to get my tools."

So it wasn't Owen. She relaxed. She smiled at him.

"Do you want me to take down the Christmas lights while I'm here?"

"I don't think they work." She glanced toward the eaves. "They went out the night of the—"

"They work. I just checked them because I was

surprised they were still up. I'll show you."

Alice followed him to the front of the mansion, watching his slender hips. She could definitely understand what Marilyn saw in him.

Owen pulled back a thick, potted yew bush on the west side of the front door to reveal an electrical panel Alice had never noticed.

"You see, they work fine." He touched a button on the panel, and the strings of bulbs sprang to life, bathing the house in Christmas splendor against the dark clouds overhead.

"Oh." Alice frowned. "I guess I misunderstood. Thank you, Owen. Please take them down and put them in the garage with the rest of the outside decorations." She turned away but then stopped. She felt sorry for Owen. He was just another staff member subject to Marilyn's whims and tirades.

"I'm sorry, Owen." She turned to face him again.

He looked at her and shrugged. "What for? You never did anything to me."

"I'm sorry you lost your job."

LILLO WAS IN THE MIDST OF preparing lunch when Alice came through the kitchen door. He stopped snapping beans, wiped his hands, and poured a cup of coffee for her. He knew just how she liked it, so she waited while he added sugar.

"Thanks, Lillo." She walked toward her office, deep in thought. Owen was off the hook. His alibi was a strong one. *Then who?* The newspaper suggested a possible intruder but offered no details. Did a burglar surprise Marilyn? Was it Javier Johnson, who seemed so angry at Marilyn the night she was killed? That weird cook Marilyn hired to prepare dinner?

A few weeks earlier, Marilyn lashed out at Trish, the maid. As the outburst went on, Alice focused on Trish's large hands as they tightened into fists. Perhaps sheer force of will had kept Trish from bashing Marilyn's face into wet paste.

Alice suspected several people who could happily have done Marilyn harm. The only person Marilyn had continued to treat with kid gloves, even through her bad moods and failing health, was her daughter, Georgia.

With her computer still in the hands of the police, Alice spent the morning responding to the mail and the telephone condolences that continued to come in. Twice, she tried to call Haydn. No answer. Did he not recognize the phone number she was using in her office? *Where the hell is my cell phone?*

A small voice in the back of her head asked if she should be worried about Haydn, but she shrugged it off.

At lunchtime, Lillo brought her a cucumber and watercress sandwich slathered with softened butter and stuffed with sunflower sprouts. Her spirits soared. She was almost through the bulk of the mail and had worked out a plan for sorting and organizing Marilyn's personal possessions upstairs.

Around two o'clock, her office phone rang. Hoping it was Haydn, she grabbed it on the first ring.

Breathless, as though she'd been running, Connie stuttered a few words that Alice couldn't make out.

"Connie, what is it? Are you okay? Where are you?"

"It's Haydn! Haydn's just been arrested for Marilyn Quinn's murder!"

CHAPTER 7

In a panic, Alice fought the midafternoon traffic all the way from Marilyn's house to the downtown police station. Dodging other drivers, she slammed the brakes, shot through open spaces, and pressed long and hard on the horn. In the parking lot on 8th Street, she cut off another driver to nab a space only a short walk from the front entrance.

The rain had come in light showers all day, and it was still cold. She ignored the pain in her knee and nearly ran, peering at the huge limestone-and-glass structure as though she would catch sight of Haydn and wave hello to him.

At the front desk, an officer told her Haydn had been booked, processed, and transferred to the Correctional Complex in Del Valle. She could, if she liked, talk to Detective Cabrera.

"But there's been a terrible mistake," she said, urgency in her tone.

The officer stepped from behind the desk. "I'm sorry, ma'am, but I can't talk to you about anyone. Let me take you to Detective Cabrera's office."

She and the officer bobbed and weaved through crowds of people down a long hall until he asked her to sit on a bench opposite a closed door. The officer had no idea when Cabrera might be available. Alice insisted she would wait.

The hard bench pinched her flesh. Her knee burned, and she rubbed it until the palm of her hand turned red. A strange, noisy parade of bodies passed her in waves.

She wanted to scream, not in pain, but in frustration. *How could Detective Cabrera suspect Haydn had anything to do with Marilyn's murder?* She shuddered at the thought of Haydn in jail.

A young girl—maybe fourteen, far too tender to be in a place like this—sat beside her. She was crying, her thin shoulders heaving under her light jacket. Alice wanted to put her arms around her, to comfort her. She forced herself to turn away. She had no feelings to spare.

A man in handcuffs shuffled past, a small, blonde female officer in uniform leading him. The man wore a hoodie and low-slung jeans that revealed several inches of frayed, gray underwear. As he passed, Alice touched her cheeks, now wet with tears—for the man in handcuffs, for the girl, for Haydn, for herself.

Then out of the crowd, a policeman turned to her. "Ms. Abbott. What a surprise to see you here."

Alice wiped her eyes and looked up at the officer, who showed her a wide smile. He was tall and unbearably thin, with a mop of red hair and a face covered in liver-colored freckles. For the first time in more than sixty years, Alice thought of Howdy Doody.

"Do I know you?" Alice said, still wiping away tears.

"Sorry. It's been a few years," the officer said, still wearing the toothy grin. "Mark Upshaw? I was in your English class at Austin High. I loved that class. *The Great Gatsby*? I've read it two more times since I graduated."

"Mark. Of course. Forgive me. I'm not exactly myself at the moment." *How many years ago could it have been?* If Mark's father hadn't been her dentist, she wouldn't have remembered him at all.

"I understand. Most people I see in here are pretty rattled, for one reason or another."

Alice nodded.

"Say, Ms. Abbott. I'm on my way downstairs to grab a cup of coffee. Do you want to join me?"

"I'd love to, Mark, but I'm waiting to see Detective Cabrera." She hoped he would take no for an answer.

"You may be here for a while. I just saw her leave the building."

ALICE SAT ACROSS FROM MARK in the cafeteria. They both held Styrofoam cups of steaming coffee while Mark chatted about his police training after high school and about a broken engagement to another of Alice's former students. She nodded, struggling to maintain polite interest while barely listening, as she tried to decide what to do next.

Alice couldn't focus on his words. Haydn had been

booked and processed. What did that mean? Cabrera was avoiding her. How could she find out what was happening? How could she—

"Ms. Abbott? Are you okay?"

"Yes. I'm sorry. You were saying?"

Mark knit his red eyebrows, his wide smile gone. He reached out and placed his big, freckled paw on her hand. "Can you tell me why you're here? Is there anything I can do?"

Alice closed her eyes and shook her head. New tears burned her cheeks. She swiped them away as she looked at Mark. "I don't know what anybody can do. You heard about the arrest in Marilyn Quinn's murder?"

Mark nodded, took his hand away from hers, and rubbed his palms together, elbows on the table.

"I worked for Ms. Quinn. The man in custody is a friend of mine. I came here hoping to see him, or—at the least—to talk to Detective Cabrera, to ask her what's going on. It's a terrible mistake. My friend didn't even know Marilyn Quinn."

"I see," Mark said.

No, you don't see. She settled the strap of her bag on her shoulder and reached for her coat. "Thank you for the coffee, Mark. It's been a pleasure to see you after so many years."

"Ms. Abbott," he said, "I was here when Mr. Lawrence was booked. I can tell you he has an attorney and he seemed to be fine. Does that help?"

"Thank you. Yes, that helps. Just to know he's okay."

Mark smiled at her, no teeth this time. "I'm glad. And I'm really sorry Detective Cabrera left the building without seeing you. That's not at all like her. I'm sure she'll get in touch with you as soon as she can. Please go on home."

"Oh. I think it's best if I just wait."

"It may be a long time, Ms. Abbott. Please go home. I'll leave a note for Cabrera to call you as soon as she can."

Unable to stop herself, Alice bent her head and sobbed. "What can I do, Mark? What can I do?"

He took a handkerchief from his back pocket and handed it to her. "I'm afraid there's nothing you can do right now but wait," he said in a soft voice. "You probably won't even be able to see Mr. Lawrence for a day or two."

Alice covered her face with the handkerchief, pressing it to her eyes.

"This is my contact information here at the station." Mark slid a card across the table. "Please call me if I can do anything."

Alice nodded, the handkerchief still covering her face.

Mark stood and rested his hand on her shoulder. And then he left.

WHEN SHE RETURNED TO THE ESTATE, Alice tried to focus on office correspondence, but it was impossible. The voice mailbox on the office landline was full.

Marilyn would have hit the ceiling, had she known.

Alice's knee throbbed. She had been vaguely aware of the pain all day, but now it turned to agony. Reaching through the morass in her shoulder bag, she touched the familiar shape of an aspirin bottle and retrieved it. She swallowed two tablets without water before she again listened to messages on the phone.

Alice noted names and phone numbers from enough messages to clear the system so it could continue recording incoming messages. Then she called Mark to thank him for his offer to stay in touch. She exhaled a sigh of relief, just to know she had a contact inside the police department.

"Officer Upshaw is not available at the moment," a pleasant woman's voice said. "May I take your name and number and ask him to return your call?"

Alice left her information. She stared at the mail piled on her desk and rotated her chair to face the garden. The sky was turning darker, promising another raging thunderstorm soon. She struggled against the tears that threatened to choke her again.

"Alice?"

She jumped at the sound of the voice. She spun around. Marilyn's daughter balanced warily on crutches in the doorway.

"Georgia," Alice said, swallowing hard. She wondered how long the young woman had been standing there.

"Hello, Alice." Georgia attempted a half-smile

that faded within seconds. "Do you have a moment?"

"Oh, my dear, of course I do. Please come in." Alice braced herself against the desk and stood, letting the pain slice through her knee. She fought to put Haydn out of her mind for now. Giving in to the knee, she limped toward the younger woman and took her elbow. Together, they managed to settle Georgia into the same armchair Ava had taken earlier.

Alice admired Georgia, who had a hugely successful modeling career. While her work kept her from visiting her mother often, Georgia's presence was palpable throughout the house in photographs and paintings and the pages of fashion magazines that Marilyn proudly, yet tastefully, displayed.

Georgia wore a slim black skirt and a simple gray cashmere sweater. She wore no makeup. Not that she needed makeup. Her strong jawbone dominated her square face and set off her large, dark eyes and full lips. She lifted her long, thin leg at the knee, just above the cast, and placed it next to the knee of her other leg so that both legs rested at a graceful angle with her torso. A photographer's dream. Not even Marilyn had that kind of poise.

A scar on the girl's forearm just above the wrist caught Alice's eye. An old scar, it seemed out of place on Georgia's perfect body.

Georgia noticed Alice's interest and touched the scar. "A horse bit me long ago," she said. "I mask it with makeup when I'm working."

Alice reddened, regretting that she'd stared. She

eased herself into the chair next to Georgia and leaned forward. She wanted to pat Georgia's arm, make some gesture of warmth and openness, but something held her back.

"How are you, dear? I'm so sorry this dreadful—"

"Thank you." Georgia reached for Alice's hand and gave it a tender squeeze.

Alice's skin tingled at the iciness of Georgia's fingers. "I have a lot of mail for you—cards and letters of condolence. Do you want it now, or shall I forward all of it to you in New York?"

"No, please. Will you handle it?"

Alice nodded.

Georgia closed her eyes and shook her head. "I can't believe she's gone."

"Well, of course. Whose life wouldn't be totally upended in the face of—"

"Yes. Upended." Georgia paused. "May I have a glass of water, Alice?"

"Of course." Alice pushed herself up from the chair and limped as fast as she could to the cabinet in the corner of her office. As she poured water into a small crystal glass, she wondered if the professional model's critical eye were assessing the extra ten pounds recently settled on Alice's behind. *I'm being unfair. She's just lost her mother. My rear end is probably the last thing on the poor girl's mind.*

Georgia's hand trembled as Alice handed her the glass. Alice stood by her side as she sipped and then placed the glass on Alice's desk. After a deep breath, she sobbed, covering her face with both hands. "I can't..."

Alice wrapped her arms around the woman and let her cry, patting her back as her thin shoulders heaved.

In a moment, Georgia pulled away and offered a thin smile. "I miss her so much." She picked up the glass and sipped again.

Alice sat on the edge of her chair, prepared to hold her again if needed. Georgia had collected herself, though.

"I know Aunt Ava has asked you to sort through my mother's belongings," Georgia said after a few moments. "I don't want to keep anything except her jewelry, and I think most of that is in her safe deposit box at the bank. I want to sell everything else. The memories make her things too painful to keep."

"I'll be glad to do that, dear."

Georgia sighed. "And the house," she continued. "Did Aunt Ava talk to you about it, about your moving in and managing things for us? Please take the yellow room in the east wing with the door that opens onto the rose garden. It's perfect for you."

"I—I'd like to help, Georgia, but I've never done anything like this before. I have no experience—"

"You'll be fine, Alice. Mother had such faith in your abilities."

Alice stiffened. *Marilyn must have said that some time ago, before her heart attack.*

Georgia continued. "Our realtor can take care

of the sale of everything, the house and all of the furnishings." She paused a moment. "I want it done quickly."

"What about David? He won't want to stay?"

"No!" Georgia raised her voice and her eyes flashed. "I want him out as soon as possible. And don't let him take a thing. Nothing, not anything of my mother's."

Alice's mouth gaped open. "But, Georgia, you don't really believe he would take... You were all so happy as a family. What a lovely Christmas you had together."

Georgia placed her hands in her lap. She shook her head, keeping her eyes fixed on Alice. "If only you knew. Mother didn't want Aunt Ava here. She only agreed at the last moment because I begged her. I needed someone to be a buffer between me and that horrible man she married."

"A buffer? I don't—"

"The police have arrested someone, but they have the wrong person." She reached for the crutches and stood. "I don't know how," she said, "but David murdered my mother."

SOON AFTER SHE RECOVERED from Georgia's shocking accusation, Alice lifted her desk phone and called Detective Cabrera. According to the receptionist, Cabrera wasn't available to take calls. Alice asked to be transferred to Mark Upshaw's line.

"Hello, Ms. Abbott," Mark said. "I was just going to return your call." He lowered his voice to a whisper. "I've been asking around for you. I'm afraid things look bad for your friend. He's going to need a really good lawyer. I see he's hired someone from out of town."

After a slight pause, Alice asked for the attorney's name.

"Sure. It's a guy from Houston, I think. Just let me find his card."

Alice bit her lip and waited.

"Here it is. Geoffrey James," Mark said. "Want his number?

Haydn's worthless nephew. Alice held the phone to her chest for a moment before she answered. "No, Mark. Thank you, but I have his number."

She replaced the phone in its cradle and walked into the garden, letting her mind wander as she assessed the damage the last storm had caused. Some of the mulch had washed away in a corner bed where an edging stone had loosened. She replaced the stone and wiped her hands on her pants.

Mark Upshaw's words haunted her: *I'm afraid things look bad for your friend. He's going to need a really good lawyer.*

And, of course, Haydn had hired Geoffrey James. Geoffrey was a joke, not a real lawyer capable of defending a murder case. He was a mooch who had used Haydn's guilt to take advantage of him for years.

Geoffrey would need her help to prove Haydn's

innocence. And that meant Alice would have to learn what she could, however she could, about the events surrounding Marilyn's death.

ALICE FOUND AVA IN the sitting room, dozing by a fire, a file folder open on her lap. Alice touched the woman's arm to wake her.

"Alice," she said, her brow furrowed at the serious look on Alice's face. "Is something wrong?"

"Yes. Something is very wrong."

"What is it?" Ava put the folder aside and sat up straight.

"It's a friend. I... I have to..." Alice swallowed and started again. "The position we discussed, managing the house and keeping an eye on David's comings and goings?"

Ava nodded.

"I'll take the job. I'll do my best to be lady of the house, to take care of it as Marilyn has."

"That's wonderful news. I know everything will be in very capable hands," Ava said, as her glance shifted to the floor where Alice stood.

Alice glanced down to find dark, wet blotches on the luxurious pile of the rug. *Oh, Lord. Great start.* She had tracked mud in from the garden.

CHAPTER 8

Early on Monday night, Alice took part of a sleeping pill, hoping to rest enough to be alert when she saw Haydn the next afternoon. Instead, the pill provoked a dream that shattered her sleep and left her wide-eyed and anxious for hours.

In the dream, she stood on a dais in a large auditorium. She smoothed the pages of a speech and smiled at the large audience before her.

"Good evening," she said. But she couldn't go on.

Something in her mouth impeded her speech, something hard and smooth, like a marble. She turned away from the podium and spit into her palm. Out came a tooth, a molar. It lay in her hand like a porcelain treasure, brilliant white, its roots long and straight.

Her tongue searched until it found the deep hole in her gum where the tooth had been. She touched her lips and drew back blood-soaked fingertips.

Turning to the crowd to excuse herself, she opened her mouth and her audience gasped.

AFTER SHE DOZED AND THEN woke again before daybreak, she couldn't get comfortable, despite relocating Arthur and punching her pillow. She pulled the comforter up to her chin when she remembered the dream. It was no surprise she was having nightmares, she told herself. She was a seventy-three-year-old retired schoolteacher with a bad knee, hoping to help a worthless lawyer prove that her best friend had not committed a murder.

The icing on the cake was that she had agreed to play lady-of-the-manor in one of Austin's most elegant mansions where her housemate—the victim's widower—was likely the real killer.

What was she thinking? She had worked with young adults her whole career, coaxing them to appreciate the value of their literary heritage, insisting that good books had insights to offer and lessons to teach. What had she learned from TS Eliot or Emily Dickinson about managing a mansion? Or fingering a murderer?

The only good coming from all this was that she still had a job, which might put her in a position to find a clue or hear something suspicious, anything to help Geoffrey with Haydn's defense.

She turned on her side and drew Arthur's warm body close to her. She inhaled at length and willed herself to relax.

And then a slice of moonlight that pressed through the blinds and danced on her bedroom wall made her think of a visit with her mother many years ago. In the small, dark room her mother shared with three other Oak Tree Retirement Home residents, Alice had focused on her mother's thick-soled orthopedic shoes. They were black, she remembered, with Velcro closures.

Her eyes riveted to the shoes, Alice listened without conviction to her mother's defense of Uncle Avery's decision to banish his sister to this piss-soaked hell of a home. "Don't be upset, Alice," her mother told her with a cheerful smile. "I'm an old woman, and Avery knows what he's doing. I'll be fine."

But Alice was furious with her uncle, and with herself, knowing she would never stand up to the man—she didn't have the temperament for such a confrontation. So she gave in, and her mother embraced a life at the mercy of overworked, underpaid employees who wrestled aching, tender bodies out of and into beds, walk-in showers, and wheelchairs.

Alice had promised herself that her own old age would be different, that she'd be independent and active and eager for new experiences. No becoming a ward of the state for Alice Ann Abbott.

That was then. In her current financial situation, she wasn't sure how long she could hold out. According to recent studies she'd read, baby boomers could expect to be hale and hearty well into their nineties.

Her mother had been lucky. Toward the end of two years at Oak Tree, death—in the guise of a staph infection—raced through the facility. As though she had been waiting for a way out, Alice's mother, a month after her sixty-ninth birthday, was one of the first to succumb.

LATER IN THE MORNING, Alice dressed and readied herself to see Haydn at the Del Valle jail. She leaned into the bathroom mirror with a tube of lipstick, but her hand trembled, so she tossed the tube back in her bag. How much would a dab of lipstick help, anyway? She hadn't been able to eat. Her breathing came shallow and irregular. Her heart raced.

Some of her misery was enhanced by lack of sleep—the nightmare imagery of the lost tooth still haunted her—but most of it was the anxiety about seeing her friend.

She paid close attention to television news reports that showed Haydn, rumpled and confused, escorted into the downtown Austin jail in handcuffs, and later read details of his arrest in the front-page article in the *Statesman*. According to the paper, on the night of the murder, occupants of the mansion were awakened by a single gunshot and then found Marilyn lying in the entryway, just inside the threshold of the open front door.

With a gasp of disbelief, Alice learned Haydn had been at the mansion that night. Neighborhood security cameras had recorded him walking through the wooded side yard toward the house at about the time she was murdered, and then running back to his car. The scratches she had noticed on his face on Friday night now made sense.

The fact that he had been at Marilyn's at all—especially at midnight—was surprise enough. As far as Alice knew, Haydn was not acquainted with, had never met, Marilyn. The only connection he had to Marilyn was through Alice. Why had he been there? To defend Alice in some crazy way that only Haydn would have thought appropriate? The whole incident was a terrible, terrible mistake.

Then she read that investigators had found the gun used to kill Marilyn in the side yard near where Haydn was spotted in the security tapes. His fingerprints were on the barrel. No other prints were found.

And then the lines of type revealed another crushing blow. Haydn not only *knew* Marilyn, but he was engaged to her many years ago in Boston, where they both grew up.

Alice dropped the newspaper to the floor and stumbled to the bedroom. She climbed into her unmade bed and drew her knees to her face, her hands knotted in fists pressed to her lips. She lay there, a woman betrayed by a lover who was never hers, and burst into tears.

IN THE JAIL'S VISITING ROOM, Alice and Haydn sat across from each other, separated by a smeared glass window. They spoke into telephones. The one Alice held was sticky. She didn't want to know why.

For the first time since she'd known him, Haydn looked old. Feeble. Afraid. The scratches on his face had formed black scabs.

Alice's eyes burned. She blinked, and fat tears splashed onto the telephone. Crying again. She wondered if these new tears were for Haydn or for herself.

Haydn smiled at her and put his hand on the window. "Alice, please. I'm sorry. I'll be out of here soon. Everything will be okay."

As if to feel his fingers, she touched the glass, trying to hold back more tears. "Why didn't you tell me about Marilyn? I don't... I wasn't—"

"I didn't know how to tell you. I was afraid if you knew, you would see a side of me you wouldn't understand."

Alice bit her lip and willed the tears to stop.

"She and I weren't right together," he went on. "We ended it, and I never saw her again."

"Did you—"

"No," he said in a firm tone. "I didn't kill her. I did go to the house that night to see if I could catch sight of her daughter."

"Georgia?"

"Yes. I know it sounds ridiculous, but I couldn't stop myself. I hoped to see her through a window? I don't know."

"But why, Haydn? Why Georgia?"

He shook his head, looked away from her as if he

hadn't heard the question. "I hid in the wooded area along the side of the house," he continued. "I couldn't see the entrance. When I heard the shot, I tried to run back to my car. The Christmas lights went out at the same time, so I was blinded for a few seconds. And then a heavy thud next to my foot." He glanced at her face and then away again. "I reached down and picked it up. It was the gun they found later with my fingerprints on it, of course. I dropped it right away— it burned my fingers—and then I ran."

Alice had no words. She sat, straining to touch his fingers through the glass, struggling to process all she had learned, trying to articulate questions that burned in her brain. Too soon, a jail guard escorted Haydn back to his cell.

Alice sat there, frozen in place, until an officer tapped her on the shoulder. She was still holding the sticky receiver to her ear.

As soon as she left the jail, Alice rifled through her wallet and found a business card that Haydn had given her years earlier to use in case of an emergency. The sun had returned and spiked the temperature. She drove to the nearest convenience store and rushed in to use one of the few remaining pay telephones in Austin. She needed to talk to Geoffrey as soon as possible.

However, a big cowboy in muddy boots and a belly that spilled over his belt was using the phone to make up with his girlfriend. Alice stood close to him and caught his eye. She was prepared to say she had an emergency and needed the phone right away, but the man glared at her and then turned his back, so she nodded and moved to a tall carousel of picture postcards to wait.

The sound system played Jimmie Dale Gilmore singing "Mack the Knife." She leaned against a cooler of beer, closed her eyes, and focused on the song, on Gilmore's haunting voice with his unmistakable Texas twang.

At the end of the song, the caller was still sweet-talking a woman he must have offended by buying another woman a drink at Donn's. That would be Donn's Depot, Alice figured, Austin's old train depot-turned-honkytonk with a small dance floor where Donn Adelman had been singing country music since the early 1970s.

How long would this guy be on the phone? Should she try to drive all the way back to Marilyn's and use the phone there?

Where is my damn cell phone?

She chewed her thumbnail and studied the post-cards on the carousel. They were all of Austin: the skyline at night, the Stevie Ray Vaughn memorial at Ladybird Lake, the food trucks on South First Street. A vertical one featured the Frost Building, which gave the city an eerie Gotham City feel at twilight, and next to it were several of the Willie Nelson statue downtown. Others depicted the state capitol,

Pennybacker Bridge, Treaty Oak, and various iterations of the massive campus of the University of Texas.

Jimmy Dale moved on to the Grateful Dead's "Ripple," and Alice hummed along absently, sucking a trickle of blood she'd coaxed from her nail.

"Jist fergit it, Crystal!" the big cowboy shouted into the telephone. He slammed the receiver against the wall and strode out the door.

Everyone froze, and silence shot through the store, Jimmy Dale's tinny voice hanging in the air like a hymn. Alice and the other patrons in the store stared wide-eyed after the man.

As voices buzzed again, Alice sidled over to the telephone, left swaying on its short cord, like a pitiful remnant. She held it to her ear. "Hello?" she said in a timid voice, in case Crystal was still on the line.

But Crystal already had forgotten whatever it was the cowboy told her to forget. The line was free.

By the time Alice dialed the number on the card in her hand, a normal volume of chatter resumed around her, the cowboy and his nasty temper all but forgotten. She hoped Haydn's lawyer, Geoffrey James, Esq., would answer right away.

The attorney wasn't available, a voicemail message told her, but her call was important to him, so she should leave a message. She didn't bother.

Instead she got back in her car and took several deep breaths in an effort to calm her frayed nerves. Her stomach turned.

The sun blazed, and she closed her eyes against the glare. Humid air hung on her like a blanket. Her head ached; her knee throbbed. She drove to the side of the store and parked.

She rested her forehead on the steering wheel and closed her eyes, hoping to focus her thoughts. Instead, images flashed like a fun-house slide show: the yellow tape cookie-cutter pattern of Marilyn's dead body; Owen arching his sweaty body between Marilyn's open legs; Ava writing a check without a care in the world; an arrogant Geoffrey James posturing in a courtroom; Mark Upshaw saying, "Your friend is going to need a really good lawyer."

Her stomach lurched. She sat back and swallowed to ease the burn in her throat. After a moment, she dropped her head on the headrest and closed her eyes again, forcing herself to focus on one thing only: Haydn.

His precious face appeared, and her mind wandered through the years of his odd relationship with Geoffrey James.

Geoffrey's mother, Meghan, was about Haydn's age and his only playmate for most of his growing-up years. When Haydn left Boston to attend college at Juilliard, Meghan stayed in Boston, lived at home, and attended Tufts. She was eighteen, and she fell in love with the first boy who kissed her.

Meghan eloped with the boy. Her parents gave her one chance to get rid of him, and when she refused, they promptly disinherited her and cut off all communication.

No one was surprised when the boy abandoned Meghan as soon as she became pregnant. Desperate, in her ninth month, she borrowed enough money for a bus ticket to Austin, the boy's hometown. She found him, but he wanted nothing to do with Meghan or the baby.

Out of money, without a car, and close to her delivery date, Meghan found help at a downtown Austin church. She delivered a healthy baby boy whom she named Geoffrey, after his father, and with continued help from the church, she raised the child alone.

Meghan sent Haydn regular updates on the boy. In the last note he received, she wrote that Geoffrey was selling shoes at Barton Creek Mall and living at home with her.

And then a few years later, Geoffrey contacted Haydn to tell him that Meghan was dying.

Haydn was dealing with the recent death of both of his parents. He had never married, had no children. In a bold, generous move typical of Haydn, he retired early, sold his home, and moved to Austin to nurse his friend.

Meghan died with Haydn by her side. Haydn promised her he would care for Geoffrey as though he were his son, the son that she and Haydn should have had.

Alice sighed, shifted her position on the car seat. She dozed for a moment and woke with a start that eased within seconds. She couldn't move. Not yet. She was too comfortable, too heavy with sleep, the sun too warm. She closed her eyes and the story continued.

Geoffrey knew all about Haydn's promise to Meghan. At his mother's funeral, he told Haydn he needed money to go to law school. Haydn gave him the money without a second thought.

After law school, Geoffrey practiced in Houston, where he built a loyal client base of repeat-offender types, mostly drug dealers and prostitutes. He never stopped coming to Haydn, though, for handouts to support a lifestyle he wanted but couldn't afford. He needed money for country club dues, a Caribbean vacation, shooting lessons, a new car. Haydn, honoring his promise to Meghan, never turned him down.

Now, sitting in a jail cell, fighting for his life, Haydn was paying the ultimate tribute to Meghan's memory by allowing Geoffrey to defend him in a murder trial. What a terrible, terrible mistake.

Alice felt herself softening in the late afternoon sunshine. She let her head roll to the side, and she slept.

A LIGHT TAPPING ON THE front window woke Alice from her little nap. Detective Cabrera smiled down at her. Embarrassed, Alice wiped a bit of drool from her cheek. After a moment, she remembered she was still at the filling station near the Del Valle jail.

"Good afternoon, Ms. Abbott. I was at the jail and stopped to get gas. I was surprised to see you sitting in your car here. Are you all right?"

"Oh, yes. I—I haven't been sleeping well."

"I understand you wanted to see me."

"I apologize for bothering you," Alice said, blinking against the bright sunshine. "Could we go somewhere and have a coffee?"

Cabrera chewed her bottom lip as she thought for a moment and then suggested Jasmine's on Highway 71. Alice started her car and glanced in the rearview mirror, tilting it down to check for signs of her recent nap. Her hair had flattened on one side where she had laid her head. The circles under her eyes seemed darker, but otherwise she saw nothing unexpected.

How can that be? Where was the hopelessness and helplessness she felt? Where was the image of her that really mattered?

"WHAT CAN I DO FOR YOU, Ms. Abbott?" Cabrera said. "I was told you know the man we arrested for the murder of your former employer."

At once, Alice realized how involved she was in this case on a personal level. She wondered if Cabrera meant to suggest that.

Alice put her elbows on the table, pushed her glasses to the top of her head, and rubbed her eyes hard. The nap had felt good, but it had left her groggy, fuzzy-headed. A waitress brought coffee. Alice added sugar and stirred, buying time while she sorted her thoughts. She trembled, which made her wonder if it was her nervous state or the steady blast of cold air whooshing from an air conditioning vent above her. The temperature outside had reached almost eighty degrees. That's when Texas places of business switched from heat to air-conditioning, no matter what the time of year.

"Detective," Alice said, folding her hands in her lap, "from what I've read and heard on the news, I can see that Haydn's actions on the night of the murder look suspicious, but I know he wouldn't have killed Marilyn. Haydn hadn't seen her in years. What possible motive could he have?"

"Ms. Abbott, you really need to talk to Mr. Lawrence's attorney about this. I'm not the one to ask about a motive."

The heat rose in Alice's neck. It was critical for Cabrera to know Haydn's situation. This was no time to be timid. "I don't know if you've met his lawyer, Detective. Haydn knew Geoffrey James's mother. He hired Geoffrey because he feels guilty about not helping the mother years ago. A murder case—especially a high-profile one like this—is well out of his reach."

Cabrera took a sip of the hot coffee, rubbed at the scar on the side of her face. "Ms. Abbott, whether or not he's capable isn't for us to decide."

Alice smiled. "I know. Thank you for that reminder."

The coffee did not set well on Alice's empty stomach, but it helped her focus, so she kept at it. She could sense Cabrera's impatience.

"May I ask if you've dismissed Marilyn's husband as a suspect?" Alice whispered. "You know that Marilyn's daughter thinks he's the murderer."

Cabrera shook her head, set her cup in its saucer on the table, and motioned to the waitress for the check. "That's something for Mr. Lawrence's attorney to look into. It's all in my notes in the investigation file, which the attorney can share with you if he chooses."

Alice took off her glasses and placed them on the table. "Thank you for your time, Detective."

"Ms. Abbott, sometimes people aren't who we think they are. This scar?" She ran her finger along the shiny white surface. "I got it from a man I was crazy about. I had known him for years. I trusted him with my life, with my children. And then, like overnight, my knight in shining armor turned into a violent, mean-spirited son of a bitch. A lesson I'm reminded of every day of my life."

Alice replaced her glasses and tried to avoid looking at Cabrera. She focused on an eye-popping pink sombrero hanging on a bright orange wall behind the detective. The toe of her shoe found a crack in the concrete floor.

The waitress placed the check on the table and Cabrera reached in her pocket. Alice opened her purse, but Cabrera waved her off.

"My point is," Cabrera said, "we never really know people. We never know their hearts, their secrets. You think you know Mr. Lawrence, but people tend to do bad and good according to their needs."

Alice's eyes darted from the sombrero to the detective. She opened her mouth to interrupt, but Cabrera held out her hand, palm facing Alice.

"I'm not saying Mr. Lawrence is guilty of anything. I'm saying you need to trust Mr. Lawrence's attorney and have faith in the system. You must stay out of it, Ms. Abbott. You could do more harm than good. And you could get hurt."

Alice nodded, defeated.

Cabrera tossed a few bills on the table. She half-rose from her chair and then sat again.

"There's something that still puzzles me, Ms. Abbott. When Ms. Quinn called you before she died, she asked a question. Do you remember?"

"Yes, I do," Alice said, as if she were dragging the words out, replaying the message in her head. She looked into Cabrera's eyes. "It was the beginning of a question. She asked me, 'Why would she—?'"

"Right. Do you have any idea what she meant by that? Who was Ms. Quinn talking about?"

Alice had almost forgotten the question. Now it filled her head again. *What could it possibly mean?*

CHAPTER 9

Wednesday was the day of Marilyn's funeral. Alice phoned Geoffrey again and left a message, although she was certain he wouldn't return her calls. Either Geoffrey didn't remember who she was or he was avoiding her on purpose. They had seen each other many times at Haydn's over the years. She was certain he remembered her.

When she arrived at Marilyn's, she was prepared to stay in accordance with the arrangements she'd made with Ava. Connie would feed Arthur and keep an eye on Alice's house while Alice lived in the glamorous estate in West Austin.

Since it was early, the family had not yet departed for services in Tarrytown, so Alice left her small suitcase in the car. She had packed enough clothes and toiletries for a week, intending to return home as needed to take care of paying bills and other household chores.

Alice planned to settle into the yellow room in the east wing, as Georgia had suggested. Under any other circumstances, Alice would have been thrilled. She adored that bedroom with its sunny décor and the

French doors that opened on Marilyn's rose garden.

When she walked through the kitchen, a short, beefy man wearing a gray suit and wraparound dark glasses seemed comfortable enough to lean against the refrigerator with his arms crossed at his chest. No doubt he was one of the security guards Ava had hired. Those guys always have a look, she thought, and this one modeled every detail, right down to the Bluetooth earpiece and the chewing gum.

Alice gave him a shy smile. No response. Maybe he hadn't noticed the smile. Maybe he hadn't noticed her at all.

She accepted a cup of sugared coffee from Lillo and headed across the entry hall toward her office, wondering why Ava hadn't canceled the security detail, now that the police had made an arrest. Did Ava suspect the police arrested the wrong person? Did she believe, as Georgia did, that David had murdered Marilyn? Or was the guard there for the same reason Alice was, to protect the estate from David's possible thievery?

As she passed the sitting room, she nodded to David, who glanced at her over a newspaper. His black suit and tie and an optic white shirt set off his tan and his sun-kissed blond hair that fell precisely as it was styled to do. *He's gorgeous. Could he really have been so cold-hearted as to shoot Marilyn?*

She shuddered, now grateful for the unfriendly man in the kitchen. She liked David, but someone had killed Marilyn, and it wasn't Haydn.

As she turned to open her office door, she spied Ava and Georgia waiting for a car at the front door. Georgia was seated and was speaking to her aunt, but Ava shushed her the moment Alice caught her eye.

They were as stunning as twins dressed in chic black suits and hats. Both women held small black Bibles. Except for the white cast on Georgia's ankle, they could be on their way to an haute couture fashion show, or—as Georgia turned her face and revealed a slash of dark red lipstick—a meeting of a coven of witches.

Georgia gave her a faint smile, and Alice lifted her hand in a small wave.

In their similar costumes, they could have been mother and daughter, not aunt and niece. Alice had never noticed their resemblance until this moment. Georgia looked more like her aunt than her mother. Alice hesitated a moment, taking in the similarity, before she closed the door.

More handwritten notes waited on her desk, a rather long one from Ava and a brief one from Georgia. Ava's note answered Alice's question about the security guard: The service would continue as long as David was in the house. Out of kindness, and against Georgia's wishes, Ava was allowing David to stay on until the house sold. He was permitted to use the SUV Marilyn had given him as long as he was living in the house. He was not to drive Marilyn's Jaguar, which would be picked up by the end of the week.

So much for Alice's hope that Ava suspected David of anything more than thievery.

The rest of the note included household instructions: Lillo would stay on to cook and Trish would remain to look after the housekeeping. Ava and Georgia would leave Austin after the funeral services in the church. They didn't plan to attend Marilyn's burial, so meals would be necessary only for Alice, David, Trish, and the guard on duty.

The next page of the note outlined business details. Most of Marilyn's current customers had been notified to contact Ava, but she worried that important correspondence could be lost, especially since the police still had the office computers. To avoid that, Ava arranged to have Marilyn's incoming email copied to Alice's personal account on her home computer.

At the bottom of the page, Ava wrote that a new cell phone would be delivered to Alice later in the day. The last sentence, Alice thought, was unnecessary:

Keep the new phone with you at all times, in case I need to contact you.

Did Ava think Alice had lost her phone on purpose to avoid getting calls?

Georgia's note said,

Dearest Alice, Thank you for agreeing to help us at this difficult time. Please begin sorting my mother's things and get the house sold as soon as possible. I found all of her jewelry in her safe-deposit

box except for her favorite pieces—the earrings she's
wearing in the portrait of the two of us in the sitting
room. Let me know as soon as you find them.
                                    Fondly, Georgia

The front door opened and closed. Alice waited a
moment and then walked out of her office to watch
Marilyn's family—sister Ava, daughter Georgia, and
husband David carrying Georgia in his arms—get
into the limousine that would take them to Marilyn's
funeral.

ALICE TIPTOED INTO HER NEW job as lady of Marilyn's
grand home. She contacted the family realtor, who
told her he would begin right away to prepare the
house for sale, although he recommended waiting a
few months before advertising the listing. Because
of the circumstances of Marilyn's death, the listing
would have to disclose the crime, so the more
distance between the time of the murder and the
announcement of the sale, the better.

A few months? Alice had not planned to be a resi-
dent for months.

On the other hand, a few months meant she would
have a job—a good-paying one—as long as she didn't
screw it up. Except for major decisions, Ava had
made clear, she didn't want to be bothered with the
house or the daily activities within it. Again, Alice
reminded herself that she was in over her head. She

dug into her bag, finding the bottle of aspirin and a chocolate bar. She swallowed two aspirin and bit into the chocolate bar before she started on the mail.

Staying for an extended period also meant she would have access to David for a longer time, and, she hoped, she would be able to keep an eye on any suspicious activities he may be involved in.

She took her glasses off, rubbed her eyes, and reminded herself that the evidence against Haydn seemed solid. Haydn knew Marilyn and knew her intimately. Who had ended their engagement? And under what—

A knock on the door derailed her thoughts. It was Trish, telling her she had retrieved Alice's suitcase from the car and unpacked her things in the yellow room.

"Trish, thank you, but please don't treat me like a guest. I'm here only to help with the sale of the house. I can take care of myself."

"You may as well enjoy the full treatment. Ava told me to treat you as I would treat Marilyn. She said you're the boss until the house sells."

Alice frowned and wrinkled her nose.

Trish smiled. "Just enjoy," she said as she backed out of the room and closed the door.

Alice readjusted her glasses and went back to working on the mail. Her goal was to get all of the bills paid and invoices posted well before three o'clock, when she planned to see Haydn again in Del Valle.

As she separated office mail from cards and letters of condolence, one small envelope caught her eye. It was a subtle beige color, with a name and address embossed on the back flap. On the front, Georgia's name and Marilyn's address had been handwritten in tiny, shaky script.

Alice glanced again at the return address. It was from someone in Boston.

Boston? Haydn and Marilyn had been engaged in Boston. Was this someone who might have known the two when they were a couple?

She reached for the letter opener and slit the top fold of the envelope.

Dearest Georgia, the note began. It was written by the same unsteady hand that addressed the envelope.

An old person's hand. Lately, Alice had noticed the same twitchy tics in her own handwriting when she posted a note or wrote a grocery list. Such a sad end for a girl who had won a penmanship prize in third grade.

You probably won't remember me, but I was your neighbor when you and your mother lived in Boston many years ago. You frequently stayed with me when your mother was working. You were such a beautiful child.

I read in the paper that your mother recently died. I have worried so much about you over the years. I hope you are healthy and happy.

"Please accept my sympathies for your loss.
Fondly,
Charlotte Bauer

Alice pursed her lips and put the note back in its envelope. Why would Charlotte Bauer be worried about Georgia over the years? Marilyn's daughter grew up with every advantage and was a fabulously successful adult.

SOMETIME BEFORE NOON, David returned from the funeral. He went straight upstairs and came back down soon after. Then he started Marilyn's Jaguar and roared out of the driveway.

"Oh, my God!" Alice cried aloud. "He's not supposed to drive that car!"

Without thinking, she grabbed her bag and rushed to her Toyota at the back of the house. David couldn't drive too fast through this neighborhood without being stopped, so she was confident she could catch him and remind him to drive his SUV.

The Toyota started on the first try, rounded the circular drive, and took her down Pascal Lane to the community gates just before Highway 360. There the Jaguar was poised to leap forward. The recent gashes in the silver paint caught her eye again.

With a sudden chill, she thought of the nasty scratches on Haydn's sweet face.

She dismissed thoughts of Haydn and made

herself focus on the Jaguar. She intended to pull up behind David and honk to get his attention, but surely he knew not to drive the car. What was she doing? She needed to get back to Marilyn's mail.

She gripped the steering wheel and slid the gear into reverse. But as David turned onto the highway, the driver behind her blasted his horn. She jumped, and caught by the seatbelt, she shoved the gear back into drive and turned onto the highway behind David.

David hadn't noticed her. The traffic was already heavy, so she passed the first opportunity to turn around and continued south, her eyes glued to the Jaguar in the lane to her left, several cars ahead of her. *Where could he be going?*

When the Jaguar signaled to exit at Bee Cave Road, Alice still lagged several cars behind. It would be easy for her to make the exit from her lane and follow him as he headed east.

At MoPac Expressway, the Jaguar signaled again to enter the south lanes of the freeway. A wave of panic surged through her due to the unavoidable conclusion that David would notice her car. She slowed, struggling to make a decision while she approached the next exit that would allow her to turn back north toward Marilyn's. At the last moment, she drove past the exit, convinced David would find nothing suspicious about her heading south on MoPac at the same time he was.

Two cars still separated them, and it didn't appear that David had seen her. Maybe he was preoccupied with thoughts about the funeral. Or about his future. Or about getting away with murder.

She followed him for miles on MoPac, wondering at some point if he was leaving town. By the time he turned on Convict Hill Road, she had all but decided to abandon her pursuit.

As luck would have it, enough traffic let Alice put two more cars between them before David pulled into Tony's, a former filling station now operating as a body shop. Alice drove past the shop, made a U-turn in an apartment complex parking lot, and crept back toward Tony's. She parked down the street and waited.

Soon, a taxi drove into Tony's parking lot. Alice watched David get in it and leave.

So he had taken Marilyn's car to be repaired. But why here? Why not at the dealership that had erased traces of Marilyn's careless driving in the past?

Alice drove into the parking lot at Tony's and inquired if she could make an appointment to have her car repaired. Tony, a thin young man with the high cheekbones and dark skin of an Aztec god, was happy to oblige her.

"Come right in, ma'am," he said, ushering her into his tiny office as he glanced at the battered exterior of the little Toyota.

While he looked through his appointment book, Alice said, "Excuse me, but that man I just saw get into the taxi? Was that David Rhodes? The husband of that poor woman who was murdered last week?"

"Yes, ma'am. It sure was," Tony said, looking up from the book. "You saw his picture in the paper?"

Alice nodded.

Tony grinned, proud of his acquaintance with a celebrity. "Mr. Rhodes is one of the richest men in town, I guess," he said. "And one of the nicest, too. He's brought that slick Jaguar in here a couple of times for maintenance. This time, it's for bodywork. Somebody keyed the hell out of it—those scratches are deep."

"Keyed?"

"Yes, ma'am. You know, somebody dragged a key across the paint."

"On purpose?" Alice said.

Tony nodded.

"My, he has suffered, hasn't he? The papers said he and the murdered woman had been married only a few weeks."

"Yes, ma'am, that's right. But he's never been rude or in a hurry. Like today, nothing but 'please' and 'thank you' and 'would you mind this or that.' Nice guy."

"Good to hear."

"Right. And not all hoity-toity, either. Do you know he sometimes hand-washes that car? And he does basic maintenance on it, too. He adds his own antifreeze. Came in here right after he moved to town and got a bottle. Said he likes to do the simple stuff himself."

"Is that so?"

"Yeah. Asked if I had any of the old formula. Said he'd take it off my hands if I did." Tony shrugged. "I'm probably boring you by talking shop." He ran his finger down a page in the appointment book. "How about next Thursday, ma'am? I could get you in for an estimate then."

Alice explained she needed something sooner and excused herself. It was getting late. She had to be at the jail at three o'clock, or she would miss her opportunity to see Haydn.

GEOFFREY JAMES WAS A LARGE man who used his impressive size to project his self-importance. He strode across the busy waiting area in the Del Valle jail like a posh yacht pushing its way through a crush of stinking shrimp boats. He wore his hair short and sported a clipped goatee that might have been shaped by a professional. His narrow shoulders, stately girth, and small feet gave him an odd, egg-shaped appearance.

Alice hurried to catch him before he left the building. "Geoffrey," she called.

He stopped and glanced at the crowd behind him. Seeing no one he recognized, he continued toward the exit.

"Geoffrey James," Alice called again, pushing her way toward him. She waved to catch his eye.

He raised one eyebrow and sighed, waiting for her to reach him.

"Geoffrey, I'm Alice Ann Abbott, Haydn's friend," she panted. "We've met several times at Haydn's home."

He held a beautiful leather briefcase in both hands behind his back. He looked down at her, his expression impassive.

Alice waited for a response. "I'd like to talk to you about Haydn's case," she said after a moment. "You see, I worked for Ms. Quinn, and I may be in a position to help you."

"Thank you. I have your contact information. I'll be in touch." He turned away from her, but she caught his arm.

"You don't understand. There are—"

He pinched the corner of her sleeve with his thumb and forefinger and removed her hand from his suit.

"I'll be in touch," he repeated.

TRYING TO TALK TO GEOFFREY had cut into Alice's time with Haydn. When she walked into the visitation room, only a few moments remained for them to be together.

Haydn appeared to be in somewhat better spirits—Geoffrey had promised he would be out on bail by the weekend.

"Haydn, do you really think it's wise to depend on Geoffrey for your defense?"

"I do, even though you don't. I realize he's taken advantage of me over the years, but this case could make his career skyrocket. At last I can do something to help him become the man who would make his mother proud."

"But, he's never even tried a murder case, has he?"

Haydn locked his fingers on the table that separated them, took a deep breath, and bowed his head. "Alice," he said in a low voice, looking at the table, "I've never forgiven myself for my absence and my lack of support for Meghan as Geoffrey grew up. I could have eased their struggles considerably if I'd sent them a few dollars here and there, visited with them, and taken an interest in Geoffrey."

"You had no obligation to do any of that."

His eyes met hers. "Yes, I did," he said. "I committed a sin of omission that haunts me every day of my life. Meghan tried to engage me over the years. I never even answered her letters. I don't talk to you about how I feel because you won't understand. You're too generous and giving, too aware of the needs of the people around you to recognize the burden I carry. It's my decision to have Geoffrey help me through this crisis, Alice, my way of having a family, of finding redemption. Please don't mention it again." He smiled at her.

What could she do but return the smile? She knew him well enough to know she couldn't change his mind.

Haydn asked Alice to bring some of his books to their next visit, so before she returned to Marilyn's, she stopped at his home in Pemberton Heights, a neighborhood in Central Austin of expensive old homes and wide, lush lawns.

Geoffrey would live in the home as long as Haydn needed his help. In addition, Geoffrey was also driving Haydn's car, which Haydn always kept in the garage. The Mercedes was now parked in the driveway.

The key she had didn't fit the front door lock. She had used it as recently as two weeks earlier to water plants when Haydn was out of town, so it didn't make sense, unless—

"Of course," she mumbled. "Geoffrey has changed the locks. I should have expected that." She pressed her thumb on the bell and held it there. "I've had just about enough of this egomaniacal bastard."

When Geoffrey opened the door, he held his hands at his sides, fuming, fists clenched. "What do you want?"

Alice explained that she needed to pick up a few of Haydn's books. He stared at her for a moment as though debating his answer, and then stepped aside to let her enter.

Haydn's longtime housekeeper, Gwen, leaned on a cane behind Geoffrey, a tenuous smile on her thin face. The woman's back was frozen in an awkward curve, a permanent posture that caused her to turn her head to the side to look into anyone's eyes. Alice never understood how she managed Haydn's house with such a pronounced physical disability. She suspected Haydn did most of the cleaning and cooking himself.

Alice touched Gwen's shoulder and walked down the hallway to the study, passing the living room on her way.

The weather had turned cold again, and a few logs burned in the living room fireplace. Alice glanced into the room and caught a glimpse of a woman—a girl, really—holding a glass of something with ice in it. She wore dark eyeshadow and shiny pink lipstick. Her glossy dark hair was cut in a shaggy style with electric blue accents at the ragged edges.

Alice bit her lip and said nothing.

Gwen followed Alice into the study and closed the door behind them.

Through a window that opened to the back yard, bright sunshine fanned across a green leather sofa and picked out metallic book titles on the shelves that lined the wall. Alice closed her eyes and breathed in the familiar scent of her old friend.

Gwen touched her sleeve. "Alice, how is Mr. Lawrence?" she said. "Have you seen him?"

They sat side by side on the sofa. Gwen, all but doubled over in the seated position, rested her hands on her cane.

Alice lowered her voice to a whisper, hoping Gwen would do the same. She had an odd feeling that Geoffrey was standing in the hallway with his ear pressed to the door. "Haydn seems to be fine, Gwen," she said. "How are you doing here with Mr. James?"

Gwen shook her head and whispered back, "He's fine, I guess. He seems nice. He puts the grocery deliveries away and eats out most of the time." She chuckled and shook her head. "The thing that drives me crazy is the way he leaves his clothes on the floor for me to pick up and take to the cleaners. He just walks out of those expensive suit trousers. He doesn't even toss them on a chair." She paused. "I miss Mr. Lawrence."

"Me, too."

They sat in silence for another moment.

"Gwen, may I ask you to help me with something?"

Gwen knitted her brow and nodded.

"I'm trying to figure out Geoffrey's defense strategy for Haydn. Geoffrey doesn't like me, so he's not talking to me."

"What can I do?"

Alice hesitated. She didn't want Gwen to become involved in anything underhanded or dangerous.

"If you see anything suspicious here in the house, will you give me a call? I wish I could be more specific, but I can't. Just use your judgment and call me." She found a notepad on Haydn's desk and jotted numbers on the top sheet.

"Your cell phone?" Gwen slipped the sheet into the pocket of her cardigan.

"My office phone," Alice said. No need to tell Gwen about the lost phone. "Let's just keep this between you and me."

"Absolutely. I understand."

Alice considered asking Gwen about the girl in the living room, but she didn't want to push the woman.

Together, they found the books. Alice checked the list to be sure she had everything: a biography of Domenico Scarlatti, a collection of Flannery O'Connor's short stories, and the latest issue of *Journal of Musicology*.

Geoffrey followed Alice to the front door. "You know you can't take those to Haydn, don't you?" he said.

"What?"

"He can't have any books in jail." His features gave her a condescending sneer.

"We know that," she said. "Haydn asked me to check some passages in them." Haydn would be disappointed that he wouldn't get his books, but she refused to let this man get the better of her, even if it meant she had to lie.

She stepped onto the porch and Geoffrey closed the door behind her, engaging the lock with a sharp click that she felt sure he exaggerated for her benefit.

"WILL YOU JOIN ME FOR a cup of coffee, Lillo?"

The new cell phone Ava had promised arrived while she was out, but instead of opening it, Alice placed the box on the kitchen counter and climbed onto a stool.

"*Carissima*, why the long face? Aren't you happy to

be in this *splendida residenza* with none of Marilyn's negative energy?"

Alice removed her glasses and pinched her eyes shut with her fingers. Then she shared her situation with Lillo, starting with her close friendship with the man accused of murdering Marilyn and continuing with her concerns about her new job responsibilities. She told him how worried she was about the worthless attorney Haydn had hired.

"I can help you keep an eye on David. I know when he comes and goes, and I see what he does in the house."

"Thanks. You're a good friend."

He poured two mugs of coffee and added sugar to hers. Before he sat at the counter, he placed a plate of biscotti next to her mug.

Alice dunked one of the almond biscuits into her coffee and munched on it for a few minutes.

"What made you leave, Lillo? After Marilyn's heart attack, you worked for Marilyn longer than any other chef."

"*Sì*. I did. She was a beautiful person—*una bella figura*. I adored her, and she treated me well until she married."

Alice dunked a second biscuit into her coffee. "Yes. She never showed her nasty temper to you." She bit off the moist end of the biscuit and chewed it, waiting for Lillo to go on.

"I don't think the heart attack changed her temper. I saw hurt in her eyes, deep and personal."

Alice frowned, then raised her eyebrows. "What do you mean, Lillo? Who would hurt her?"

He shrugged. "After she married, she became a *strega* to me," he said. "A witch. She started complaining about my cooking."

"What? You're a fabulous chef. Everyone knows that. Did she have a specific complaint?"

"*Pazza!* Said I put too much sugar in everything. *Che esagerazione!* It started right after she came back from Paris with that gigolo. No one else made a fuss, but she insisted. I tried to reason with her, but in the end, she disrespected me. I got my things and walked away. I think she needed me to quit. She didn't want to fire me."

"Why not? She'd fired lots of other chefs."

"It was the agency. They wouldn't send any more people here."

"I thought Marilyn fired the agency. Sounds like it was the other way around."

"Yes, that's true. After I left, they were done with her. When I heard from a friend that someone was needed here again, I hoped you'd still be working for the family. I took the job."

"Thank heavens for that. Have you heard about the cook Marilyn hired after you left?"

"Trish told me. She said David knew him. What a *disastro*." He turned his head and pretended to vomit.

They laughed.

"Thank you, Lillo. I needed that. I haven't laughed

since before Marilyn died."

Alice reached for another biscuit. "It might be helpful to know the truth about where Marilyn found that cook. Do you think you could ask around? See if any of your colleagues know anything about him."

"Sure. Trish told me his name is Bill Wilcox. I didn't know him, and I can tell you he's not a local. At least, not someone who does in-home service. I know everyone in the area who works privately." Lillo stared hard at her. "Alice, you're not trying to do the work your friend's lawyer should do, are you?"

Alice sighed. "I only hope his lawyer will listen to me if I happen to stumble onto something."

Alice dunked yet another biscuit into her coffee, but she stopped before she raised it to her lips. "Oh, my God," she whispered. The heat flashed up her neck.

"What, *Cara*? What?"

She spoke in measured phrases, expressing a realization that had only just occurred to her. "Geoffrey is living in Haydn's house, driving Haydn's car, has access—I'm sure—to Haydn's bank account." She looked up at Lillo. "Geoffrey is living on easy street as long as Haydn stays behind bars. If Haydn is convicted of murder, Geoffrey hits the jackpot. He's Haydn's sole heir."

CHAPTER 10

When Javier Johnson, Marilyn's next-door neighbor, rang the doorbell at dusk, Alice couldn't have been more surprised. After all, Jasper Estates wasn't the sort of community where neighbors dropped in unannounced to borrow a cup of sugar or share a coffee and a slice of pie.

The temperature had taken a plunge when the sun went down, but Johnson wore only a long-sleeved shirt and a light cardigan with his jeans. His bald head was bare. He was pacing when Alice opened the door. He seemed angry about something.

The man was tall, thin, and slump-shouldered. His long nose and small eyes made Alice think of a rat.

He elbowed his way past her into the entryway and called, "David? Caitlin?"

Javier whirled around to Alice, his face inches away from hers. "Where are they?" he barked at her.

"Mr. Johnson, David isn't here. Even Trish is gone. It's just the chef and me, and he'll be leaving soon." She didn't mention the security guard. She never saw the guard and often forgot he was there. "Can I help you with something?"

As though he just that moment realized what he was doing, he stepped away from her and rubbed his head with the flat of his hand, smoothing phantom hair. He took a deep breath. "I'm sorry. I'm from next door. Javier Johnson." He offered his hand.

Alice took his hand. She wasn't surprised he hadn't remembered her. While they'd never been formally introduced, they had seen each other many times, including the evening Marilyn was murdered. Alice had opened the front door that night, greeted Javier and his wife, and invited them in.

"I'm Alice Abbott. I've worked for Marilyn for several years. Marilyn's sister asked me to stay on to help with the logistics of the sale of the home."

"Yes, I remember you now."

He dragged his hand over his head again, but he kept his eyes on her. "I guess I've been a little nervous about coming here so soon after the—" He looked down. "After the other night."

"What can I do for you, Mr. Johnson?"

He looked up, but not at Alice. His eyes darted around the room.

"I think I, uh—I lost a cufflink when my wife and I were here for dinner. Would you know if anyone has found it? I hate to bother you, but the pair were a Christmas present from my daughter, and I'd really like to retrieve the missing one before she notices I'm not wearing them."

"Your daughter?" she said, trying to calm his nerves.

"Yes. She's visiting for the holidays." Javier pulled his wallet from the back pocket of his jeans and opened it to a photo of a girl standing on a beach in a bathing suit. "This is Caitlin. Have you, uh, have you seen her?" Again, his eyes skittered around the entryway and up to the second floor landing.

Alice took the wallet and gazed at the attractive girl's features. Something about her looked familiar.

"I don't think so. Why?"

"She knows David, and I thought you'd met her."

Ah. So Javier suspected his daughter and David were together. She would ask Trish about that.

"She's lovely," Alice said, handing back the wallet. "And I completely understand why you want to find the cufflink, but I haven't the first idea where to look. Trish, the housemaid, will. She'll be back early in the morning. Shall I ask her to call you?"

"Thank you. Uh—it could be in the garden if it's not in the house." He walked to the door and then turned back to face her. "My wife and I are still unnerved over what happened that night. We were here for dinner." He glanced at Alice. "But you already know that." He wiped his hand over his mouth, as if to shove the words back in.

"Yes."

"Of course, of course. The police talked to us. Both of us. For a long time." He took a deep breath. "I think they suspected we had something to do with Marilyn's death."

"The police questioned almost everyone Marilyn

knew," Alice said. "And they've arrested someone, so I don't think they'll bother you anymore."

"We've been so upset." He stared at the floor. "Neither of us has slept. I had an argument with Marilyn at dinner. The police were very interested in that."

Javier needed to talk, maybe get something off his chest, something that could help Haydn. "What did you tell them?" she said. "The police, I mean."

"It was only a misunderstanding about a business venture." Javier lifted his palms toward the ceiling in a gesture of exasperation. Then he stiffened, lowered his hands, and peered at Alice through narrowed eyes. He crossed his arms. "Why do you want to know what I told them? What business is it of yours?"

Alice swallowed and shrugged. She knew better than to push.

"No reason," she said. "I'm as worried as everyone else. Do you remember the meal that night, Mr. Johnson?" she said, hoping to change the subject.

When Javier answered, it was clear he intended to be in charge of the conversation. He was no longer an anxious father looking for a cufflink his daughter had given him. He was in control, an aristocrat talking to a peon.

"Not until the detective reminded me," he said. Tension built between them as he went on. "My wife complained about it as soon as we got home, but I didn't pay much attention. It must have been pretty bad."

"It was." Alice smiled to diffuse the stress she felt.

"Poor Marilyn. She hadn't dined with the family in so long because of her stomach problems. And the one night she does, the meal is inedible."

"Yeah, well," Javier said, "Marilyn didn't eat anything. My wife said she didn't drink anything, either. She just kept going back and forth to the bathroom to throw up. I was too whacked to notice." He moved toward her, his face inches from her own. "Sometimes it's best not to notice too much—don't you agree?"

Alice looked at the floor, wondering if he was threatening her. Her neck burned. She glanced at Javier. "I'm sorry the evening was such a disaster."

He started toward the door, flung it open, and turned to give her one last, disgusted look.

She followed and closed the door behind him. She locked it and leaned against it, trying to recover. Her neck was on fire.

Was the man's bullish behavior a personal strategy he used in dealing with his inferiors, or did he intend to scare her?

Would he come back? How would she handle him if he did?

Handle him? She'd never handled anyone in her life, except for the few teenagers who disrupted her classes over the years. She'd been dropped into a totally different league with the likes of Javier Johnson.

WHEN HER BREATHING SLOWED and the flush in her neck faded, hunger pangs took over. She took a moment to wash her hands and to pat some water onto her cheeks, and then she found Lillo in the kitchen.

"You're still here?" she said.

"*Certo*. I have stayed to serve you dinner."

"Lillo, you could have left something for me to pop into the microwave."

"I'm glad I was here and you were not in the house alone with that man."

Lillo had waited to protect her, standing around the corner the whole time Javier was in the house.

"Tonight you deserve to be pampered," he said, taking her elbow and escorting her into the sitting room where he had started a fire. He stopped at the sofa and seated her. Then he presented her with a crystal old-fashioned glass with two fingers of single-malt scotch and one cube of ice, just as she liked it. He told her that dinner would be served in fifteen minutes.

"It's been a long time since anyone served me a scotch, Lillo. Thank you."

Lillo bent forward at the waist.

"I'd rather not see David. Maybe I should eat in my room, or my office," she said, sipping from the glass.

Lillo shook his head. "He told me he'd be out tonight. Please remember to lock your bedroom door when you go to bed."

She sighed, relieved. She couldn't deal with David tonight. "I will. Will you have dinner with me, Lillo?"

"No, *Signora* Alice. Tonight you need some peace." He turned and left the room.

She stared at the bright fire and wondered if Javier Johnson was involved in Marilyn's murder. Georgia had accused David. Was Geoffrey James looking at Javier and David as possible suspects? Would he step up as a good attorney and help Haydn, or would he see to it that Haydn never left jail?

So far as she knew, Haydn was everyone's target. The police had closed their investigation and handed it over to the district attorney. Haydn was on the security-camera footage fleeing the scene. They had his fingerprints on the gun. All they needed now was a motive, which shouldn't be too hard to create, given Haydn's past relationship with Marilyn.

A strong sense of fair play, or justice, swept over her. Alice would have to find an alternative suspect among a group of people who lived in Marilyn's world, people with money and brazen self-confidence, people like Javier Johnson. God forbid she would have to confront him, or anyone like him, again. She didn't have the nerve.

Alice's eyes traveled from the crackling flames in the fireplace to the portrait above the mantel. She glanced at Marilyn's face and then looked away, back at the fire. After a moment, she took a deep breath and raised her gaze to Marilyn's face again. She stared into Marilyn's eyes and sipped her scotch.

CHAPTER 11

A light knock on her bedroom door woke Alice from the first good sleep she'd had in over a week. She yawned and stretched before she called, "Come in, Trish."

The door opened and Trish bustled in with a tray of coffee, buttered toast, and the morning paper. She set the tray on the low table in front of the silk sofa at the foot of Alice's bed.

"How did you sleep, madam?" she said as she pushed aside the draperies to reveal an intimate flag-stone terrace lined with velvety, cherry-colored rose bushes. A clear blue sky promised a beautiful morning.

"Oh, Trish, can you please, please, please help me? I need to figure out how to take this bed with me when I leave. It. Is. Heaven."

Trish's shoulders jerked straight back at Alice's suggestion. Her smile vanished. "I'll just get your towels," she said as she walked into the bathroom.

Did I say something I shouldn't have? Could Trish think Alice meant they should steal the bed?

Alice's bare toes found her slippers. They felt good to her, homey in spite of all the splendor that surrounded her.

"Trish, did you know that Javier Johnson has a daughter?"

"You mean Caitlin, the slut?" Trish called from the bathroom.

"What?"

Trish appeared in the bathroom door with a few towels draped over her arm. "You don't see it because you're in your office, Alice, but I do. That girl's here all the time. She follows David around like a dog in heat. He won't have anything to do with her, of course, but she doesn't give up. Someone needs to teach her a lesson."

Alice nodded. Her suspicions were right about yesterday. Javier wasn't hunting for a missing cufflink. He was looking for his daughter.

"How did Marilyn feel about Caitlin spending so much time around David?"

"What do you think?" Trish shifted the towels to her other arm. "Caitlin and Marilyn despised each other. I never mentioned this to anyone, but I saw Caitlin key Marilyn's car one afternoon after Marilyn threw her out of the house."

So that's how the beautiful car had been scarred.

"How do I miss all this drama?" Alice said.

"You work with your door closed, your head stuck in that computer monitor. Marilyn and David fought as much about Caitlin as they did about Houston."

"Houston?"

"David and Marilyn argued all the time about him spending so much time there."

"Did you tell Detective Cabrera about Caitlin's interest in David?"

Trish shook her head.

"Did you mention the arguments Marilyn and David had about Caitlin, or about Houston?"

Trish shook her head again as she walked to the door. "No. No one ever asked about any of that."

Great, Alice said to herself, watching Trish leave the room. More possibly critical information that a jury would never hear.

She opened the terrace door and for a moment considered taking her coffee outside. Enough chill in the still air made her close the door and settle herself on the sofa.

The coffee was hot and strong. She took a bite of the toast and snapped open the newspaper.

Marilyn's murder was still the front-page headline, although the story revealed no new information. On an inside page of the front section, a sidebar featured Geoffrey as the defendant's attorney. The article mentioned he had attended law school in Las Vegas. Why Nevada? He was a Texas boy, so he would have paid out-of-state tuition in Nevada.

She shook her head. What difference did it make to Geoffrey how much his tuition cost? Haydn had footed the bill.

LATER IN THE DAY, Alice went to the kitchen for coffee and passed one of the security guards walking through the entryway to the front door.

Lillo smiled at her and shrugged. "These security guys, they're like *fantasmi*, no?"

"Yes. Just like ghosts."

He studied Alice's face. "Are you okay, *Bella*?"

"Much better after that fabulous meal you served me last night. And the scotch."

She sat at the counter. Lillo rested his elbows on the counter across from her and ran his big hands along his powerful upper arms.

"What's that, Lillo? A tattoo?"

"This?" He lifted the left sleeve and showed her a bright red, beautifully rendered image of an elaborate flower about the size of her fist. "It is the symbol of my city, *Firenze*, the *giglio*."

As Alice tried to repeat the word, failing miserably, they both laughed.

"No. *Gillio*," he said again. And then more slowly, "GEE lee oh."

"But Florence is in Italy. That's a *fleur-de-lis*, the emblem of the French monarchy."

"No. *Guarda*, look more closely. You can see the difference here."

She studied the tattoo. It did differ from the *fleur-de-lis*, which she remembered as a simple flower figure with three petals, the central one upright and the other two arching outward. A plain band created a base for the flower.

The stunning image on Lillo's arm was much more elaborate. The arching petals formed sinuous curves ending in hook shapes that bore flowers, and between the petals, two elegant stamens emerged at graceful angles, their tips also bearing flowers. Beneath the band holding the flower, three graceful leaves protruded.

Alice touched it, tracing the image with her fingertips.

"Giglio," she said.

"*Giglio*, for the iris flower that grows in the fields around *Firenze*," Lillo said, pride blanketing his tone. "It represents *verita* and *purezza*, truth and purity. My name 'Lillo' comes from it."

"You must miss Florence very much."

"*Sì*. I miss my family. My home. In Italy, everything is about home and family."

"You're lucky. I always wanted a family."

Lillo's eyes grew soft. "I'm sorry, Alice. But you have many friends? A home you love?"

No need to share her financial problems with this dear man. She shrugged.

"And Sofia?" Alice said. "You must miss her most of all."

"Sofia is my home, my family."

Alice had seen photos of Lillo's slender, gorgeous fiancée and knew most of the details about next year's wedding plans. It would be a grand affair in Florence, financed entirely by Lillo's work in Austin. Alice was invited, but the chances of her having enough money for a plane ticket to Italy were about as slim as Sofia.

As she and Lillo chatted, Trish rushed in from

the mudroom, an air of panic surrounding her. "You know that white winter coat Marilyn always kept in the closet?" she panted.

"That luscious cashmere?" Alice said. "Like it's forgettable? What about it?"

Trish wrung her hands. "Well, I just noticed that it's missing. I've looked everywhere, and I don't know what to do about it. I sure don't want to be accused of taking anything."

"Missing? Maybe Ava took it. Or Georgia," Alice said.

"Maybe Marilyn was wearing it that night," Lillo offered.

The women looked at him. He shrugged.

"Yeah, maybe so," Trish said. "I read in the paper the door was open when the police arrived," Trish said. "I thought she may have been wearing it, too. But it was still so warm that night. It wasn't cold and rainy until the next day, remember?"

"It was midnight," Lillo said. "She probably just had her nightgown on. Maybe she wanted to cover herself."

"That woman never wore a nightgown," Trish scoffed. "Maybe a little see-through robe, or something, but she slept buck naked."

Lillo and Alice exchanged smiles.

Trish continued. "I'm serious, you two. I'm really afraid Ava will accuse me of taking that coat."

"That's insane, Trish. Why would she accuse you of stealing?" Alice said. "Is anything else missing from the closet?"

"No... I mean, I don't think so. I just noticed the coat is gone because it took up so much space. You don't know Ava like I do. She can be vicious. Just like Marilyn."

Alice reached for one of the tiny Italian pastries Lillo had placed on the counter and then put it back. She stared hard at one of the veins in the marble counter, trying to tease out a reason for how the coat could be missing.

If Marilyn had come downstairs and gone through the kitchen to the coat closet, that meant someone could have followed her downstairs, slipped out the front door, and waited for her outside on the veranda. Whoever killed Marilyn was here in the house that night.

She and Lillo exchanged glances. Was he thinking the same thing?

"Trish, Marilyn must have taken the coat that night. The police probably have it," Alice said.

"Okay," Trish blurted. "When do we get it back? As I said, I don't want to be accused of stealing anything."

Alice said, "I'm not so sure we want it back."

"Why not?" Trish said, her tone harsh.

Alice pictured Marilyn splayed inside the front door, unnatural and already cold. Under the gray moonlight, spatters of blood and brain tissue would appear black, not red, against the plush white cashmere.

BACK IN HER OFFICE, Alice had an opportunity to have a look at the new cell phone Ava sent her. All charged and ready for use, it was a much newer model than the flip phone she had lost, and some of the features puzzled her.

Her first call was to be to Mark, but she paused when she noticed a message in the voicemail inbox. Who would have called her? No one knew this new number.

It was Ava.

Alice, don't follow David. I didn't ask you to do that. Just watch him and keep notes. Don't stick your nose in someplace it doesn't belong.

The last comment was a stinging rebuke that turned Alice's face hot and red. She had overstepped her authority in this new job, realizing she'd made a fool of herself when she dashed out of the home after David.

She listened to the message again and wondered how Ava knew she had followed David. David must have detected Alice's car tailing him and complained to Ava.

She stared at the new phone. She was so rattled now that she couldn't remember whom she was going to call.

ALICE DIALED MARK UPSHAW'S number and told him about the missing coat. He would have to do some inappropriate sleuthing, he told her, but he would find out what Marilyn was wearing when she was killed. Alice left her new cell phone number with him.

She convinced herself she should try one more time to talk to Geoffrey. Maybe after lunch. For Haydn's sake, she would put her pride behind her and hope for the best.

When she finished with the mail, it was well after noon, just enough time to squeeze in a visit with Arthur before she had to be back at Marilyn's to meet the realtor. She stood up, stretched, and turned to the window behind her desk.

A young woman was crossing the yard at the far end of Marilyn's lot. She wondered if it was Javier Johnson's daughter, but the girl wore a dark hoodie that covered her face. Would Javier be following close behind, making sure that she wasn't off to rendezvous with David?

Owen had removed all the debris from the last storm and remounted the trellis on the back wall. She could have found a new gardener, but since Owen knew the place so well, she had called him instead. He was happy to come back to work at the mansion.

She walked to the front door and opened it, hoping to catch him clearing the beds. He was there, bent over a young mountain laurel that had taken a beating from strong winds and rain.

Hugging herself against the cold, she left the door open and walked down the drive. "Owen, you are a magician. Everything seems to thrive in your care."

"Thank you, Ms. Alice. I appreciate your calling me."

"Of course. You appear to have survived the

trauma of being fired by the pickiest woman in the neighborhood."

He looked up from the little bush. "It wasn't so bad. It was actually Georgia, not Marilyn, who fired me, so I missed out on the screaming."

"I didn't know. Good for you."

"Yes, she said her mother was ill and had asked her to speak to me. She was very nice. I was just checking the panel controls for the outdoor lighting when she opened the door. She was probably waiting for me to finish that job before she told me to get lost." He laughed.

"I don't know, Owen," Alice said. "I could believe that, if it had been Marilyn, but not Georgia. Why did Marilyn want to let you go?"

Why did I ask that? Her face flushed red hot. Surely the firing had to do with Owen's role as Marilyn's lover.

Owen looked away. "It was partly personal," he said, patting mulch at the base of the bush. "But why did she let anyone go? She liked that role of power, you know?"

He stood and brushed his hands on his jeans. "When Georgia talked to me, she said Marilyn wanted to change the garden design and would hire someone new, someone more attentive to detail." He drew air quotes around the last few words and shrugged.

"Well," Alice said, "it could just as easily have been me she fired, you know."

"Alice, may I talk to you about something?" he

said, his tone turning serious.

"Of course."

"Right after the murder, everyone in the neighborhood let me go and never hired me back, even though the police confirmed my alibi. I guess I understand why. They want to protect themselves, protect their families. But that leaves me without work." He hesitated. "Uh, will you talk to a few of them, please? Tell them I'm hoping they'll reconsider their decision, now that I'm in the clear?"

"I would, but the only neighbor I know is Javier Johnson next door."

"I'm still working for Mr. Johnson. He never said a word to me."

Alice nodded. Her gaze lingered on the glossy green leaves of the mountain laurel. Would it rally in the spring, she wondered, and dress itself in clusters of purple pea flowers that smelled like grape Kool-Aid?

"I'll see what I can do, Owen," she said, knowing she was unlikely to follow through.

Owen went back to work on the bush, and Alice watched the muscles in his strong back. Javier hadn't fired Owen, as the rest of his neighbors had. Why not? What made Javier so certain Owen wasn't a murderer?

IT FELT GOOD TO BE OUT of the house and away from her desk. Alice spread her arms wide and breathed deeply, her face to the sun. She needed just a bit longer outside before she returned to work. Her knee felt strong, so she set out for a short walk, just to the garage and back.

The building was detached from the house and set back on the wooded lot. According to Trish, Marilyn had planned to convert part of it into a stable. All the family women—Marilyn and Ava and Georgia—loved horses and loved to ride. During her high school years, Georgia had competed on a national level in dressage.

Marilyn kept a photo in her office of Georgia at one of the competitions. She sat tall and perfectly poised in the saddle on a wide-eyed, jet-black mare. The girl's hair was tucked under a black helmet, and she wore a black cutaway jacket over a bright-white, starched shirt. Her leggings appeared to be painted onto her slender, athletic legs. In her right hand, Georgia held a leather quirt at her thigh just above knee-high black boots.

The image conveyed complete control and discipline. The girl and her horse were poetry. Ava took the photo, Trish had told Alice. But, according to Trish, the horse was found dead, poisoned in its stall just days after the photo was taken.

Alice glanced across the horizon beyond the garage. Marilyn's plans had extended past the stable, Trish told her. Marilyn wanted to add a spa and a room for private yoga lessons. And plans were already drawn for two additional buildings she wanted to construct on a lot next to hers. One of the buildings would be an indoor shooting range for target practice. The three women loved to shoot as much as they loved to ride, although Alice had never seen guns in the house.

Had Marilyn lived, the property would have become a stand-alone resort. With her good taste and unlimited funds, she could have created the perfect retreat, a haven for her family and guests. How sad, Alice thought, that Georgia wasn't interested in keeping the house, in seeing her mother's plans completed.

When she reached the garage, she stuck her head in and looked at a perfectly clean and uncluttered area. As she suspected, Marilyn had not let Owen go for his inattention to detail. Marilyn simply didn't want an ex-lover around her handsome new husband.

She turned to leave when a plastic bottle on a shelf at the back of the garage caught her eye. It had fallen on its side among several other standing containers of various sizes and colors. She walked to the shelf and placed the bottle upright.

It was antifreeze, probably the antifreeze David had bought at Tony's. Funny, Alice mused, the jug was opened, but only about half full. Her local garage always drained the entire bottle into her car.

What an odd thing to remember, she mused as she walked back to the house.

IN THE KITCHEN, Lillo called over his shoulder that lunch would be ready in twenty minutes and that he himself would be serving on the pool terrace, unless she preferred to eat at her desk.

"You're serving?"

"Trish has an appointment," he said.

"Sounds lovely, Lillo," she told him on the way back to her office.

At her desk, she used the new cell phone to call her sister. Twyla had left a message on Alice's landline the day Marilyn was killed, saying she was flying home from Buenos Aires. She would be rested from her flight by now. Although she always traveled first class, long flights left her exhausted.

Twyla wrote for a popular travel magazine, so she spent a lot of time out of the country on assignment. She and Alice didn't see each other often, but they spoke on the phone at least once a week. They were only fourteen months apart, and they had been close since they were toddlers.

Twyla sounded tired, defeated. Leaving her husband had taken a toll.

"Can you come to New York, Alice," she said, "at least until I get through this legal razzle-dazzle? It would be such a comfort to have you here with me."

Alice reached under her glasses and pressed her eyes tight. Tears slipped down her cheeks.

"Twyla, Haydn's in trouble." Alice explained the situation and hinted at her own oblique involvement in his defense and her new work responsibilities.

Twyla adored Haydn. Alice had introduced them a few years earlier during one of Twyla's visits to Austin. Connie from next door had joined the three of them for long, happy evenings of cooking, drinking wine, and playing bridge. Twyla gasped when she learned Haydn had been arrested for having done something so totally out of character.

"Please let me know if there's anything I can do from here, Alice. And keep me updated."

"Same here, Sis."

"When everything's back to normal after this divorce, I want to slow down a little. Maybe write a book. I'm thinking of settling in Austin."

"I'd love that." It was the best news Alice had heard in weeks. She wiped her cheeks.

"Let's hope Haydn's in the clear by the time I get there," Twyla said. She paused a moment. "Alice," she said almost in a whisper, "will you think about the possibility of us living together? We can find someplace where we can both be comfortable. It's time we think about what we'll do with the rest of our lives."

This didn't sound like her overly confident sister at all. There was something Twyla wasn't telling her.

"Of course, Twyla. We always talked about being roommates when we got old, remember? I guess we've arrived."

They laughed and said goodbye. Before her financial problems got so bad, Alice had loved the idea of living with Twyla. What could she contribute to a joint household now?

Later, she told herself. She would explain her circumstances to Twyla later. She couldn't take on another impossible situation right now.

On the pool terrace at the back of the house, Lillo had set places for two under one of the outdoor gas heaters. He had decided to join her, she thought with a grin. How many more beautiful days like this one would they have before the next winter storm?

She paused to gaze at the infinity pool that appeared to spill into the Colorado River. The back terrace had been a favorite of architectural designers from around the world when Marilyn had it built. Now, infinity pools were rather common in this neighborhood, or so Alice had heard.

"Nice view, huh?" someone behind her said.

She whipped around.

David stood gazing in the same direction. He gestured toward the table. "I hope you don't mind if we have lunch together."

She waited for him to smile, but his features were rigid. In truth, she *did* mind, quite a lot. As she sat in the chair he pulled out for her, a weak feeling rushed over her. Old and afraid—and embarrassed because she was afraid. She glanced over her shoulder for Lillo. Where were those damned security guards?

David sat in the chair facing her but refused to meet her eye. "I've been wanting to talk to you." He poured cold sparkling water over the ice in their glasses and took a long drink from his glass.

"What is it, David?"

"Well—" he stopped as soon as Lillo walked onto the terrace with two plates of cold, curried salmon and fresh, steamed vegetables.

"Will you have wine, Mr. Rhodes?" Lillo said.

"Yes. Please choose one for me."

Lillo bent from the waist and backed away from the table.

Alice looked down at her plate.

"I wonder if you have access to Ava's or Georgia's email addresses, Alice. I was hoping—"

Lillo returned with a glass of wine, setting it at David's plate. Whatever David had to say was not meant for Lillo's ears.

"Will there be anything else?" Lillo said.

Helpless, Alice looked at her friend, hoping he wouldn't go too far.

David was silent. He stared at the pool until Lillo left them.

"I was hoping you could help me move on with my life," he said, placing one elbow on the table and resting his chin on his fist. "I'm having a hard time doing that because of the box Ava has put me in."

"'Box?' What do you mean?" Alice struggled to control her quavering voice.

Their eyes met, and he studied her face. "You don't know about the loan, do you?" he said. "The loan Ava has to pay back. The reason Marilyn was so angry all the time."

Alice found herself leaning forward, fighting her fear. What was David trying to tell her? "What loan? Was it money? What loan did Ava have to pay back, David?"

David turned his head toward the pool. He wasn't going to answer her questions.

After a moment of silence, he turned to her again. "The security guy who lurks around? He's here because of me. They've arrested someone for Marilyn's murder, but I'm the one being dogged as if I'm guilty." He raised his wine glass to his lips. His hand trembled. It occurred to her that he was afraid, too.

"Marilyn," he whispered as he replaced the glass on the table. He fixed his eyes on the glass and whispered, "Marilyn—I can't—I don't—" He pushed his chair back and stood for a moment, hands in his pockets.

"It wasn't supposed to happen this way," he said. He stared at his shoes. "I've got to get out of here, but they're not going to let me leave."

"David, please. What are you talking about? Why was Marilyn angry about a loan Ava had to pay back? What does all of this have to do with Marilyn?"

"Nothing!" David was almost shouting.

Alice stood and backed away from the table, but he stepped closer to her.

"Look at this, Alice." He turned so she could see him slide something out of his pocket.

"If Ava asks you about me," he said, "tell her I have this. We had a deal, and now they've left me out." A small gun with a bright red trigger rested in the palm of his hand. "I'm going to blow the top off of everything. I don't care what it means for me."

"David! What are you thinking?" she gasped. "What are you talking about?"

Lillo appeared. *"Tutto bene?"* He must have been watching them from the kitchen.

David shoved the gun back in his pocket.

"We're fine, Lillo," Alice squeaked. "Thank you." David was confiding in her, and she wanted to hear more.

Lillo glared at David, who had turned his back to the big man. Lillo glanced at Alice and backed away toward the kitchen.

"Use it on Ava, David? You're threatening Ava?"

"They're following me." He was pacing now, between her and the pool. "There's always someone parked across the street, waiting for me to drive out of the driveway. I tried to get back to Houston after the police arrested that guy for Marilyn's murder. Some brute met me at the airport and told me to think again if I thought I was going to get out of town."

"Was it one of the security men? Ava hired those people, David. Why would she want to keep you in Austin?"

"She is not what you think, Alice. She—" David snatched up his wine glass and drained it, spilling a drop on his chin.

He reached for Alice's arm and grasped it hard in his fingers. "Alice, please don't tell the police about the gun. My life depends on it."

Alice shook her head.

"Just give me one day. That's all I ask. I need to

work a few things out, and then I'll tell you everything I know. I'll go to the police with you. The man the police arrested isn't the one who killed Marilyn. He was just in the wrong place at the wrong time. Please." Without waiting for an answer, he whirled around and rushed into the house.

What was going on here? Alice took a deep breath. *Is the man insane? Is he the killer? What did he know about Marilyn's murder?* Could he provide information to prove Haydn was innocent? Would he really go to the police with her?

If what David said was true, her job of watching him for Ava had just been shaken out of focus. David had acted in an awkward manner with the gun, anxious about having it. That didn't seem consistent with someone who had shot his wife dead a few days ago.

Ava had told Alice she wanted to be rid of David, so why would she hire guards to make sure he didn't leave Austin?

Alice now understood how Ava knew that Alice followed David to Tony's body shop. Someone else had been following David, too.

CHAPTER 12

Soon after lunch, Mark Upshaw called Alice to tell her that he had news for her.

The bright-red trigger on David's gun was burning a hole in her brain. Should she tell Mark about it? He would have to report it, wouldn't he? David said he'd tell her everything if he could have just one day without police interference.

Mark suggested they meet at Magnolia Café on South Congress. Alice glanced at the clock on the wall opposite her desk and told him she'd be there. If traffic wasn't too bad, she'd have plenty of time to see Haydn, meet Mark, and stop by the house to check on Arthur. She didn't mention the gun.

Lillo tapped on the door and stepped into her office with a tray holding a coffee service. He told her David had left in a taxi without saying where he was going. Lillo hadn't noticed if a car followed him.

"What scared you earlier, Alice? At lunch? I was afraid he was going to hurt you."

"So was I. David thinks the family is trying to keep him here in Austin against his wishes," she said, wondering if she should tell Lillo about the gun.

No. The gun was her secret—a dangerous one, but

one worth keeping. At least for a day. That's what David asked for.

In her office, she rifled through her desk drawer for the note Ava had left her the previous day, the day of Marilyn's funeral. She needed to reread the part about David. Had she misunderstood Ava's intentions about him?

The note was written in a steady hand on several pages of blank printer paper.

Dear Alice, the note began.

I can't tell you how much I appreciate your staying on to help us work through all the details involved in settling Marilyn's estate. It's such a relief to both Georgia and me to know that our interests—and Marilyn's legacy—are in the best of hands.

I expect David will stay in the house until it sells, as he has no money and has burned too many bridges in Las Vegas to return there. Georgia believes letting him live in the house is far too generous, so I am authorizing it without her approval. Please do not mention it to her.

David was not included in Marilyn's will, so it's important for you to understand that nothing in the house or on the grounds belongs to him, and thus he has no authority to take, sell, destroy, or otherwise act as owner of any real estate or property belonging to the estate. This, of course, includes Marilyn's car, which will be picked up by the end of next week, and the SUV he's been driving. He is not to drive Marilyn's car.

That was it—the sentence that had made her leap to her feet like a fool and follow David to South Austin. She poured coffee and read on.

He may use the SUV for as long as he lives in the house. Please notify me if he appears to break any of these restrictions.

I have no intention of putting you in harm's way, so I have employed a full-time security service to help you keep track of David's actions. I do not know David—I think it's safe to say none of us knows him. In fact, I doubt my sister knew him when she married him. I suspect he married her for her money, and now that he finds his plan to live a life of leisure and luxury has been foiled, I can't imagine what his next move will be.

I have notified all of Marilyn's primary business contacts to send all correspondence to me. However, I don't want to close Marilyn's email account right away, so I've had her mail also copied to your personal email account. Please check your inbox every day so we don't lose any important messages.

Enjoy the house. I have asked Lillo and Trish to stay on to ensure your comfort. Trish will keep house for you and David. Lillo will cook for you, David, Trish, and the security guard.

I think this does it for now. If you have questions, please call me on the cell phone I'll have delivered to you later today."

And then the sentence that offended Alice: *Keep the phone with you at all times in case I need to contact you.*

> *With much gratitude,*
> *Ava*

The tone of this note was polite and grateful—different from the dramatic phone message Ava had left on Alice's new cell. *Don't stick your nose in someplace it doesn't belong,* Alice recalled Ava saying.

"What is it with this woman?" Alice muttered.

The note verified Alice's understanding about David: Ava had no interest in forcing David to stay in Austin. Had David been hallucinating? Or was there someone else who wanted him to stay put?

She glanced over the handwritten note again. One of the comments in the note caught her eye: Ava wrote that David had "burned too many bridges in Las Vegas" for him to return there. She remembered the newspaper article that stated Geoffrey had gone to law school in Las Vegas. David and Geoffrey both with links to the same glitzy city.

What's in Las Vegas?

MARK WAS STANDING UNDER the "Sorry, We're Open" sign at Magnolia Café when Alice drove into the parking lot. He didn't look any less comical in his jeans and button-down than he did in his police uniform. She smoothed the smile from her lips as soon as he looked her way.

He waved and flashed his toothy grin when he saw her car.

She had spent only a few moments with Haydn, who told her Geoffrey was working on trying to have him released by the end of the day. That had raised his spirits as well as hers. Having access to Haydn outside of jail would make it easier to persuade Geoffrey she could be a valuable addition to his defense team. Seeing Mark gave her an extra boost of positive energy.

She took the last parking space available. Mark opened her car door and bent low to give her a brief hug when she got out of her car.

"How are you holding up, Ms. Abbott?" he said as they slid into a booth at the front of the restaurant.

A waitress appeared and took their orders—a Diet Coke for Alice, a Topo Chico mineral water and Magnolia nachos with ancho chicken for Mark.

"Please call me 'Alice.' I'm okay, I think. I want you to know how much I appreciate your help."

"Well, I'm happy to do whatever I can, but I'm afraid I have to know why you need the information I have for you. You know Mr. Lawrence's attorney has access to all the case files."

"Yes, I do." Alice went on to explain Haydn's relationship with his attorney, Georgia's accusation that it was David who killed Marilyn, and her role working for Ava.

Their order arrived. Mark pushed the nachos toward Alice. She shook her head.

"Geoffrey James is living in Haydn's home. He's Haydn's heir. What earthly motivation does he have to prove Haydn's innocence?"

Mark pulled a chip from beneath a mound of beans, melted cheese, avocado, and sour cream. Distracted, he took the whole of it into his mouth and chewed.

"Ms... Alice," Mark said, elbows on the table as he rubbed his big hands together. "This sounds really dangerous to me. If Ms. Quinn's husband is the killer, you could be in his sights if he gets desperate. As an officer of the law, I'm required to tell you that you need to leave this matter to the police."

"I know, Mark, I know. But what would you do in my position? Haydn is my friend, and I know he isn't a murderer."

Mark concentrated on the nachos. In a matter of minutes, the plate was empty. He wiped his lips, took a long draw on the bottle of mineral water, and pushed the plate away from him.

"Well," he said, glancing over his shoulder at a lively crowd that had arrived for happy hour, "I can tell you that Ms. Quinn was naked under a thin silk robe. She had a heavy white coat draped over her shoulders as she walked to the front door. She was barefoot. She was carrying a set of keys and a cell phone that were found next to her body. She used the cell phone to call you just before she was shot." He paused. "The killer got her with one shot, smoothly through the left eye."

Alice grimaced as she traced the rim of her glass with her fingertips. She had been right about the coat.

"There is no film footage of any activity at Ms. Quinn's front door," Mark went on. "Marilyn's security camera at the front of her house was disabled."

"So the only film is from the neighborhood cameras on the street, and they show Haydn in the woods at the side of the house."

"Right." Mark paused for a moment. "There's something else, Alice. The killer apparently kicked the body several times."

"Kicked?" Alice said.

Mark shrugged. "Gruesome, isn't it? Bad enough to shoot someone in the face, but to do that to a corpse?"

Alice took her glasses off and rubbed her eyes. "Anything else?"

"Yes. A neighbor standing in his yard heard the shot. He said that the same moment the gun fired, he looked toward the house because the Christmas lights went out."

"Yes, Haydn mentioned the lights, too," Alice said, replacing her glasses. She stared at the wall behind Mark's head for a moment. "David asked me for Georgia's and Ava's contact information. I found that surprising, that he can't even contact Marilyn's family. What do you think?"

Mark shrugged. "Makes me think of a line from some Russian writer you quoted in class one day about families. You know the one I mean?"

Alice smiled, proud of her student. "Yes, I do. It's the opening line from *Anna Karenina*, by Leo Tolstoy: 'All happy families are alike; each unhappy family is unhappy in its own way.'"

"That's the one." He tore a slip of paper from a small notebook and wrote on it. "This is my cell phone number. Please call me if you need me. It'll be better for us both if you don't call the station anymore."

Mark gave her a tight-lipped grin. The Howdy Doody show was over.

BY THE TIME ALICE and Mark left the café, it was late afternoon and would be dark soon. She slipped her key into the door lock of the Toyota. A man across the parking lot appeared to be watching her. She glanced toward Mark's car, but he was already pulling onto South Congress Avenue. She shook her head. *I've become paranoid. David and me, two peas in a pod.*

At the stoplight at Live Oak Street, her cell phone rang. She answered the call, then punched the "speaker" icon so she could hear without holding the phone to her ear.

"Hi!" It was Haydn.

"Where are you? Are you out?"

"Yep," he said, in a merry tone. "I'm on my way home with Geoffrey. The guy did as promised and got me out of the hoosegow."

"Oh, Haydn, I'm so happy for you. I'm in the car on my way to check on Arthur, so I'll head to your house in thirty minutes, okay?"

After a brief silence, Haydn said, "Maybe in an hour or so? Geoffrey and I need some time to discuss a few things."

ARTHUR RUSHED TO WELCOME Alice when she got home, his soft, fat belly swinging like a hairy metronome as he ran. He cried in a high pitch and wound his thrumming body tightly around her ankles, bunted his head against her shins and stretched his long tail straight toward the ceiling. He was thrilled she had come home. Alice would have been flattered, but the big cat welcomed everyone—friend and foe, neighbor and stranger—in the same way.

Alice bent to scratch his chin, encouraging his enthusiasm with one hand while she wiped his long white hair off her pant legs with the other.

Connie had stacked the mail on the kitchen table.

Alice sat and sorted through the pile, making way on her lap for Arthur.

Bills, a few ads, a Target flyer, and more bills. Such a joy to come home.

She sighed, stroked Arthur, and wished she didn't have to leave him again.

"Do you want a kitty-cookie, sweet baby?" she cooed.

He did. He jumped off her lap, landed with a thud on the linoleum floor, and ran to his cookie jar by the kitchen door that opened to the backyard. Pushing herself up from the table, Alice noticed that the door was partially open, that the jamb had been splintered and the latch wedged open.

"My God!" she cried out loud. Someone had broken into her home.

SHE WAITED FOR A REPAIR service to reinstall a lock on the back door. Alice didn't own anything that was worth stealing, so it didn't surprise her to find nothing missing. Just another lark for local teens who didn't have enough supervision at home. Thank god she wasn't teaching anymore. She feared she'd have come to blows with some of the snotty kids she'd seen around town of late.

She nibbled on cheese and crackers and part of an apple while the lock was being fixed. Around 8:30, Alice was in the Toyota again, this time headed to see Haydn. Exhausted now, but eager to see her friend, she found herself smiling when she parked in Haydn's driveway.

Twin sconces flanking Haydn's front door flooded the porch with enough bright light to help visitors find the entry through the lush greenery that surrounded the home.

Alice rang the bell, still smiling.

When Geoffrey, not Haydn, appeared in the doorway, the smile vanished.

"Oh," she said. "I expected—" Alice strained to see inside, hoping to catch a glimpse of Haydn, but Geoffrey's girth was too wide. His body filled the doorway.

"He's sleeping," Geoffrey told her in a bored monotone. "I suggest we not wake him until morning. He's going to need all the rest he can get." He had no intention of inviting her in.

"Yes. I understand," she said. "But maybe you and I can talk? As I told you, I have some information that may be useful to your case."

"I'm sorry, but I have company at the moment. Tonight is inconvenient for me. Perhaps another time?" He pushed on the door.

Just before the door closed all the way, Alice lowered her eyes, giving in to fatigue and defeat. And then, right there before her, attached like tiny Post-It notes to Geoffrey's jet-black trousers, were patches of long, white hairs. Cat hairs.

ALICE STUMBLED OUT TO her car. Why would Geoffrey break into her home? She had tried so many times to meet with him, to offer to help, and he always refused her.

She drove back to Marilyn's in a stupor, trying to make sense of the day's disturbing events. But the image of long, white cat hairs caught on stark black fabric pushed any rational thought from her head. Geoffrey wouldn't have noticed them beneath the width of his torso.

As she approached the community gates off Loop 360, intense white LED lights brightened the night sky ahead. She edged her car up to the guard gate and asked what was happening.

"Not sure," the guard told her, "but there is some big-time commotion up there."

Alice drove through the gateway and toward Marilyn's home, toward the lights. They led her straight to Marilyn's driveway. Police cars, an ambulance, neighbors crusing past, creeping by, straining their necks to see some morbid follow-up to last week's brutal murder.

She stared slack-jawed at the flashing red and blue lights, white lights, handheld lights... Lights of every kind and size articulated the house and its yard against the indigo darkness of the evening.

Alice parked her car as close as she could to the property. She walked toward the driveway, until a police officer stopped her.

"I live here," she told him.

He looked at her, doubtful but only for a second. Then he took her elbow and guided her through throngs of uniforms to face Detective Cabrera. In a daze, she waited while Cabrera nodded at the officer, who then hurried Alice onward to the house.

As they walked, Alice turned and stared in horror at a motionless figure at Cabrera's feet. It was a woman. Her face had been battered—kicked?—beyond recognition. As the officer pulled Alice away from the scene, her gaze settled on the girl's beautiful dark hair. It was cut in a shaggy style with electric blue accents at the ragged ends.

A few feet away, a tight assembly of uniforms gathered near Marilyn's Jaguar and a man in civilian clothing. Alice sensed some recognition of the man. It wasn't until he turned that she saw his hands were cuffed.

The man was Haydn.

CHAPTER 13

Detective Cabrera led Alice into the kitchen, where they sat on bar stools at the counter. Alice sat bolt upright, eyes wide, lips parted. She pressed her purse into her chest, her fingers locked tight on the strap.

"Did you know her?" Cabrera peered into Alice's eyes. "The young woman outside? The officer with you said you saw her."

"I... I—Yes! I mean no. I didn't know her." Alice took shallow breaths, trying to focus on Cabrera's question and force down rising bile. She wasn't aware of much, but she knew she didn't want to be sick right now.

Cabrera nodded. "Was this the first time you saw her? Out there, on the drive?"

"No, no. I saw her at Haydn's." Alice covered her mouth with her hand. "Someone shot her? What happened to her face?"

"When did you see her at Mr. Lawrence's home?"

"While Haydn was in jail, I dropped by his house to pick up some books for him. She was there with Geoffrey. They were having drinks. Geoffrey—" The words tumbled out of her mouth. She couldn't think.

Two uniformed officers entered the kitchen. One of them leaned close to Cabrera's ear and whispered something.

Cabrera listened, her eyes still locked on Alice. Then she stood. "Thank you, Ms. Abbott. We'll finish this later."

"Haydn didn't do this, Detective!" Alice cried as the detective turned to walk away. "David... David Rhodes has a gun. Find him."

Cabrera stopped and spun toward Alice. "David Rhodes has a gun?"

Alice's eyes darted from the uniformed officers back to Cabrera.

"Yes, he showed it to me at lunch on Marilyn's terrace." She swallowed. "He had it in his pocket. He was... he was afraid of someone. He intended to protect himself."

Cabrera walked back to the counter. She didn't sit. "Protect himself from what?"

"I don't know," Alice said. Her eyes were saucers. Was she in trouble?

One of the officers touched Cabrera on the shoulder. She held up her hand toward Alice, palm outward. "Stay right here, Ms. Abbott. One of my officers will wait with you."

AN HOUR LATER, ALICE collapsed into her desk chair, slipped her fingers under her glasses, and rubbed her eyes. Cabrera had left her at the kitchen counter, where an officer placed a catalog of handguns in front of her. She turned the pages one by one until she identified the weapon in David's hand, a Ruger Custom LCP. The red trigger stood out like a flag.

Why had Haydn been at Marilyn's again when Geoffrey told her Haydn was sleeping?

A blinking light on the base of her desk telephone in front of her caught her eye. In a kind of trance, she pushed the "Play Message" button.

Hi, a voice said in a Texas accent even thicker than Alice's own. *This is Vivian at Brush Salon. Marilyn Quinn was a client here. I am so sorry to hear about the recent tragedy that took her life. Please accept my condolences.*

Alice sighed heavily and held her head in her hands, elbows on the desk. She rubbed her eyes again with her fingertips.

I'm not sure what to do with the cell phone Marilyn left with me a couple of weeks ago, Vivian went on. *I just received a bill addressed to her for the phone, but at my salon, and I'd like to get both the phone and the bill to someone who can take care of them. The salon is on West Avenue. Just ask for me when you come in. Thanks!*

CHAPTER 14

After a short, sleepless night, Alice felt disoriented, as though she were coming down with a cold or the flu. Her knee ached; her head throbbed. Neither Trish nor Lillo had come in, so she made herself a cup of weak tea and took it to her office. As she drew the cup to her lips, her hand shook.

It occurred to her that she wasn't suffering from a physical illness. This was fear.

She placed the cup in its saucer and reached in her pocket for her new cell phone. The pocket was empty, but she was too exhausted to think twice. She reached for the desk phone and dialed Connie's number.

"I want to come home," she said when Connie answered.

"YOU'RE A WRECK," Connie said as she helped Alice into the passenger seat of her car. Alice sat without stirring while Connie fastened the seatbelt and closed the door.

Connie had left a note on the kitchen counter in

the mansion explaining that Alice was ill and that she would be in touch with someone as soon as she felt better.

Slipping behind the wheel, Connie paused before she started the car. She was dressed in red scrubs. Scrubs meant she had been working when Alice called.

"Are you comfortable?" Connie said in a soft voice.

"No," Alice answered. "I... I—"

"It's okay. Let's get you home."

"But my car—"

"I'll have someone get it later today."

Alice managed a weak groan and let herself relax in the passenger seat. Within moments, she fell asleep.

At Alice's house, Connie toasted a bagel she found in the freezer. She watched as Alice spread butter on it and then stared at it.

Connie placed a glass of water and two capsules next to Alice's bowl. In her best bedside manner, and with the kind of authority only a doctor can assume, she pointed to the pills. "You'll need sleep, and I'm starting you on some antibiotics, just in case. You don't look well."

"Tell me what you've heard about Haydn first, Connie. I haven't seen a newspaper, listened to any news."

Connie looked at her with half a frown, weighing the impact of what news she had to share.

"Please," Alice said. "I want to sleep, but first

please tell me the latest."

Connie's news matched Alice's worst fears. Haydn had been arrested again.

"It's pretty clear the police think he had something to do with the girl's death," Connie said. "But they arrested him for violating the terms of his bail. He wasn't supposed to be anywhere near the Quinn mansion."

"Why was he there, Connie? Why would he go back there?"

Connie shook her head. "Why does Haydn do any of the strange things he does?"

Alice closed her eyes and swallowed two large gulps of water to wash down the pills.

Arthur followed as Connie walked Alice down the hall to the bedroom. Alice sighed. The sheets had been changed and her warmest duvet had been draped across the bed. The draperies were closed, and the room was dark and cozy.

Alice slid between the sheets and exhaled at length. Arthur settled himself on the pillow next to hers.

"This feels good."

Connie stroked her friend's hair and pulled the duvet under her chin.

"Just one more thing," Alice said as Connie turned to leave. "How is he doing? Is he coping?"

Connie sat on the side of the bed. "It's a good thing I can still get in to see him. He's not doing well," she said. She frowned. "The jailers are giving him his meds, but he doesn't sleep, doesn't eat the right things. I worry about his diabetes."

Alice hadn't considered the effects of being in jail on Haydn's physical health.

Connie went on. "I've asked Geoffrey to see if there's a possibility he can be released because of his age and his health issues. I hope he can do something."

Yes, Geoffrey would have to come through. He would have to do the right thing.

Connie stood. "I'll be in the living room." She closed the door with a soft click.

It felt good to have someone else take control. She was comfortable. She was safe.

CHAPTER 15

Eleven hours later, Alice walked into the living room and found Connie dozing on the sofa.

"Hey," she said, nudging Connie's shoulder. "I brought you some coffee."

Connie sat up and stretched more than once, arching her body in all directions and then reaching her fingertips toward the ceiling. "Thanks. Are you feeling better?"

Alice settled herself into the recliner, making a nest in her lap for Arthur. She had taken two aspirin, but she had no relief yet from the sharp stabbing in her knee. "A little," she said as she raised the hem of her nightgown and kneaded the sore area with both her hands.

"It hurts, doesn't it?" Connie said, glancing at the knee. "I can see it's swollen. Let me get you an appointment with a good specialist. It's time to take care of it."

Alice studied her hands as they coaxed blood flow into the joint. She wouldn't have a job. No income. And now a possible surgery that would keep her from finding work. It was time to face the end of life as she had known it.

"Yes," she whispered. "Please take care of it for me."

They sat in silence. Alice considered telling Connie about the cat hairs on Geoffrey's pant legs and the gun that David had showed her, but she didn't care about any of that anymore. She didn't have the energy, or the stamina, or—hell—maybe if she were younger. She reached for her coffee.

Connie set her cup on the table beside her and leaned close to Alice.

"I have to be honest with you, Alice. I know how much you care about Haydn. I care about him, too. Neither of us thinks that Geoffrey is the right person to defend him, but Haydn is resolute about having him on the case. I've tried to talk to him, but he just clams up."

Alice stared at her coffee.

"Geoffrey has complained to Haydn about what he called 'your meddling.' Haydn's very upset about it."

"Meddling?" Alice said. "I've done no such thing! I've only—"

"There are things you simply shouldn't be doing at your age. It's devastating to watch our friend go through this ordeal, but you have to stay out of it. It isn't up to you to save Haydn from his own bad choices."

Alice tightened the grip on her coffee mug. Connie was right. Haydn was upset with her, and for what? She had gotten nowhere trying to help him.

"Haydn is innocent," Connie went on, "and things will work out." She softened her voice. "You have to let this go. I had a friend bring your car home from Marilyn's. When you feel better, go get your other things from there and come home."

Alice hung her head. She felt totally foolish, totally defeated.

ALICE DROVE TO MARILYN'S IN the afternoon to pick up her personal belongings. She agreed with Connie that she had to abandon her involvement in Haydn's trouble. She would call Mark later and apologize for dragging him into her insanity, and that would be the end of it. She worried about Haydn, but she was helpless.

Still a bit groggy, she stopped at a 7-Eleven along the way to buy a cup of coffee. She stood at the machine waiting for her paper cup to fill while she flipped through a newspaper someone had left behind. She hadn't found her usual morning delivery in her yard at home. Connie had taken it, she assumed, probably to keep Alice from reading it.

In front of her at the register, a woman about her age waited to pay for a loaf of bread. She and Alice exchanged glances.

Alice leaned against the coffee counter and focused on the front page of the paper.

"Investigations Ongoing into Murders at the Quinn Mansion," the headline read. The story was still above-the-fold, front-page news, but it wasn't the featured article. A photograph on page three showed a gathering of police officers standing around a roped-off area on Marilyn's front lawn where the body was found. Alice blanched when she thought of the poor girl's battered face. Mark told her that Marilyn's face had been kicked by her murderer, too. Had the same killer vented his rage at this victim as well? She swallowed and forced herself to read the article.

The dead girl, according to the reporter, was Caitlin Johnson, daughter of Javier, Marilyn's neighbor. Alice caught her breath. Haydn Lawrence, the suspect in the first death at the mansion, reported the murder. He was being held by the police, not in connection with the murder, but for violating a bail agreement related to the murder of Marilyn Quinn. No murder weapon had been found at the scene.

So the dead girl, the same girl Alice had seen having drinks with Geoffrey James in Haydn's home, the same girl who had pursued David with romantic intent, was Javier Johnson's daughter. Javier had shown Alice the girl's photo the night he was in the house looking for a lost cufflink.

The girl in Javier's photo was somewhat pretty, but also plain, with long, straight, brown hair. No wonder Alice hadn't realized she was the same heavily made up, dark-haired woman she saw with Geoffrey.

Alice searched for other articles related to the murder. On page six, a piece on Javier Johnson, father of the girl, described him as a used-car magnate with huge lots in Austin and Las Vegas. A photo of Javier at a company board meeting accompanied the article. Seated next to him, but turned away from the camera so that only a part of his face and a good deal of his immense frame had been captured, was Geoffrey James. The meeting had been held in Las Vegas, according to the photo caption.

She stared at the photo, trying to see a connection among David, Geoffrey, and Javier, all of them having found their way from Las Vegas to Austin, and all of them in some way connected to the same two murders, murders they had somehow pinned on Alice's best friend. The idea of these smart, well-heeled con men taking advantage of Haydn's sweet nature infuriated her. Her neck flushed.

She folded the newspaper and placed it on the counter where she found it. The paper cup was full. As Alice reached for it, a raucous burst of laughter came from a clique of teenaged boys at the back of the store. The boys jabbed and pawed at one another, inching their way toward the front register, where the woman with the loaf of bread was next in line.

One of the boys held a bottle of Dr Pepper and a sleeve of salted peanuts. He elbowed the woman out of his way and shoved a few dollars across the counter.

Alice glanced at the woman, who had backed away from the ruckus and lowered her head to focus on her shoes. The shoes were black, thick-soled orthopedics with Velcro closures, the same shoes her mother had worn.

Alice squared her shoulders, pushed her way past the boys, and stomped out of the store. She wouldn't be shoved aside. She wouldn't abandon Haydn. And she'd be damned if she'd ever wear those shoes.

CHAPTER 16

Alice didn't expect to feel good to be at her desk again, back in a place where she could try to protect Haydn's best interests, but she did. Connie would be upset; that couldn't be helped. She worked all afternoon, then had a light dinner with Lillo and the security guard, who ate without saying a word while he stood at the kitchen counter. That night in the yellow room, she slept undisturbed by anything, not even her own thoughts.

The next morning, Trish tied the heavy draperies back from the windows with silk cords, and sunshine spilled through the windows like melted butter. Alice rubbed her eyes and grabbed her glasses from the bedside table. She glanced at Trish. She had been crying.

"Trish, what is it?" She threw back the duvet and rushed to Trish's side. The woman crumbled, broke into tears, and covered her face with both hands.

"I'm scared, Alice," she said between sobs. "Especially when you're not here. I know you've been gone because you were ill, but I can't handle this on my own. Marilyn's death was enough. And now this girl. God knows she wasn't a likeable person, but..." She wiped her eyes and took a deep breath. "And

David's been acting so weird."

Alice put her hand on Trish's back and shushed her as she helped her to the sofa. She pulled some tissues from a box and placed them in Trish's trembling fingers. "I know, Trish, I know. I'm sorry I was away. Shhhh." Alice stroked the maid's hair and let her cry.

After a few minutes, Trish sat up and ran her hands over the starched lap of her uniform. "It's not your fault. I can't do it anymore. I just told Ava I'm done at the end of the week." She blew her nose into the wad of tissues. Alice handed her more.

"Ava was furious with me," Trish went on. "But I don't care. Being in this house terrifies me." She ran the back of her hand under her nose like a child.

"You told Ava you're leaving your job? Ava's here?" Alice's shoulders tightened.

Trish nodded. "She and Georgia arrived late Thursday afternoon."

"Huh. I didn't know they were coming. Were they here when the girl was found?"

Trish nodded.

"A few moments ago you said David was acting weird. What did you mean? Weird how, exactly?"

Trish dabbed at her eyes and shrugged. "When Ava and Georgia are here, he's fine," she said, "but when they leave, he paces. It's like he's in a cage, waiting for something. Or someone."

"Well, he's pretty stressed, don't you think? After all that's happened? I guess I've acted weird lately, too." She wondered if she should tell Trish that Georgia had accused David of murder, but dismissed the thought in the next instant.

"No, not like him. He drinks. A lot." Trish paused for a moment, sniffed, and kneaded the tissues into a ball. "I think he's afraid of something. Friday after lunch I took a new floral arrangement into the sitting room. His back was to me, and he was talking on his phone. He was angry. Whoever he was talking to must have hung up because he threw the phone across the room. When he turned, he shouted at me to get out. His eyes terrified me."

Alice nodded. "I surprised him once, too," she said to Trish. "Same reaction."

"Yeah?" Trish's eyes opened wide, fully engaged in whatever Alice was going to divulge.

Alice ignored the invitation to share details. "Was it like a warning, do you think, what David said to the person on the phone?"

"Maybe. I think he's in trouble."

Alice sipped her coffee. "Were you here when Caitlin was found on the front lawn?"

"Yes, I was. Mr. Johnson had been over here looking for her earlier, mad as a hatter," Trish said. "What about your friend? Haydn Lawrence? What was he doing here?"

Alice ignored the question. "Did you ever hear David or Javier mention Las Vegas?"

"No. It's not like they talk to me. What's in Las Vegas?"

Alice put her cup back on the tray. "It's probably nothing."

Trish dabbed at her eyes again. "I almost forgot," she blurted. "Ava said she'd been trying to call you. She thinks you lost your phone again." She smiled. "I may not be the only one she's unhappy with."

"Too bad," Alice said, anxious, but smiling for Trish's sake. "She'll just have to get over it, won't she?"

"I wish I had your courage and strength, Alice," she said. "You don't seem to be afraid of anything." She patted Alice's knee and left the room.

Alice blinked. She stared at her knee for a moment before she picked up the newspaper.

No news on the murder. Did she dare think that was good?

She wondered how long she would have to wait to see Haydn at the jail today. She had done some computer research the night before on Javier Johnson's business holdings and discovered that the used-car lots in Austin and Las Vegas were operated by a parent company called RA Enterprises. It was no big surprise to learn Geoffrey James was listed as the general counsel for the company. Haydn needed to know that his attorney was somehow involved with people who knew both Marilyn and Caitlin. David's connection to Las Vegas remained unclear.

She drained her cup of coffee, had a bite of toast, and stood to stretch her back.

So where was the damned cell phone that Ava

had bought for her? No wonder Ava was irate.

She scooped out two handfuls of the contents of her bag and studied what remained inside. The phone was not there.

She looked around the room and then pawed through the few things she had placed in the cherry dresser when she first moved into the beautiful yellow room. Was it weeks ago? Months? She held up her fingers as she counted. She had first stayed here last Wednesday. Could it have been less than a week?

She dropped the T-shirt she held and looked again around the room. Why was she having such a hard time keeping track of a cell phone? Younger people seemed to have cell phones attached to themselves like prostheses. Alice could put hers down and forget she ever had one.

At the thought of having to face Ava, Alice's heart raced. Trish had said she was on the warpath. Could Alice handle a tongue-lashing without bursting into tears as she had when Marilyn laid into her about the year-end bonus?

As soon as she was dressed, she stole across the entryway and into her office. Just as she reached for the desk telephone, it rang.

"This is the estate of the late Marilyn Quinn," she said in a low voice. "I am Alice. May I help you?"

"Alice, it's Mark Upshaw. Are you all right?"

"Oh, Mark. I was going to call you. Things, as you know, are not good. Haydn's back in jail and—"

"I know," Mark said. "I've been calling your cell

phone, but I always get voicemail, and I can't leave messages. I thought I'd try your office. Can we meet?"

"Of course. When? Where?"

"There's a parking lot at the wine bar on Glenview Avenue in Bryker Woods. Do you know it?"

"Yes, I do."

"Can we meet there right away?"

Mark's anxious tone worried Alice as much as whatever it was he wanted to tell her.

ALICE CALCULATED HOW SHE MIGHT slip out of the house with as little trouble as possible. She edged past the sitting room where Georgia sat reading a magazine. Nearing the kitchen, she held her forefinger to her lips to stop Lillo's booming voice from calling out his usual "*Buongiorno, Bella.*"

The chef looked at her with his permanent scowl, but his eyes told her he was concerned. She hadn't spoken to him alone since before the death of the girl. They needed to talk. He would want to know her plans.

He followed her out to the driveway, where David had just returned from a run. No time for a private conversation with Lillo now. The chef stood at Alice's side as she wished David a good morning.

"You and Georgia are early risers this morning," she said.

"Yeah," he said, shaking his hands at his sides in the last of his cool-down. "I need to go up to see her."

"She's in the sitting room." Alice wondered for a

moment who had carried her down the stairs, if not David. She tried to imagine the delicate woman in Lillo's beefy arms.

David slapped Lillo on the back in the spirit of good-natured intimacy and asked him for a cup of coffee. Lillo flinched at his touch and flashed a sour glance at Alice.

David was in a great mood this morning. Just as Trish had said, David was delightful when Ava and Georgia were in the mansion with him. Maybe today he was also happy about getting away with murder. Twice.

BRYKER WOODS IS AN OLD Austin neighborhood just south of 35th Street and west of Lamar Boulevard. Alice arrived at Olive and June, a wine bar and restaurant that didn't open until early evening. Mark's personal car, a black Maxima by no means new, but spit-shined and detailed to near perfection, was already there. He got out as she pulled up. He was not in uniform.

Before Alice had time to turn off the engine, he was in the passenger seat next to her, his body at an awkward angle so he could look squarely into her eyes.

"Alice, you had me worried sick! This second murder—"

Alice apologized and explained about her cell phone. "I'm going home after we talk to see if it's there. Thank you for your concern. I'm fine."

"Thank God. Now listen to me."

She looked at him, looked at the protruding ears, the red hair, the freckles. Today, his face contradicted the comical image it usually presented. This was a strong, confident man speaking to her, a police officer.

"You're going to get out of this mess, Alice. You're going to quit working for Ava Sauvage and move out of that house. We'll both hope for the best for Mr. Lawrence, and I'll keep you informed of any new information I hear about, but this is dangerous business, and you're totally out of your depth."

Alice stared at him, her jaw clenched. First Connie and now Mark. She had almost given in to Connie's demands to fade into the background, as any old woman should do. She wouldn't consider that option again.

"Officer Upshaw," she said, back in the classroom speaking to an impudent student, "I have broken no laws, so you have no right telling me what to do. I know you are concerned for my welfare, but I have explained my relationship to the man who is accused of murder and I have also explained that he has no one except me to help him prove his innocence. I have asked for your help, but I totally understand if you refuse. Now get out of my car, please."

She started the car and turned away from him, waiting for him to leave. He opened the door and slid out.

"You're going to do this with or without me, aren't

you?" he said, bending low to speak through the open door.

She didn't answer or even look at him.

"You know, if David Rhodes were the killer," Mark went on, "Detective Cabrera would be all over him. But there's no evidence against him. You have no idea who has killed two women or what you're dealing with."

Seconds passed. Silence.

"Damn it!" He folded his tall frame back into the car and slammed the door.

More silence as they sat side by side, both of them staring ahead over the hood of the car. After a few moments longer, Mark shifted his weight in the seat and rubbed his big hands together, the rough skin of his palms rasping like sand paper.

"What's the situation at the house?" he said.

Alice let herself relax. She leaned over to kiss Mark on the cheek. "Thank you." There were no more words for the gratitude she felt. Having his continued support filled her heart.

ALICE TOLD MARK ABOUT the photograph of Geoffrey and Javier Johnson in the paper.

"I found a connection between Javier's used-car business here in Austin and another one in Las Vegas," she said.

"Right," Mark said. "I found that, too. And get this: David Rhodes worked at the Las Vegas location before he met and married Ms. Quinn."

"What?"

"Yes, he worked there until late October last year. He was selling used cars."

"But... but he met Marilyn in New York... at a conference," Alice sputtered. She shook her head in disbelief, then raised her brows. "Selling cars?"

Mark ducked his chin and closed his eyes. "It gets better," he said, opening his eyes and peering into hers. "David Rhodes was already married to another woman when he married Marilyn."

"What?"

"Yeah. There's no chance he's gonna inherit anything. His marriage to Marilyn was illegal."

Alice gasped. She held her hands to her lips and stared out the windshield. The same sense of disorientation she had in a funhouse mirror when she was a child washed over her. The skin on her arms prickled. What tricks were being played here? What funhouse had she unwittingly walked into?

"Are you okay, Alice?" Mark said.

She swallowed and ran her fingers through her hair. "Who are these people, Mark?"

Mark shook his head. "Bad people, I think."

"Poor Marilyn. She didn't deserve this."

"Exactly." Mark gazed into the distance and nodded. "David has to be involved in her murder if he wed her under false pretenses, knowing she would die before she discovered the marriage was a sham."

"But why would he go through all that if he doesn't

inherit anything?"

"Maybe someone paid him to kill her?"

"Maybe," Alice said, dragging her words out. "Wouldn't all of this be in the electronic file at the station? Doesn't Geoffrey have this information?"

Mark nodded.

"But Geoffrey isn't doing anything. Haydn is still the only suspect."

"Well, David Rhodes's only crime so far is polygamy. Your friend Haydn was at the scene of the murder and his fingerprints are on the gun that killed Marilyn. The gun has no manufacturer markings, so it's untraceable."

"What about Caitlin? Will Haydn be accused of her death, too?"

"I haven't heard anything yet about that investigation."

Alice squirmed in her seat. "We know there's a parent company for the used car lot businesses called RA Enterprises, and we know Geoffrey James serves as general counsel," she said. "If nothing else, that smacks of conflict of interest to me, especially if Haydn's attorney is involved with the murder, or a coverup. Haydn has to be told."

"How does the argument between Javier and Marilyn on the night of her death fit in?"

She shook her head. "I wish I'd heard what it was about." After a pause to think it through, she told him about the break-in at her house and the cat hair on Geoffrey's pants.

And then, she told him about the red-triggered gun.

Mark's jaw dropped when he heard about the gun, but he stopped short of reminding Alice about the danger she was in. His recovery was quick and smooth. "We've got to share information more often, Alice. Not only for your sake, but for mine. Does Cabrera know about the gun?"

"I told her the night Caitlin was killed. David promised to tell me what was going on if I let him have one day before I talked to the police. If I had told you about the gun, you would have been obligated to report it."

Mark nodded, took a deep breath to say something, but checked himself again. He waited a moment before he went on. "When David showed you the gun, his words were 'Tell them I'm going to blow the top off of everything'?"

"Yes."

"And Ava and Georgia are back in Austin? Do you know why?"

"No idea."

"Okay. You have to let Detective Cabrera know about the break-in. That needs to be a part of the investigation."

"I can't say anything about Arthur's hair. If Geoffrey can wriggle out of my accusation, and all he has to do is deny it, Haydn will think I'm trying to discredit Geoffrey. Kids have been breaking into houses in my neighborhood for a couple of weeks. I don't want to be seen as hostile to his attorney."

Mark nodded. "I understand. Just let the police know that someone broke into your house."

"I'll phone them today."

"What do you think Geoffrey was looking for? Was anything missing?"

"Not that I can tell. It looked like someone may have poked around in the desk drawers." She told him about Caitlin pursuing David and about Javier's veiled threats the night he said he was looking for a cufflink.

Mark looked away. They sat in silence, both of them trying to sort out the events of the past few days.

"Marilyn and Javier had an argument at dinner," Alice said. "He could have called her later that night and waited for her to appear at the door."

"That call would have been on Marilyn's cell phone. We didn't find it."

"She and David had been fighting about David's trip to Houston. Maybe he told her to go downstairs and he waited for her with the gun—"

"Alice, you're not making any sense. Marilyn was sick. Something spectacular had to happen to make her leave the house."

"You're right. She was so very sick."

She paused. "What about Caitlin? Trish says the girl was pressing David for a physical relationship, but he kept brushing her off. Could she have gone too far, made him snap? We know he has a pretty short fuse."

Mark shook his head, lost in thought. "Maybe," he said. "If he killed Marilyn, he could probably kill a second time. And the girl's face had definitely been kicked or beaten, just as Marilyn's was. Except Caitlin was shot from behind."

"She was shot from behind?"

"Yes. Sorry, I meant to tell you that."

Mulling over the details, Alice said, "It makes sense that whoever shot Marilyn was in the house, or somewhere close by."

"Like hiding in the woods?" Mark added, reminding Alice that the police had a reasonable suspect in custody.

Alice ignored the comment and continued. "Ava? But why would Ava want her sister dead? Ava has plenty of her own money. Not Georgia—she loved her mother, and she makes oodles as a model. Besides, Georgia couldn't get down the stairs on her own with that broken ankle. Geoffrey? He's in this somehow. And he knew Caitlin. Maybe he was jealous of Caitlin's interest in David?"

Mark nodded his head. "Trish?"

"Don't be ridiculous," Alice said with a sigh. "Oh. I almost forgot. Marilyn's hairdresser called. She has a cell phone Marilyn asked her to keep. Wants me to pick it up at her shop. I'll try to get there today."

"Okay. And something else I almost forgot. The reason Haydn was at Marilyn's the night Caitlin was found? He said he hoped to see Georgia Quinn."

"Haydn told me that, but he didn't say why or –"

"Alice," Mark said, "Haydn thinks he may be Georgia's father."

Alice stared at Mark, unable to speak.

A sharp sound broke the tension between them. It was coming from inside the car.

Mark looked around for a moment and then reached under his seat. He pulled out a cell phone, still ringing, and offered it to Alice.

"Not mine," he said. "Must be yours."

ALICE LOOKED AT THE CALLER identity on her phone and let it ring as Mark walked to his car. She was in no state to talk to Ava.

Ava, however, was in the mood to talk to Alice. There were three more calls from her in rapid succession.

Alice had never seen Ava when she was angry. She expected Ava's ability to express herself and her fury was equal to that of her sister's. Alice placed the phone on mute and shoved it into her purse.

She sat still for several minutes.

Georgia would be the right age to have been born during or soon after the time Haydn and Marilyn became engaged. If there was a physical resemblance pointing to a father-and-daughter relationship, Alice couldn't see it.

Who but Haydn would lurk outside Marilyn's home in hopes of a glimpse of a woman who might or might not be his daughter? Of all the boneheaded things Haydn had done over the years, this had to be the worst.

She sighed at length and shoved her fingers under her glasses to rub her eyes. She thought about trying to find Geoffrey James, but she dismissed that thought in the next second. This time, she knew how she could help.

IT WAS A BEAUTIFUL JANUARY afternoon, and Alice let herself enjoy the sunshine as the Toyota sped along Route 2222 and then down to Loop 360 to Marilyn's. The temperature display on her cell phone read sixty-five degrees. Another cold front would arrive by tomorrow with a high in the thirties. She liked a bit of winter weather in January, Austin's coldest month of the year. She held vivid memories of the January day back in the early '70s when the temperature topped ninety degrees. That could happen again.

Things seemed calm at Marilyn's when she arrived. The Jaguar had been moved from its perennial perch at the front entrance soon after Caitlin's murder. A quick look revealed no sign of David's SUV. She drove to her car's hiding spot in back of the house.

Lillo met her with coffee as she walked through the kitchen. "I'll bring you a tray," he said.

"Thanks, but I'm not hungry. It's quiet. Where is everyone?"

"Everybody went to lunch. Together, if you can imagine. I thought David was *odiato*—" He struggled to find the word in English, his big hands twirling in front of him as if they would help his lips give birth to a word he had probably never heard spoken. In bewilderment, he raised his hands, palms up, expressing the international gesture of defeat. "I thought they did not like him."

"I thought so, too, Lillo. I wonder what's changed. Do you know why Ava and Georgia are here?"

"No. But," he said, shaking his huge head, "I heard Ava tell Trish she needs to see you *subito*."

"Immediately, right?" Alice said. "Yeah, I'm not her favorite person at the moment. I'm prepared for a long, harsh lecture. Fortunately, I have found the topic of her ire..." She held the cell phone up for Lillo to see. "...and I'm prepared to tape it to my body so I won't lose it again."

Lillo looked at her curiously. "*Ire?*" he said. "What is *ire?*"

ON THE SEAT OF HER DESK CHAIR, Alice found a note from Ava scribbled on a sheet of printer paper. "I need to see you ASAP!" it read. No expensive stationery this time, no careful script. Ava meant business.

"Soon, madame," Alice said, speaking to the note. She set her jaw, folded the note in fourths, and dropped it into the wastebasket under her desk.

With a smile, she realized she was calmer than she should have been about seeing Ava. *After all*, she said to herself as she plowed through stacks of mail on her desk, *how much worse could things be?*

"Bring it on, baby," she muttered to herself,

forcing an attitude of bluster that felt new to her.

"Bring what on?" Trish said from the doorway.

"Oh, Trish, come in. I need to ask you for a favor."

Alice told Trish about Haydn's long-ago engagement to Marilyn and his suspicion that he could be Georgia's father. Maybe she and Trish could put his mind at ease, at least about that.

"Do you think you can collect something of Georgia's that has her DNA on it? Q-tips? Hair? Kleenex? I have a friend who can do the test pretty quickly, I hope."

"Are you kidding me? That woman is a slob in private. Her room is an obstacle course. Her clothes, her makeup, her nail polish, her handbag, her stockings, her cast, her magazines, her shoes, her hair accessories. I can't believe anyone can live that way," she said, in a smug tone. "You bet I can get something for you."

Alice reached for the phone. If Connie could do this one thing for her—testing Haydn's and Georgia's DNA—Alice would feel as though she were helping her friend in some way. If the test returned a positive result, Haydn could be certain he had fathered a beautiful, successful child. He would have a daughter. A family.

IT WAS ALMOST 2:30 WHEN Alice glanced at the time. She grabbed her purse and rushed out of the house. There was one more thing she wanted to do before she met with Ava.

On her way to Vivian Lombard's downtown salon, she called Connie, who agreed to do what she could to persuade a friend at a testing site in Dallas to rush the DNA results. Now all Alice needed was a sample from Haydn.

She drove to the back lot of Vivian's salon and parked among several luxury cars waiting for their polished and coiffed owners to emerge re-polished and re-coiffed from the exclusive establishment, which opened on Sundays only for special clients. This was exactly the kind of place that Alice avoided. She would feel humiliated the moment she stepped through the door.

But she was eager to know why Marilyn had left a phone with Vivian, so she had to retrieve it. Alice paid five phone bills—one landline for the office, another landline for the home, a cell for Marilyn, a cell phone for David, and the old flip phone that Alice lost before Marilyn was murdered. The cell here at Vivian's was not one Alice knew about.

She took a deep breath on the front steps of the spa. As she expected, several heads turned to stare when she entered. She was out of place in this oasis. She was a blight on a landscape of tanned, beautiful women who waited for their turn to be made more tanned, more beautiful at the hands of Vivian and her talented staff.

Alice smiled at the floor, as the usual flush made its way up her neck, and shuffled to the front desk.

"I'm Alice Abbott," she mumbled to the receptionist, a thin, golden-haired girl with dark, smoky eyes and impossibly plump lips. "I'm here to pick up a cell phone that Vivian is holding for Marilyn Quinn."

A polite murmur erupted behind Alice. She had not spoken in as low a voice as she had intended.

"Of course," the golden-haired waif said in a breathy whisper. "Vivian said someone would be coming by. One second, please."

As promised, the waif reappeared after only a moment. She handed Alice a small box.

"Is this the phone?" Alice said.

"Yes. And a note of condolence from Vivian." The girl cocked her head, and her lips formed a heart-shaped pout that told Alice she was being dismissed.

Alice turned and would have shuffled back toward the door when one of the seated clients caught her sleeve with plump fingers that glittered with jewels. The woman wore an expensive black tracksuit and white tennis shoes. Her massive legs were crossed at the ankles.

"All that trouble at Marilyn's," the woman said to Alice. "That young girl. And Marilyn herself. It must be devastating to lose someone like that."

Alice froze. The woman held on, pinching Alice's sleeve between her fingers as she turned to speak to the other women in the room.

"I saw Georgia in Houston just before New Year's Eve," she said. "We ran into each other in Neiman-Marcus in the Galleria."

All eyes were on the woman now, and she dropped Alice's sleeve. "It's a pity we were both in such a rush," she said with a shrug. "We only hugged and then rushed off in opposite directions."

The other women stared in awe, as though this oblique brush with the recently dead were some sort of coup.

Alice backed away. The woman had manufactured the story to call attention to herself. Georgia wouldn't have rushed away from anyone with that cast on her leg.

BACK IN HER LITTLE CAR, relieved to have escaped from the spa with her self-respect at least partway intact, Alice tossed the box onto the passenger seat and turned on the ignition. But something made her pause before she backed out and onto the street.

She reached for the box and opened it. Inside was an envelope and what she supposed was the cell phone wrapped in thin tissue paper tied with a red ribbon. She picked the package up and pulled the end of the ribbon. When the paper fell away, Alice's old flip phone—the one with a break in its face from a drop on Marilyn's marble floor, the one that had gone missing several days before Marilyn was killed—lay exposed in her hand, its charger line wrapped tightly around its middle.

"WHAT A BITCH," Alice seethed as she spun away from the spa. "Marilyn knew perfectly well where my phone was while she was making me feel like some demented fool for losing it."

She was driving too fast. She turned south on the expressway, willing herself to take deep breaths. She needed to cool off.

Alice exited at Bee Cave and parked at P. Terry's Burger Stand. Still angry, she slammed the car door, stormed into the restaurant, and ordered a large Diet Coke. As she turned to leave, her handbag caught on a newspaper the man behind her had tucked under his arm. She apologized, but the man had turned away to read the menu board.

"Slow down," she muttered to herself.

Back in the car, she examined the phone. No surprise that the battery needed to be charged, but otherwise it seemed okay. Why had Marilyn kept it? If her purpose was to mortify Alice, why not just toss it in a garbage can somewhere?

She shook her head in frustration and took a long drag on the straw in the Diet Coke before she opened the envelope Vivian had placed in the box with the phone. Inside were several pages of paper that she spread across the steering wheel. One was a bill for the flip phone addressed to Vivian's salon.

Why would Marilyn change the account information for the flip phone? She glanced at the call log and then focused her attention on one of the other pages, a brief, handwritten note.

Dear Ava: My heart breaks for you and dear Georgia. Marilyn was a longtime friend and client. I will miss her.

I know this tragedy hits you at a particularly hard time. I was both surprised and saddened to hear that you sold your clothing boutique in Santa Fe.

Ava sold her shop? *When?* Alice wondered. And more important, *why?*

Marilyn left this cell phone with me a couple of weeks ago, the note went on, *so she could use it, she said, for private calls. She changed the billing address from her home to my business. I enclose the bill with the phone.*

> *Sincerely,*
> *Vivian Lombard*

The call log on the bill showed incoming call numbers she recognized. Those calls had been made to Alice before the phone had gone missing. Most of them were from Haydn and Connie. There were also calls from Marilyn and a few from a woman in Alice's bridge group.

One or two of the incoming calls were from a number she didn't recognize. The area code was 713. Wasn't that Houston?

Alice recognized the outgoing calls she herself had made while the phone was still in her possession. The other outgoing calls, perhaps made by Marilyn, were to the number with the 713 area code.

Marilyn hadn't taken Alice's phone to make Alice look foolish. She took it to make and receive private calls to someone in Houston.

ALICE MADE A SUDDEN DETOUR to her house and right away plugged the flip phone in to charge. She fed Arthur and glanced at the new lock on the back door. Her knee ached, so she found some Advil and took two, swallowing them with water she cupped in her hand at the tap in the kitchen.

She sagged onto the sofa and stopped the blinking on her landline phone when she touched the play button.

There were three messages from Rosemary Richards asking Alice to play bridge. The women Alice played with must be eager to learn all she knew about Marilyn's murder.

And—she was surprised to hear—there was a message from Geoffrey James. Alice's spirits rose when she heard his voice. At long last, he was reaching out to her.

Ms. Abbott, this is Geoffrey James, his deep, southern voice boomed. *I am calling you on behalf of my client, Haydn Lawrence, who gave me this number. Mr. Lawrence asks that you not attempt to contact either him or me by telephone, personal visits, or in writing. We both need to focus on his upcoming trial, and your presence and your repeated interruptions create a distraction that diminishes that focus. Have a good day, Ms. Abbott.*

ALICE LISTENED TO GEOFFREY'S message twice before she rested her head on the back of the sofa. How long could Geoffrey keep her away from Haydn? By isolating him, Geoffrey would have full rein over what Haydn would hear about his own defense.

Arthur pasted his thick body on her thighs. Grateful to be at home with him, she buried her fingers in his fur, and after only minutes they slept.

Two hours later, Alice crawled along with rush-hour traffic to Marilyn's. When she arrived, she expected the house to be filled with the aromas of some devilishly divine meal that Lillo was preparing for dinner, but the kitchen was dark. Trish was nowhere in sight. David's SUV wasn't in the driveway. Now, if Ava and Georgia were out, she would have the house to herself.

She was famished. She went straight to the refrigerator to see what Lillo had left for her.

He never disappointed. Waiting at eye level was a serving of baked salmon with what appeared to be his mustard-lime sauce and a serving of new potatoes with parsley butter. Attached to the potatoes, a small note in Lillo's tiny, feminine handwriting read, *Please heat for 2 min in micro.*

On the counter next to the refrigerator sat an open bottle of Chardonnay and a single chocolate cupcake with dark chocolate frosting.

She popped the potatoes and fish into the microwave and poured a glass of wine. When the buzzer sounded, she gobbled the food and then put the dishes in the dishwasher as she chewed the last bite of the fish.

She felt better. Much better. She took her glass, grabbed the bottle of wine, and tucked her purse under her arm. The cupcake could wait.

No note from Ava had been left on her office chair. Alice wasn't sure if that was a good sign, or a bad one. When she spotted an envelope on her desk, she sat, placed her glass on a coaster, and poured more wine before she opened the envelope. Inside, she found two cotton swabs and four strands of long, dark hair. Trish had come through with specimens from Georgia's room for the DNA test.

She now realized that getting a test sample from Haydn would be nearly impossible. She had lost access to Haydn's home, thanks to Geoffrey James.

She sat back in her chair and sipped the wine. What Vivian's note said about Ava selling her boutique in Santa Fe buzzed in her head like a gnat. Did that have anything to do with the loan David mentioned when he showed her the gun with the red trigger? The loan she needed to pay back? The loan that had made Marilyn so angry?

She tried to find a way through her muddled thoughts. David was terrified of something when Alice talked to him on Thursday. Then when Ava and Georgia returned to Austin, his demeanor changed 180°. Even Trish had commented on it.

That brought her to the fundamental question about David: How did he go from selling used cars in Las Vegas to becoming involved with an Austin millionairess in New York City?

CHAPTER 17

Alice woke up early on Monday morning. Even though she'd napped during the previous day, the couple of glasses of wine she drank the night before had ensured sound and peaceful sleep.

The weather was nasty, a disappointment after yesterday's lovely afternoon. Low temperatures and a dark sky meant morning traffic would be even worse than usual. When the rain began, traffic would barely move, but there was something she had to do.

She showered, dressed, and opened her bedroom door without making any sound. The house was still except for noises in the kitchen, where Lillo was working. She could smell coffee.

She and Lillo exchanged pleasantries in hushed voices, and he handed her a mug of coffee.

"You're up early," he whispered. "Eggs?"

"Nope, but thanks. I'll be back soon." She sipped at the coffee and set the mug on the counter.

She was out the door and on her way home by 6:30.

ARTHUR WAS WAITING AT the door to greet Alice. She picked the big cat up and hugged him tight.

"Help Mommy find something very important, okay?"

She dropped him to the floor, and together they rushed to the kitchen. Her eyes searched every surface, tabletop, counter, refrigerator, oven, microwave. She opened the cabinet below the sink and looked in, moving bottles and jars aside so as not to miss anything.

Frowning, hands on her hips, then squinting, she had a sudden moment of clarity. She snapped her fingers and rushed to the bathroom. Reaching into the dirty clothes hamper, she pulled out a dishtowel that was stained with bright red blotches.

"Aha, Arthur!" she said, waving the towel like a flag. "Thanks to the cheese grater, we have Haydn Lawrence's DNA."

WHEN ALICE DELIVERED THE TOWEL, the cotton swabs, and the strands of hair, Connie told her she wasn't sure her friend would accept the blood sample on the towel to use in a paternity test. Her tone of voice hinted at a dismissive temperament, Alice believed, because she had decided to stay on at Marilyn's

"And two of these hair samples won't do because the roots aren't attached."

Alice's face fell. The one helpful surprise she thought she could present to her friend now looked doubtful.

"Whatever the results are, they won't be official.

You understand they won't be of any use in court, right?"

"Understood."

"You have a key to Haydn's house, don't you? Can't you get his toothbrush?"

"No," Alice said. She flopped onto the sofa and rubbed her knee hard as she told Connie about Geoffrey's phone call warning her to stay away from both him and Haydn.

"Damn it, Alice," Connie muttered, keeping her eyes on the floor. "Here's my offer: I'll have your samples looked at if you will promise..." She looked up and stared at Alice hard. "...*promise* that this paternity test will be the end of your camping out at the Quinn estate."

Silence.

"Say it."

"I promise."

THE RAIN HAD STARTED AND so had rush-hour traffic. Alice tried to coax the car radio to work—sometimes if she pressed down hard on the dashboard in just the right spot, the signal cleared—but no luck today. She looked in her rearview mirror and gasped at the unending, melted ribbons of lights behind her. It would be a while before she arrived back at Marilyn's.

She should call Lillo or Trish, she told herself. Her purse was in the seat beside her, so she shoved her hand in and grabbed for her phone.

But she touched two cell phones. The new one Ava had given her and the flip phone Marilyn had taken from her and left at Vivian's. Alice had left them on the coffee table to charge and grabbed both of them on her way out of the house.

Traffic was at a complete standstill, so she turned the flip phone on. The Messages button indicated that there were four.

The first two were from her sister, Twyla, before she gave up and called Alice's home phone.

The third was from Haydn. He had called late on the Friday night he made an omelet for her, the night after Marilyn's death. She pressed the Listen button.

Hi, Alice. It's me. I—I have something to say to you. I wanted to tell you when we were together, but you were so tired and upset.

*It's—this is hard to say after so long—*He coughed and cleared his throat and then whispered, *I love you, Alice!* A pause. *If I get out of all this, I want you to be my wife.* He cleared his throat again.

I know it's stupid to say after all these years, with all this mess about Marilyn, but—well... Another shallow cough. *I had to tell you because I may be in a lot of trouble. Things I've done, stupid things.*

Don't try to contact me. I'm too embarrassed to see you. Just please try to understand how I feel. How terribly messed up my life has been and how foolish I feel for not saying something to you earlier.

A powerful flash of lightning cracked the sky, and—for an instant—Alice could glimpse the place she held in the endless throng of traffic that struggled to move forward. She pressed the phone close to her ear, straining to hear every word of Haydn's message against an explosion of thunder.

This was the message Haydn had asked about the morning Marilyn was killed, the morning Alice called him to tell him about the murder. She placed the phone in her purse and lifted her foot off the brake to inch forward with the traffic. A declaration of love and a marriage proposal left on a voicemail message? Would she ever get accustomed to Haydn's sometimes surprising, childish behavior?

BY THE TIME ALICE ARRIVED at Marilyn's, the temperature had plunged. She darted from her car to the kitchen door, and still she was soaked through when she stepped into the house.

Why wasn't Lillo in the kitchen?

She dashed to her bedroom, stripped out of the dripping clothes, and stepped into a hot shower, still thinking about Haydn's bizarre phone message.

A few moments later, she walked into the bedroom, drying her hair with an expensive, fluffy towel she had pulled from the warming rod next to the shower stall. God, she'd miss living here.

Trish was waiting for her in the bedroom. "I was worried about you."

"The weather." Alice shrugged. "Where's Lillo?"

"Shopping. He should be back soon." Trish raised her eyebrows. "Did you get the things I left on your desk? Will they do?"

"They're perfect. Thanks."

"Well, Ava and Georgia have left, and David told me he won't be back until dinner," Trish said as she turned to leave.

Alice reached out to stop her. "What are you going to do when you leave here, Trish? Do you have another job? Can I help you find something?"

Trish looked at her, hope filling her eyes. "Do you know of something? I don't have another job, and I have to find a cheaper place to live."

Alice sat on the bed and patted the space next to her.

Trish sat down. "I know it was stupid to quit this job before I have another one."

"It's okay, Trish. We'll find something for you. Meanwhile, why don't you stay with me? You don't mind cats, do you?"

"I love cats! Are you sure, Alice? I can help with expenses a little—my Social Security isn't much, but it'll be all I have."

"Not to worry. I'll be leaving here at the end of the week, too. It'll be fun to have a roommate."

Trish folded Alice in her long, strong arms and

held her close.

"Thanks, Alice," she said. "All we need now is Lillo."

AVOIDING A CONFRONTATION WITH Ava didn't mean Alice had escaped the tongue-lashing she expected. After a couple of hours of working at her desk, she looked up. One of the security guards, a tall man in a black suit and dark glasses, stood in the doorway. As soon as he caught Alice's eye, he walked to her desk and handed her a note from Ava. Then he stepped back into the doorway.

Dear Alice, Ava's note began. *As you know, I have tried unsuccessfully to contact you for some time by calling the number of the cell phone I gave to you and by leaving messages with others on staff. To say I am disappointed with your non-response is an understatement of the maddening frustration I feel in trying to work with you.*

I realized during this visit that you have done absolutely nothing to sort through my sister's personal things. In fact, it was heartbreaking to watch Georgia's face when she saw that her mother's belongings are still as Marilyn left them.

It was true, Alice admitted to herself. She simply hadn't had the time to get upstairs to deal with

Marilyn's clothing and jewelry. It was the first time in her life she hadn't done what she had been paid to do.

Poor Georgia. It had to have been a shock for her to see her mother's things untouched.

The note went on: *We have collected all of the jewelry from the bank. Marilyn's favorite earrings, the pair Marilyn is wearing in the portrait in the sitting room, were not with the pieces at the bank and were not in Marilyn's room. Please talk to Trish about this serious issue and ask her if she knows where they are. I understand this is not the first time Trish has worked for someone who lost expensive jewelry during her employment. I haven't said anything to the police yet, but if the earrings aren't returned by the end of the week I'll call Detective Cabrera.*

I want both of you out of the house immediately. I have asked someone to help you remove your personal belongings. He will inform me as soon as you have left the house, at which time I will have a personal check for the remainder of your month's salary mailed to your home address. This check will mark the end of your employment with my sister's estate and with me.
Ava Sauvage

A harsh cough made her look up. The security guard watched her from the doorway. She realized why he was there.

"Oh," she said to the dark glasses, "I'll just be a few moments."

"*Now*, ma'am," the dark glasses growled. "I've done all your packing for you. The maid is waiting in the driveway." He moved to the side of the doorway to allow her room to leave.

"Of course," Alice breathed. He had been in her room and packed her things? The man frightened her.

She grabbed her bag and slipped out the door, turning sideways to avoid brushing against the suit. As she hurried toward the driveway through the kitchen, her heart sank. Lillo wasn't there. Outside, she found Trish huddled against the Toyota, staring into the rain.

BY THE TIME ALICE DROVE HOME, Trish had worked herself into a complete frenzy. Ava had flat out accused her of stealing Marilyn's earrings.

Trish gave Alice only a few details about her previous employer's missing jewelry. Between long, shuddering sobs, Trish managed to explain that she agreed to take the fall for the employer's son. The boy had been in trouble before and was already facing prison time. Having stolen his mother's jewelry would have put him away for years.

Trish was arrested, and then the employer dropped the charges. When Trish left jail, the employer paid her a handsome amount, and then fired her.

"But, Trish," Alice said, "you had no record. You could have found work anywhere. Why stay with Marilyn after she began treating us all so badly?"

"I couldn't leave her," Trish sobbed. "Marilyn contacted me right after I was fired and told me she knew what happened. She said she completely understood the situation, she offered me a job, and I took it. It was only later—after her heart attack—that she said she'd tell any new employer I was a thief if I ever dared to leave her."

So that's why Trish had put up with Marilyn. And that's why she was so anxious about Marilyn's missing cashmere coat. Marilyn had been blackmailing her.

Alice called Connie on the way home, so Connie was waiting for them when they arrived. She had turned up the thermostat, started a fire, and made hot cocoa. The most helpful tool in Dr. Connie's bag of tricks was the Valium she brought with her. One of those and a cup of chocolate was all it took to calm Trish and send her off to sleep.

After they tucked Trish into the bed in the guest room, Alice and Connie crept back to the living room to finish the cocoa. Alice collapsed into the recliner and helped Arthur settle in her lap, then rubbed her knee.

"Finally," Connie said, "you're back home. Even though it did take getting fired to blast you out of that hellhole. I'm leaving a Valium for you, too, by the way. And I have a call into a specialist to look at your knee."

Alice's neck burned. All she needed was another lecture from Connie.

"How is Haydn?" she said, ignoring the not-so-gentle advice. "Anything new on getting him released based on his health issues?"

Connie shook her head. "He's not doing well. And no, Geoffrey hasn't had any luck with a release."

Alice frowned. She wasn't surprised, but she wouldn't mention Geoffrey's motives to Connie again. "I'd like to talk to you about something else if you have the time," Alice said.

Connie sat forward and listened to Alice relate the mysterious disappearance and reappearance of her old flip phone.

"Marilyn took it and never told you?" Connie said. "Why couldn't she get private calls on her own phone? The woman was mad as a hatter."

"You're right. But I charged the phone, and there was a message from Haydn that really surprised me."

"What? What was the message?"

Alice shook her head, put her cocoa on the table, and sat up straight. "He said that he loves me." She looked at Connie. "What does that mean?"

Connie shrugged. "It means he loves you." She leaned over and took Alice's hands in her own. "He has for years. Haydn just couldn't say it. When you retired, he told me how he felt. He asked me then if I thought you'd marry him. I assured him that you would, but he said he was afraid, and you know how foolish he can be. Haydn cares so much about you that he didn't want to lose you if you didn't feel the same about him."

Alice said nothing. Could she trust him? Haydn had been engaged to Marilyn. Why would he want someone like Alice, someone so different in every way?

"I'm thrilled he finally told you," Connie went on, "but rather disappointed he did it in a phone message. Haydn's really just a little boy in so many ways, isn't he?"

Alice said nothing.

"What would you have answered, Alice? Do you feel the same about Haydn?"

A ring on Alice's cell phone saved her from a reply. She should have left it at the mansion for Ava, but she had been ushered out of her office in such a hurry she didn't think of it. She reached across the sofa to answer it.

It was Lillo, calling to make sure she and Trish were okay. His voice was more measured than usual, as though he were trying to slow his breathing.

"May I call you back in a few minutes?" she said.

Connie stood and stretched. "I'm on duty in a few hours," she said. "I've gotta try to catch a nap."

"Thanks, Connie. I don't know what I'd do without you."

"I'm seeing Haydn tomorrow. Apparently, I'm still on Geoffrey's good side." Connie smiled. "Any message I can give him?"

Alice thought for a moment. "No. No message."

CHAPTER 18

A fter her friend left, Alice put the cups in the dishwasher. Connie had left her a pot of split-pea soup, some cornbread, and several bottles of wine in the refrigerator. Alice hoped Trish would eat later. She would need all the strength she could muster to deal with Ava's accusations.

She looked in on Trish, who slept on her back and snored like booming thunder. The down throw she and Connie had set out earlier was too short to reach her feet. Alice got another blanket from the closet and covered them.

When she was sure she was alone, she returned Lillo's call.

"Alice, you were fired, *vero*? You and Trish? So was I."

"Lillo, I'm so, so sorry."

"I can always find work," he said. "I have something for you. Can I come to your home?"

WHEN ALICE OPENED THE DOOR about thirty minutes later, Lillo thrust a large mailing envelope into her hands. He was soaked to the skin, water streaming

218 - ⬡ - Susan Toalson

from his heavy mustache, his eyebrows, and his trembling hands that clutched the envelope. The envelope was dry, except for where his fingers touched it. He had probably carried it inside his vest.

"Come in, sit by the fire," she said. "You must be freezing."

She stumbled over Arthur, rushed to the bathroom, and returned with two thick towels that she draped over his shoulders, standing on her toes to reach them. He had placed the package on the table in front of the sofa, never taking his eyes off of it.

"Look inside," he said.

"What's the matter? Are you all right?"

He pointed to the envelope.

Alice's name was written on it, printed in block letters with a wide, black Magic Marker. She lifted the closed end and emptied the contents onto the table.

A single item slid out. A gun with a bright red trigger.

DETECTIVE CABRERA WAS AT Alice's house in a matter of minutes. Alice wondered if she'd been nearby when she called, or if she sped down the wet freeway with her siren screaming at cautious drivers scrambling to get out of her way.

What did it matter how Cabrera got there? The detective had come to pick up an envelope with a gun in it that had been delivered to Lillo's house but had

Alice's name on it. This was serious.

Before Cabrera arrived, Alice told Lillo what she knew about the gun. Now the two sat next to each other on the sofa, where Alice held Arthur close to keep him out of the way. Cabrera had made a call to the station that brought several uniformed officers, as well as a couple of men in civilian clothing, who poured over the envelope and its contents as if it were a relic from an Egyptian sarcophagus. Cabrera asked if she or Lillo had touched the gun.

"No," Lillo said. "I looked in—it wasn't *sigillata*, erm, closed—to see if it was important and I needed to take it to Alice right away. I didn't touch it."

"Sealed, Mr. Cambria?" Cabrera said. "It wasn't sealed?"

"*Sì.* No tape, no glue, nothing."

Cabrera turned to Alice, who shook her head. "No, I didn't touch it, either. But this is the gun I told you about, the one David showed me. The one with the red trigger."

Had Lillo seen anyone near his house, Cabrera wanted to know, who may have delivered the envelope? At what time had he noticed it was there?

"Is there someone else here, Ms. Abbott? Anyone besides you two who may have handled the gun?"

"Oh, yes. I almost forgot. Trish, Ms. Quinn's maid, came home with me. All three of us..." Alice glanced in Lillo's direction to include him. "...were dismissed this morning. Trish hasn't come out of the bedroom. She took a sedative, and she's been sleeping."

"All of us. Fired." Lillo nodded.

"By whom?" Cabrera said.

"Ms. Quinn's sister," Alice said. "I, uh, guess she's planning to close the estate until she can put it on the market."

"Is David Rhodes still living there?"

"As far as I know, Detective. I haven't seen or talked to him since he showed me the gun."

Cabrera turned to Lillo.

"I'd like to meet you at your home, Mr. Cambria," Cabrera said, "to see exactly where you found the envelope. Can you be there in an hour?"

"*Certo*. Of course."

Then two officers took statements, one from Alice where she sat in the living room with Arthur and one from Lillo in the kitchen. When Lillo walked to the kitchen, he left behind a huge dark spot on the sofa. His clothes were still wet.

AFTER CABRERA AND HER officers left, Lillo sat again on the wet sofa next to Alice.

"Shit," Alice said, wrapping her arms tight around his huge bicep. She realized only now that he wasn't wearing his kitchen whites. The deep blue, cable-knit sweater he had on under a down vest—still wet— emphasized his strong arms and large chest.

"*Sì. Merda*," he echoed. "What do we do now?"

"We don't do anything. We wait. What else is there for us to do?"

He shrugged. The muscles flexed in his arm.

He stared at her for a long moment. "There's something else."

"What?"

"David. He called me. He wants you to meet him. He says he has information for you."

"What? Why does he want to see me? Why didn't you tell Detective Cabrera? Why doesn't he go to the police?"

"He said, don't notify the police. But I can call her now if you want. I didn't know what to do."

Alice hesitated. Her anxiety turned to fear. "Lillo, he could be a killer."

"I will call Cabrera now," he said, reaching into his vest for his cell phone.

"No, wait. I'm the one who has to do this. David won't tell Cabrera anything."

"He wants you to come alone, but I will be there, Alice. He won't see me."

Alice leaned forward and rested her elbows on her knees. She rubbed her eyes.

"He said to tell you that he did not murder anyone," Lillo went on, "and your friend in jail did not murder anyone, either. He said he needs your help."

Alice turned to look up at him, her eyes wide and bright. "David told me he knew who the killer was. He has to tell the police. Why does he need my help?"

Lillo shook his head. "I don't know. You don't have to go, *Bella. Ma chi sa?* Maybe he can help your friend."

Alice looked away.

"I will go, too," he said. "Different car so he won't know I'm there. Panera Bread on Route 2222 at 1:30 day after tomorrow. I will watch from outside. If he tries anything, I will help you. I will go early. You go early, too. Take a seat facing where I am outside in the car so he won't see me, but I can see both of you."

He stood. "I must go now."

"Thank you, Lillo."

"*Prego.*"

And then he was gone. Alice stared at the damp spot next to her and rubbed her knee.

AFTER LILLO LEFT, ALICE stoked the fire and settled into the green recliner with Arthur, who fell into a deep, heavy sleep in her lap.

At 5:00, she turned the TV on to watch the evening news. She was grateful the newscaster didn't mention Haydn's name in the update of the murders at Marilyn's mansion.

The weather forecast followed headline news. Rain would turn to snow and sleet sometime before midnight, a beautiful young woman told her. Schools and government agencies would be closed the next morning due to ice buildup on bridges and over-passes. Roadways often turned icy in Austin winter storms, but snow was a rarity. The weatherwoman knitted her lovely brows and cautioned Alice to be careful. "It can get dangerous out there."

"You have no idea how dangerous, dearie," Alice said. Then she pressed the OFF button on the remote and placed it on the table beside her cell phones. Two cell phones.

She picked up her old phone. Dare she listen to Haydn's declaration of love again? Could she bear it? Would she ever forgive him for waiting so long to tell her how he felt? Years. They could have had years together.

She pressed the phone messages icon and listened, dry-eyed this time. No surprises anymore. Just disappointment.

She listened to him say it. "I love you." And then she smiled as he called himself foolish for not having told her long before. He pleaded with her to leave Marilyn's and then the message was over.

She stared at the phone, realizing the hopelessness of the situation.

A brief click on the phone and then, *Message Four.*

Alice had forgotten there had been four messages on her flip phone. The final one had been recorded on January 6. It was for Marilyn.

Ms. Quinn, this is Marta Rodriguez in Jay Pierce's office, a woman with a slight Spanish accent said. *I'm calling to tell you that Mr. Pierce has had a fatal heart attack. I am closing his agency for the family.*

I see that he had a paper copy of your case file delivered to your address on West Avenue on

January 1, but I still have the electronic file. Please advise me how to proceed. I can simply delete it, or I can send it to you by text and then delete it.

I know you don't have the photos that Mr. Summers took to accompany the file. They are on Mr. Pierce's personal computer, and I don't have a password to access them. In accordance with your directions, I will text those to you as soon as possible.

The woman left a phone number with a 713 area code. It was the Houston number Alice had seen earlier on the bill Vivian Lombard had returned with the phone.

Agency? A case file that Marilyn had picked up on January 2, when she drove herself to the beauty shop? That was the day of the dinner party with the Johnsons. What case was Marta Rodriguez talking about? What was Marilyn working on?

She called the number right away and waited for someone to answer.

After a few rings, an answering machine picked up. It's late, Alice remembered. Of course they've closed for the day.

You have reached the office of Jay Pierce, private investigator. Please leave a message at the tone.

Private investigator?

Beep.

"Hello," Alice said, quickly gathering her thoughts for the message she would leave. "Erm, I'm returning your call from last week about the electronic file and photos you have. I'm terribly sorry to hear about Mr. Pierce's heart attack."

She swallowed, pressed her left eye with her fingers, and tried to focus on what she needed to say.

"Will you please text that file immediately to this number? And I'll expect the photos by text as well, as soon as you have access to them."

She paused. "Thank you."

AT ABOUT 6:30, TRISH trudged into the kitchen to join Alice. The woman had only enough energy to lean against a chair at the table.

Connie's soup bubbled on the stovetop. Alice's table was set for two, wine glasses included. Arthur lingered at attention at Alice's feet, his tail sweeping the linoleum floor. Except for a quick glance at Trish, his eyes remained glued on Alice.

"I smell cornbread."

"Sit. You're up just in time to join me."

Alice had heated the bread in the oven instead of the microwave to warm the kitchen. She slathered the squares with butter and filled two bowls to the brim with Connie's thick, rich split-pea soup. Trish poured Chardonnay into the wine glasses. Except for Arthur's pitiful cries for a handout, they ate in silence, too hungry to chat.

At last, Trish dabbed her lips with a napkin and sat back in her chair. "Delicious," she said. She took a sip of her wine. "You know, I've been meaning to tell you, I think the chef who was at Marilyn's the night she died lives in this neighborhood."

"What?"

"Yeah. I've seen him driving around."

Alice froze but within seconds recovered. "Right. You served the meal he prepared the night Marilyn was killed. I don't even know what he looks like, so maybe I've seen him, too. What kind of car does he drive?"

Trish shrugged. "Some kind of van. A dark one. Big." She scraped up what little soup remained in her bowl and licked both sides of her spoon. She wiped her lips again. "Alice, I'm so grateful to you. I can't imagine what I'd do, where I'd be, if it wasn't for you."

"Hey, we're in this together. I don't have much to offer, but what I have is ours. Please don't think I'm doing something selfless. I need you as much as you need me. Let's not say anything more about it."

Trish grinned. "Okay," she said, "but you've got to let me hold up my end, starting now. I feel so much better. I'll clean the kitchen—you go get comfy in the living room. I'll join you soon."

"You'll want to join me *very* soon. Now that the oven's off, the kitchen will get cold in a heartbeat."

Trish winked. "I'll work fast."

THE WOMEN SPENT THE EVENING in the living room in front of the fire, each of them huddled under woolen throws and sipping wine. Arthur was a hot, swollen lump in Alice's lap.

Alice told Trish about Cabrera's visit but didn't mention the gun.

"You mean I slept through that?"

"Sure did. My friend Connie knows how to put a woman down for a few hours, huh?"

Trish worried about getting her things from her apartment, but they agreed they would wait until the worst of the storm was over before they attempted that.

Alice said nothing about the private investigator in Houston. Best to protect Trish from as much as she could. Her thoughts were so wound up in the missing earrings that she would be no help anyway.

Around 9:30, ice pellets bounced against the windows. Alice emptied the last of the Chardonnay into their glasses.

"Do you have any family, Trish?"

"Two brothers and one cousin. One brother is here in Austin, so we see each other a lot. The other one is divorced, raising his granddaughter in Port Lavaca, down on the Gulf Coast. The cousin is in North Carolina. You?"

"A tango-dancing, hot-mama sister," Alice laughed. "Twyla. She's just left her most recent husband in Buenos Aires. I expect we'll see her sooner rather than later."

"Twyla sounds like fun. Are you close?"

"About as close as oil and water can get. We love each other dearly and get along beautifully, but it's really hard to believe we're related, and impossible to see us as sisters."

"Have you ever been married, Alice?"

"Once. Many, many years ago. You?"

"Same. Many years ago. He's also in North Carolina, same town as my cousin, which means I get to hear about him frequently."

"I take it that's not a good thing?"

"No. I really don't care which waitress or topless dancer he's making miserable these days. He's one of those guys who's as bad as he is good-looking." She sipped her wine. "We took target practice together once, hubby and I. More than once I thought about using him as my target."

They laughed. It made Alice happy to think of Trish on the arm of a good-looking husband.

"I'm calling it a night," Alice said. She drained her glass and unwrapped herself and Arthur from the throw.

"Me, too. Talking about my ex always exhausts me."

CHAPTER 19

S ometime in the night, Arthur jumped on Alice's bed. Only half-awake, she turned on her side and made room for him to curl into a ball next to her belly.

When the alarm broke into her dreams, the bedroom was still dark. The rain had stopped, but Alice's clock radio told her that Central Texas remained in the grip of below-freezing temperatures, and roadways were slick with ice.

Weather like this brought Austin to its knees. Public schools were closed. The universities and state agencies wouldn't open until noon. Flights were canceled at the airport. Parts of Interstate 35 and the expressway were shut down.

The sun was expected to make an appearance at ten o'clock or so.

She fumbled for her glasses and her phone with one hand, eased Arthur's body away from her with the other. Ava would want the phone back, she thought as she picked it up. Until she heard otherwise, or until service was disconnected, Alice would have to rely on it. There were too many people who had this number to change it now.

Cramming her glasses onto her nose, Alice squinted at the bright light of the phone. She had missed a call from Mark.

Alice, I have news about the gun that was delivered to your friend Lillo, the gun you said was David Rhodes's. First, it is the gun that killed Caitlin Johnson. Mark took a deep breath and let it out in stages. *David's fingerprints aren't on the gun, though. Haydn Lawrence's are.*

"My God, Haydn!" she said aloud as though he were in the room with her.

Mark's message continued. *That's not good news, of course, but it's something you need to know.*

After another pause, Mark went on: *There's something else. I left a package for you at Summer Moon Coffee House. I wanted to bring it by your house, but I don't have the time. We can talk about it later if you see anything interesting in it.* The message ended.

Haydn's prints were on David's gun? How? She didn't think Haydn and David knew each other. What new muddle had Haydn created?

Trish's bedroom door was closed, but she'd left coffee in a thermos bottle on the stovetop and oatmeal warming in a slow cooker. Alice was going to enjoy having a roommate.

The newspaper was outside. It must have been delivered on time despite the weather. With the sidewalk glistening with ice, Alice decided to wait before she ventured out to retrieve it. She often felt unsure walking on uneven surfaces. Icy surfaces were the worst.

She spooned hot cereal into a bowl and stirred in generous amounts of butter and brown sugar. This was one of her favorite meals.

She poured a cup of coffee and shuffled to her recliner, nudging Arthur away from her feet. Since he was a kitten, Arthur had understood that anything eaten in the living room was at least partly his. He could be disappointed in the kitchen, but never, never in the living room.

"Please, Arthur," she said to him. "Let me have a few bites first."

He sat erect at her feet and howled until she put the leftovers on the floor next to her. His entire head disappeared into the bowl.

"That'll keep you busy for a few minutes."

"What will?" It was Trish. She had showered and put her uniform back on. It was all she had to wear, Alice realized. She had to be miserable in that outfit, but it would be impossible for the large woman to fit into Alice's clothes. Alice decided it was best not to offer.

"I'm talking to Arthur. I do that a lot."

At the sound of his name, the cat raised his head. It was ringed with a brown syrupy goo. He licked his lips and dived back into the bowl.

Trish sat on the sofa. "Your house is so comfortable, Alice."

"Thanks. I think we can get your stuff today. You must be sick of that uniform."

"I am. I've always felt like a joke in this thing," she said, holding the skirt out with two fingers. "I think Marilyn liked that I looked so silly."

"She was always the belle of the ball, wasn't she?"

"The belle of everything," Trish sneered. "On a lighter note, I called my brother, Thomas. He has a truck, and he said he can help me move. You're off the hook."

"That works out great. I'm looking forward to meeting him."

Trish grinned as she stood. "I'm headed out to have coffee with Connie. She thinks she knows of a job I can get right away."

"Fantastic. Careful crossing the lawn. It's slippery out there."

ALICE WAITED UNTIL MOST of the ice had melted before she drove to Summer Moon. The barista handed her the envelope Mark had left for her. She thanked him, ordered a tall coffee, and climbed onto a barstool facing the parking lot.

The envelope held several pages of an Excel spreadsheet oriented horizontally and stapled in the upper left corner. On top of the first page, Mark had attached a large Post-it note explaining the pages.

This is a list of the people who called in to offer information after Marilyn Quinn was murdered. You'll see that they were all contacted, but no one had anything substantial to say. Some of the calls are from nut-jobs who phone in after every brutal murder, hoping to get some attention. It probably won't help, but I just couldn't throw it in a trashcan. Mark.

She was alone in the coffee shop, except for the barista, whose head was buried in a book, and a man who came in after her and sat across the room reading the newspaper with his back to her. The quiet suited her mood, so she settled in to drink her coffee and look through the pages.

The spreadsheet comprised four columns: Name and Contact Information; Date of Call; Notes; Need for Follow-up. The callers' names were listed in alphabetical order.

She first scanned the Need for Follow-up column. A neat row of marks indicated none of the calls had yielded any information deemed worthy of investigation. So many lonely people, she thought. How sad.

One entry read, "Caller in hospital, not expected to live." She glanced across the page. The caller's name was Charlotte Bauer, and she lived in Boston. Alice looked up from the page and furrowed her brow. Why did that name sound familiar to her?

According to the interview notes, the day after

Marilyn was killed, Charlotte Bauer had left a message, asking to speak to someone about the murder. When an officer returned Ms. Bauer's call the next day, the woman's nephew answered the call. Ms. Bauer, he informed the officer, had suffered a heart attack and was in the hospital. The nephew did not expect his aunt to survive.

Heart attacks, the bane of the elderly. Heart attacks and cancer, Alice mused. She thought of Marilyn. Heart attacks and cancer and murder. Alice scanned the other names on the spreadsheet. She was sure she had never seen or heard of any of them.

She looked again at Charlotte Bauer's name and then closed her eyes tight, willing herself to remember why it looked familiar. And then it came to her: It was the woman who sent the handwritten note of condolence to Georgia, saying she had been Georgia's babysitter many years ago in Boston.

"Yes," Alice whispered to herself. "That's it. The woman who said she'd been worried about Georgia over the years."

What information could Charlotte Bauer have to contribute to Marilyn's murder investigation? It must have been years since she had even seen Marilyn. What was she planning to tell a police officer?

On a whim, Alice dialed the number listed next to Charlotte Bauer's name. After three rings, someone answered.

"Hello. This is Charlotte," a wavering, breathy voice said.

"Oh, Ms. Bauer," Alice sputtered, trying to think of what to say. Was it too late to end the call? "I, uh, I understood you were in the hospital. I hope I'm not disturbing you."

"Please call me Charlotte," the frail voice said. "You're not disturbing me at all. In fact, it's good to have a distraction. My nephew lets me keep the phone in bed to play online bridge. He's told all my friends not to call—he's worried I might get agitated—but I miss talking. What can I do for you?"

"Uh, well, I see that you called the Austin Police Department with some information you have about Marilyn Quinn's murder? I—"

"Yes, I did call you. And the next thing I knew," Charlotte chuckled, "I was in the hospital."

"I understand. I'm not actually—"

"My nephew will be back soon, and he'll take my phone away. Please listen while I tell you what I know."

Alice hugged the phone tight to her ear while Charlotte Bauer spoke in clear and blunt terms, pausing often to take shallow breaths. The effort was tiring the woman, but Alice couldn't bear to stop her. What Charlotte Bauer knew about the Sauvage girls was remarkable. And frightening.

MARILYN AND AVA LIVED IN THE brownstone next door to Charlotte Bauer in Back Bay, Massachusetts, from the time they were adopted by their grandparents until the sisters sold the home forty-some years ago. Charlotte struggled to remember the year of the sale but dismissed it, as she said, "in the interest of time."

"Ava was six and Marilyn four when their father committed suicide in a seedy motel room where they were living in Los Angeles," Charlotte said. "I was only ten at the time myself, so of course I didn't know all the details. Years later I learned the girls were in the motel room, listening to their father kicking against the bathroom door until the rope around his neck took his life.

Alice gasped. Her hand covered her lips.

"I say *they* were listening," Charlotte went on. "Someone told me a few years ago that Marilyn slept through the whole thing. She was so young. I'm sure she had no idea what was happening."

"Anyway, Ava knew, and she called the front desk when the kicking stopped."

Alice realized she was holding her breath, shocked by Charlotte's story.

Charlotte inhaled before she continued. "Their mother had died of a drug overdose soon after Marilyn was born, so when the father died, the children were placed in a foster home. Sooner or later, the father's parents, who had been estranged from their son, were located. The grandparents welcomed the granddaughters with open affection and right away whisked them off to Boston to live in their lavish home next door to my parents."

Alice exhaled and waited.

"You can imagine the emotional trauma," Charlotte said, "being plopped into that grand mansion after all they'd been through. They were shell-shocked."

Charlotte paused to catch her breath. "Our brownstone shared a small front courtyard with theirs, and the first time I met them... was when I happened to see them hiding in a corner of the courtyard... under some boxwood shrubs. They were so painfully thin that they appeared to be all eyes, huge black eyes."

"Are you okay, Charlotte?" Alice said. "Shall we finish this another time?"

"No. We'd better finish it now, dear. I may not be here another time," Charlotte chuckled, "and I want someone in the police department to know what I have to say."

"Charlotte, I'm not really—"

A burst of ear-splitting laughter from the back of the coffee shop stopped Alice in midsentence. She turned to shush five teenaged girls who had taken a table behind her, but none of them noticed.

"The sisters were inseparable," Charlotte said, "but they soon began to reveal distinctly different personalities. Ava, the older one, the one who was aware what her father was doing in that motel room, acted out in nasty, violent ways, especially against her sister. I watched Ava from my parents' front window pinch and bite her sister, kick and slap her. I remember seeing teeth marks on Marilyn's cheek and black and blue spots on her thin arms and legs."

The last words were only a whisper. Charlotte's energy was giving out, despite her wish to tell this shocking story.

Alice couldn't help but think of her own sense of abandonment and dislocation when her father left her. For years afterward, she struggled with the urge to lash out, to hurt someone else, to make them suffer as much as she did. A feeling of pity for Ava washed over her. She pressed a napkin to her eyes.

In a moment, Charlotte took a breath and continued. "Marilyn was quiet, calm. She never fought back. Once or twice, I tried to play with them, but they wouldn't talk, wouldn't laugh, didn't know how to play." Charlotte was silent for several seconds.

"Charlotte?" Alice said.

"Yes, just let me rest a moment."

"Of course."

"It wasn't long before Ava began acting out against the grandparents. Neighbors watched in horror as she slapped and scratched and kicked at the old couple."

Alice winced.

"But the Sauvages refused to believe Ava needed anything more than unconditional love to change her behavior. Black eyes and broken bones were dismissed as accidents. A puppy the grandparents bought the children died of a broken neck. The Sauvages insisted the dog had caught itself in the iron fence in the back garden."

A muffled cough. A wheeze, and Charlotte pushed on. "When the grandparents died, the girls were in their mid-twenties and continued to live in the brownstone, which they inherited. A few years later, Marilyn married Walter Quinn. He moved into the brownstone with the sisters, but he left soon after Marilyn became pregnant. The rumor was that Marilyn had caught her sister in a compromising position with Walter."

"Do you mean—"

"Yes. In bed with him!" Charlotte raised her voice, indignant. "Ava was mean." A slight pause. "Dangerous. Under all that expensive makeup and those designer clothes, she was cold and cruel. The way she treated the servants was..." Another cough. "...despicable."

Where, Alice wondered, did Haydn fit in to all of this? Did he know Walter Quinn? Why would Haydn think he had fathered Georgia? Was he seeing Marilyn while she was married to Walter? Was Marilyn pregnant when their engagement ended?

"Ava treated Marilyn's daughter so badly, Officer."

"Charlotte, I'm not—"

"Marilyn had started an interior design business, and it took off. She was so successful that she was known all over the world. Sadly, she left Georgia with Ava, who used the child as her personal punching bag. Ava ignored Georgia, punished her for little things that all children do. Spilling milk. Wetting the bed."

Someone tapped Alice on the shoulder. "May

I take this, ma'am?" he said, indicating her empty coffee cup.

Alice handed it to him.

"I could see that it was a kind of jealousy," Charlotte was saying, "an extension of the way Ava treated Marilyn when they were children. I finally said to Marilyn that I'd be happy to have Georgia stay with me a few afternoons a week."

"How did that work out?"

"She was an angry, anxious child. I tried to get her to open up to me, but she simply couldn't. And she had trouble in school. The rumor at the time was that Georgia had been expelled, so Marilyn sent her away when she was seven or eight. I've worried about her so much over the years. My parents—someone—should have reported the abuse."

A long pause turned Alice's breath shallow. "Hello? Charlotte?"

"Yes," Charlotte said. "I'm here... I'm so happy Georgia grew up to have a career."

Charlotte's voice was becoming fainter, her speech slowing. Alice pressed the cell phone closer to her ear and strained to listen.

"I used to follow her... in fashion magazines. So beautiful. I haven't seen her... in any of the magazines for several years. Has she... retired from modeling?"

Alice hadn't bothered to look at the dates of the magazines at Marilyn's, but no one had said anything about retirement.

"I have to stop now," Charlotte muttered. "That's all I know… Ava Sauvage was a monster… when I knew her. I don't expect her to be any less than a monster today… Marilyn was murdered. Your number one suspect… should be her sister."

ALICE SAT WITH THE CELL PHONE at her ear until a car drove into the parking lot and stopped where the sun struck its front window. The bright reflection snapped her out of her stupor.

She struggled to process all that Charlotte Bauer had told her. Could what she said possibly be true? Or had Alice just listened to the ramblings of an old woman with an axe to grind for some bizarre reason?

Her instinct was to believe Charlotte, who hadn't rambled; in fact, she'd expressed herself with quite a degree of eloquence.

My God, the story of Ava's and Marilyn's early lives! They were babies left in the care of drug-addict parents. How was that allowed to happen?

Marilyn may have escaped the worst part, not hearing her father commit suicide in that horrid way, but both girls had to be affected by such an abysmal start to their lives.

Alice could sympathize with Ava's pain but not with her physical abuse and punishment of those around her. The dead dog was most worrisome. She'd learned in teacher training that animal cruelty was one of the best predictors of later violence.

Alice ran her fingers through her hair. That beautiful black horse, the one in the photo in Marilyn's office, had been killed. Poisoned. Could Ava have—

Was Ava still punishing Marilyn? Had she done it for so long that taking the next step—killing her—would be reasonable to expect? Had Charlotte Bauer been right when she accused Ava of such an unimaginable act?

Alice tried to push the questions into some kind of order, but they had taken root where they landed and now blossomed with more questions.

If Ava had a motive to kill—a big *if*—she also had the perfect opportunity. Ava was in the house the night Marilyn was killed. Georgia told Alice she had to beg her mother to allow Ava to join them for the holidays. Had the sisters argued upstairs, engaged in their final, hateful exchange before Marilyn tried to walk away? If Ava knew her sister was leaving the house that night—another big *if*—she could have run down the stairs and waited outside for Marilyn to open the door.

Too many ifs. Alice needed proof.

And, as though she could forget, another murder had occurred while Ava was in Austin. Would Charlotte say that Ava was capable of murdering Caitlin, too? Ava was, in Charlotte's words, a monster.

But that was a huge leap. Why would Ava kill Caitlin?

The coffee shop was filling with people on lunch breaks. They brushed against Alice's back as they moved toward the bar to order. She looked around her, surprised at how crowded the place had become. The man in the suit with his back to Alice, however, hadn't noticed. He still had his nose buried in the newspaper.

Alice stuffed the printed pages and her phone into her shoulder bag and walked to her car.

ON HER WAY HOME, Alice answered a call from Connie.

"I've just seen Haydn in jail. He wanted me to give you a message. Can you meet me at your house at 2:00? I'll only have a few moments."

"If this is about the love message he left on my flip phone—"

"It's about the DNA results. And the gun with the red trigger."

CHAPTER 20

"So that explains why his prints are on the gun," Alice sighed.

Connie sat on the sofa in the living room, and Alice perched on the arm of the green recliner, facing her.

Arthur installed himself on the floor and stared at Alice, trying to catch her gaze. It was dinnertime, and he wasn't willing to be put off.

"Yes. When you first went to work for Marilyn, you mentioned she had a daughter. From that moment, Haydn wondered if he could be the father. He suspected Marilyn was having an affair with Walter Quinn while he and Marilyn were engaged. When Marilyn ended their engagement, Haydn was so devastated that he never saw or spoke to Marilyn again. He didn't know about the child. So, you see, either of the men could be Georgia's father."

Alice pressed her eyelids with her fingertips.

"When Haydn learned Georgia was in Austin, he went a little crazy trying to see her. After he was arrested," Connie continued, "he contacted her through Geoffrey. He wanted her to know he would be helpful if she needed him. You know how he can be, Alice."

Alice ran her fingers through her hair and sighed. "Do you have the results of the DNA match yet?"

"Yes. There is no match. Since you can't see Haydn, I've already told him he's likely not Georgia's father."

The women looked at each other. Alice rested her elbow on the back of the recliner and let her fist support her head at the cheekbone.

A plaintive cry from Arthur distracted them. Alice reached out to scratch under the cat's chin.

"Let me see if I have this right," she said. "Georgia called Haydn the night Caitlin's body was found— the same night he got out of jail—and asked him to help her get rid of a gun. She had gone to lunch with David before Caitlin's body was found, noticed the gun in the car, and, without thinking, she jammed the gun into her purse before David realized she'd seen it."

"Right."

Alice frowned. Georgia and David had lunch together? Georgia detested the man. She suspected him of killing her mother. Why would she go to lunch with him?

"And then," Alice continued, "Haydn rushed to Marilyn's to get the gun from Georgia. He wanted to put it back in David's car. That's why Haydn was at the estate, on the lawn, where he found Caitlin's body."

Connie nodded.

"He didn't think to wipe his fingerprints off the gun?"

"He said he thought he did."

Arthur bellowed.

"How is Haydn?" Alice stroked the cat's back.

"Not well. I told him you heard his message, since you found your old flip phone."

Alice straightened and looked at her.

"He wonders what you think about it," Connie said with a shrug. "You need to tell him something."

Alice's mouth twisted upward on one side. Connie had acted so demanding the last few days, insisting she abandon Haydn, and now this order to respond to his voicemail marriage proposal. Her instinct was to push back, but she knew her friend cared about her. On several occasions, Connie had even told Alice she loved her as much as she had her own mother.

And Connie was right. Alice did need to respond to Haydn's phone message/marriage proposal.

The women sat in silence as Alice recalled the only time Haydn had held her in his arms, the night of Marilyn's murder when he surprised her on the back porch. She'd longed for that tenderness and warmth since she met him. He had been awkward that night, though, ready to release her long before she was ready.

Alice thought of the quiet boy she had married many years ago. Her relationship with him had been passionless, too, but Alice had convinced herself the boy was too shy to touch her, that he would change as they became more comfortable with each other. That had never happened.

Alice exhaled at length. "I can't marry him, Connie. I know I'm well past my 'sell-by' date, and I've always longed for a family of my own, but Haydn and I will never be more than friends."

Connie took Alice's hands in hers and pressed them tight. "Friends *are* family, aren't they, Alice?"

TRISH BROUGHT HAMBURGERS FOR dinner. She and Alice sat at the kitchen table and ate from the waxed paper wrappers, Arthur hugging their ankles in anxious anticipation of any random, tiny bite that might fall from the sky. Alice piled a huge mound of French fries on one of the bags between them. She coaxed ketchup from a nearly empty bottle she found at the back of the refrigerator next to a metal ring attached to the back-gate key she'd been looking for since Christmas. Red-faced, she slipped the key into her pocket, hoping Trish hadn't noticed.

"We need to do some grocery shopping," Trish said, her mouth full of fries. "Maybe we can make a list after dinner?"

"I was just thinking how good pickles would be on this burger," Alice said, smiling. "I haven't bought a jar in years because I wouldn't be able to open it."

"Arthritis?"

Alice nodded. "Yeah. My thumbs. They're not as painful as my knee, but that's probably because I don't try to open pickle jars anymore." She pushed her chair away from the table, and Arthur jumped into her lap.

"I'm beat tonight, Trish," she said, pinning the cat to her body to keep him away from what was left of her meal. "I'm going to take a shower and go to bed. Let's do the list tomorrow. How did your chat with Connie go?"

The hospital where Connie worked was hiring custodial staff. Connie promised she'd put in a good word for Trish.

"It's good pay and good benefits, Alice. And now that Marilyn's out of the way, I don't have to worry about her lying about me anymore."

The big woman's shoulders sagged; her smile vanished. "Do you think Ava will do to me what Marilyn was doing? Will she blackmail me, too?"

She dropped the last bite of her cheeseburger on the paper and held her head in her hands. "Why am I even thinking about getting a job? If Marilyn's earrings don't show up, I could go to jail."

"They'll show up." Alice reached across the table to touch Trish's arm.

Would they? Were they really missing? Or was Ava toying with Trish for some reason, because the maid had no resources, no way of defending herself?

Trish wiped her eyes and popped the last bite of the burger into her mouth. Then, despite Arthur's attention riveted to her fingers, she finished the fries. She offered to clean up, so Alice took a quick shower and crawled into bed early.

Alice pulled a notebook from the nightstand drawer and fumbled for a pencil until her fingers closed on one. It was a yellow mechanical pencil, the kind Cabrera used. Maybe it would bring her luck.

It was time, she thought, to get straight what she knew and what she *needed* to know about the two recent murders that she'd lived through. She fluffed a few pillows behind her back, placed the notebook on her bent knees, and took a breath. Arthur settled on her stomach.

Alice wrote "Victims" at the top of the page, looked at the word, and scoffed. Who did she think she was, Agatha Christie? She erased the word and wrote in its place, "Dead People I Know." Then she drew a vertical line halfway down the page to create two columns. One column she named "Marilyn," the second "Caitlin."

Where the vertical line stopped, she drew a horizontal line and wrote "Possible Killers" at the top of the line. Below the line, she created three columns and named them "Ava," "David," and "Javier." She looked hard at the three names and then created two more columns, crowding them into the side of the page. "Geoffrey," she wrote on one column and— after a brief hesitation, her pencil hovering above the page—she wrote "Haydn" on the other.

Then she took a deep breath and filled in the columns with all the details she knew about each of the people she had named.

CHAPTER 21

In half an hour, or so, the page was full, but Alice didn't feel any more clarity about the associations among the names than she had before she started. Her back and her knees ached. She folded the paper and slipped it and the pencil into the pocket of her robe at the end of the bed. Then she turned the lamp off, and she and Arthur settled in for the night.

The next morning, Alice woke up again to the sound of sleet slapping at the windows. This winter could turn out to be one of the worst in Austin's usual mild-weather history.

She made coffee, turned the thermostat up, and then lit a fire. Coffee in hand, she collapsed in the green recliner. Arthur landed in her lap with a dull thud and rolled onto his back, as if luxury were his only aim.

She rubbed her knee and sipped coffee. For no particular reason, a tear slid down her cheek.

What a difference these last two weeks had made in her life. She had done things, seen things, said things that she could never have imagined, yet Haydn's situation kept getting worse. She had collected bits of information that someone with the right skills could put together and come up with a reasonable way to explain his innocence. Cabrera could do it, but the detective had insisted that Alice deal with Geoffrey. Geoffrey could probably do it, if he had any actual interest in helping Haydn. But he wouldn't talk to her, either.

Not even Haydn was talking to her.

She was tired. Used up. After two weeks of her best efforts, all she had were pieces of a puzzle in a plain box with no image of a finished picture to guide her. Besides, a good many of the pieces were missing.

She crossed her legs, for a moment disturbing the big cat. The scratch of a folded sheet of paper in the pocket of her robe made her reach into her pocket and bring out the yellow pencil and the page she had created the previous night. She straightened her posture and unfolded the page.

Something occurred to her as she examined the blocked-off sections of text. It *was* a puzzle, and the pieces had to fit together somehow.

It seemed reasonable to connect names of the Possible Killers to names of the Dead People based on their relationships. She drew a solid line from Haydn to Marilyn and solid lines from Ava to both of the Dead People. She stared at the names on the page. This was getting her nowhere. She drummed the tip of the pencil on the paper. She was missing something. What was it?

She tried to picture Marilyn opening the front door to the killer. She was not even halfway dressed, anxious, from the sound of her voice on the message she had left Alice, and very sick. Whose face did she see? Whose face—

Wait! Maybe Marilyn hadn't seen a face. One of Marilyn's neighbors heard the shot and said that the Christmas lights had gone out at the same time the shot was fired. The shooter must have been waiting at the electrical panel that controlled the lights.

How far was the panel from the door? Maybe ten yards—or more? And Mark had said one shot was fired and it hit Marilyn in the left eye. That would take a pretty good shooter, wouldn't it?

Alice had never shot a gun in her life.

Neither had Haydn, as far as she knew.

Ava had, though. Marilyn and Ava and Georgia all loved to shoot—Trish had told her Marilyn planned to build an indoor shooting range behind the house. She looked back at her list, at Geoffrey's name.

Years ago Geoffrey had asked Haydn for money for shooting lessons. Haydn joked that he probably needed a gun, considering his clientele, and he mailed Geoffrey a check for $500. At that price, Alice remembered thinking at the time, they must have been really good lessons.

ALICE WAS ALMOST OUT of the door on her way to meet David when a curious beeping sound came from the living room. Following the sound to her recliner, she lifted the seat cushion and found the flip phone that

Marilyn had left at Vivian Lombard's spa.

She had forgotten about the phone. Who could be calling?

"Hello?" she said, wariness edging her voice.

"Oh, Ms. Quinn. This is Marta Rodriguez in Jay Pierce's office. I was about to hang up. I'm so glad you answered," the female voice said. "I'm still working on closing Mr. Pierce's office. In response to your request, I texted a copy of your file to this phone number. Have you received it?"

My God—she'd neglected to follow up on the private investigator file.

"Hello, Marta. Will you hold one moment while I have a look?" Alice pressed the text icon on the phone. A file had been received. "Yes, Marta, I have it."

"Perfect. It'll be hard to read on your phone, but I've made the file print-friendly. I apologize about the photos that should accompany the file. As I said, Mr. Pierce downloaded them to his personal computer, and I'm still having a bit of trouble locating the password. I'll send them along as soon as I can."

"Thank you, Marta."

The file Marta sent was a document on office letterhead entitled "Confidential Surveillance Investigation Report, submitted by Jaydon Pierce." The report was dated January 1. The client name, Marilyn Quinn, appeared right under the date.

Reaching behind her for the arm of the recliner, she lowered herself to sit as she scanned through a text file that swam before her eyes on the tiny screen of the phone. She re-oriented the screen to horizontal, which provided a somewhat better view. Later she'd change the ink and add paper to the printer.

The report was arranged under bold headers. Alice's eyes locked on the text beneath Identification of Subject. An unmistakable description of David Rhodes followed.

Under Nature and Scope of the Investigation, Alice read that Marilyn had suspected David of infidelity, of meeting a woman for sex on his visits to Houston.

Alice held the phone to her chest and stared at nothing for a moment while she caught her breath. She rubbed her temples with her free hand and shoved her glasses tight onto her nose.

Toward the end of the report, under a header entitled Summary, Alice read:

Jay Pierce followed Subject from the airport when Subject arrived in Houston at 3 o'clock PM on Tuesday, December 31, until Subject boarded a flight back to Austin at 10 o'clock AM on Wednesday morning, January 1.

Subject took a cab from the airport to a Lexus dealership on the Katy Freeway, where he met with P.H. Sanders in Sanders' office from 5 o'clock PM until 5:45 o'clock PM. According to Mr. Sanders, the general manager, subject was interviewing for a job at the dealership.

So David hadn't been working in Houston? Ava had told her that he had no job and no money.

Subject took a cab from the dealership to the Sofitel Hotel on Sam Houston Parkway. He checked into Room 213, where Room Service delivered a cart with meals for two diners, a bud vase with a single red rose, and a bottle of champagne at 7:30 o'clock PM. Room Service removed the cart at 9 o'clock PM. Neither the bud vase nor the wine bottle was on the cart.

Her eyes ached. She would print the file later to make it easier to see. For now, she squinted past the pain and continued reading, riveted to the text.

At 5 o'clock AM on Wednesday, January 1, a slender, well-dressed woman with long, dark hair left the room.

At 8 o'clock AM on Wednesday, January 1, Subject left the room. He took a cab directly to the airport and boarded the flight back to Austin at 10 o'clock AM.

A well-dressed woman with long, dark hair? Ava? He was traveling to Houston to meet Ava for love trysts? Ava. Ava, who had slept with Marilyn's first husband, Walter Quinn, according to Charlotte Bauer. What qualms would she have about sleeping with David?

Marilyn had picked up a hard copy of this very report at Vivian's salon the day she died. No wonder she was furious that evening at the dinner party.

BY ONE O'CLOCK, ALICE WAS splashing along the highway through half-melted ice, mixed with sand the city had spread to help provide traction on the glassy surfaces. She would be early for her meeting with David, which was what she and Lillo had planned.

The university and all state offices had made announcements that they would be closed the entire day, so Alice was almost alone on the road.

At FM 2244, she exited the freeway with caution and pulled into a parking space at the entrance to Panera Bread. David's SUV was nowhere in sight. Thank God, Lillo was there, huddled in the driver's seat of a car she didn't recognize. He held a newspaper in front of his face as soon as he caught Alice's eye. He must have borrowed the car, believing David would recognize his black Chevy pickup.

She ordered coffee and took a seat at a table for two so David would have his back to Lillo. Then she took a deep, ragged gulp of air and sipped her coffee, holding the rim against her bottom lip to keep her trembling hands from spilling it.

How would this confrontation go? She wanted answers from David, and she was determined to get them.

At 2:00, she wondered if the weather had caused problems for David. She ordered another coffee.

At 2:15, just as she watched a familiar SUV pull into the restaurant parking lot, her cell phone rang. It was Mark.

"Alice, I have something for you. Caitlin Johnson wasn't killed at Marilyn's. She was shot somewhere else and left on Marilyn's front lawn."

"What? Where—"

"We don't know where yet. I'll keep you informed."

Alice pressed the phone to her ear, trying to make sense of this most recent development.

"There's something else, Alice," Mark said. "David Rhodes was in an accident sometime early this morning. He was apparently really, really drunk, and he lost control of his car. He's in the hospital."

"No! I'm waiting for him. I've got to get over there. He wanted to tell me something. I've been waiting for him!"

"Don't go to the hospital, Alice. People will know you heard about the accident from me. The ID hasn't been released yet. And he wasn't hurt that bad. He'll probably be back at Marilyn's soon."

A family in the booth next to her was ordering burgers and drinks. One of the children begged for ice cream.

"It's getting harder for me to cover my tracks in the department, Alice," Mark was saying. "Someone is going to figure out I'm accessing files that I'm not officially authorized to see."

"Please be careful, Mark."

ALICE AND LILLO SAT IN THE borrowed car, staring at the restaurant's wall of windows in front of them. She told Lillo about David's accident. Lillo said nothing. When he started the ignition and turned the heater fan to high, Alice realized how cold she was. She glanced at the table where she had waited and noticed she'd left her coat on the back of her chair.

"*Vado io*. I'll get it," Lillo said in a gentle voice.

She watched him enter the restaurant—a big man with a big heart, a friend who was standing by her in this most difficult situation of her life. Just as he reached for Alice's coat, her cell phone rang. It was Mark again.

"David wasn't drunk, Alice."

"Can I see him, talk to him?"

"I'm afraid not. He died about five minutes ago."

"What?" She gasped. "But you said the accident wasn't bad."

"He didn't die because of the accident, Alice. He was poisoned. One of the ER docs was suspicious of something when David was brought into the hospital. They're following up now with blood tests for ethylene glycol, which made him appear to be drunk."

"I don't—"

"Antifreeze, Alice. Looks like someone poisoned him with antifreeze."

ALICE INSISTED SHE DRIVE home alone. Lillo wanted to stay with her. Someone out there was dangerous, and, he reminded her, they still had no idea who.

In the end, Alice convinced him she would be safe until he returned later in the day to prepare dinner. She could use the time to think, and he needed to return the car he'd borrowed before the next storm arrived.

Trish had delivered several boxes from her apartment and left them against the walls of the living room. A stack of books—most of them were about rose gardening and interior decorating, to Alice's surprise—had fallen over and scattered across the floor. The arrangement lent an uneasy, lonely feeling to the room, as though the home were being abandoned.

She needed to warm the room. With the last of the wood outside the back door she started a small fire. She made a cup of hot chocolate and settled with Arthur into the green recliner.

She closed her eyes and pictured the bottle of antifreeze on the shelf in the garage at Marilyn's, lying on its side among a row of neat upright containers of oils and other automotive elixirs. She had set it vertical. It was opened, but only a part of it had been used.

Who else would know about the antifreeze? Owen, of course. Javier Johnson, who had searched in the garage for the tools he needed to fix Alice's car. And David, who, according to Tony at Tony's Repair Shop, had bought antifreeze to put in his car.

So what? Anyone could have walked by the garage and seen it. Unless it was raining, Owen always left the doors open when he was working.

And maybe David wasn't paranoid, after all. He had shown Alice a gun and said he wanted Ava to know about it. Did he threaten her? Someone murdered him. Was it Ava? Javier Johnson, who probably blamed David for Caitlin's death?

When he showed her the gun, David had told her he was ready to blow the top off everything. She moved herself from under Arthur, spilling his body onto the chair cushion, and carried her chocolate to her desk. Her old computer wheezed and flickered, but managed to take her to *Antifreeze Poisoning*.

In a few moments, Arthur jumped onto the desk and walked across Alice's keyboard. Alice stared at the screen as though she didn't see the cat. With no response from his mistress, Arthur walked across the keyboard again and sat on it. Still no response. Unperturbed, the big cat turned twice and lay down, his big fluffy butt hanging off the space bar.

Alice sat frozen in her chair. Her mind reeled over what she had read about antifreeze poisoning, in particular about the symptoms: nausea, vomiting, dizziness, fatigue, headache, slurred speech, unsteady walk, weakness, leg cramps, and blurred vision.

In the weeks before she was murdered, Marilyn had presented all of those same symptoms.

"HOW DO YOU POISON SOMEONE with antifreeze?" Alice paced the floor in front of Connie, whom she called soon after her Google search. Connie had agreed that Marilyn's symptoms could be related to ingestion of ethylene glycol.

"Well," Connie said, "with the kind made before governmental regulations, you could put it in someone's food, probably more likely in a drink. It could be done very easily by administering small amounts over a long period of time." She wore leopard-print silk pajamas. It was her day off.

"Before what regulations?" Alice wrung her hands. She sat for a moment to rub her knee. Then she stood again.

"Regulations that have changed the taste. Animals and children used to die from drinking it because it was sweet. The newer stuff tastes bitter."

Alice lowered herself into her chair, at once still. "My God," she whispered. "Lillo could be in trouble. I told Cabrera that Marilyn complained about his food being too sweet."

"Wait, Alice," Connie said, placing her hand on Alice's arm. Her long, elegant nails were painted black.

"The symptoms you describe could also be caused by the drugs she was taking," Connie continued. "Maybe lithium. Was she manic-depressive? Bipolar?"

"Dear God, I don't know. She took a lot of pills."

"Any number of psychotropic drugs could cause those symptoms," Connie said, thoughtful for a few seconds. She crossed her long legs and went on at length, elucidating various scenarios as she spoke. "If someone wanted to kill a person taking one of those drugs, the old, sweet-tasting antifreeze would be the way to go. Even normal autopsy results would show the drugs but wouldn't separate out the antifreeze. It would take an independent test to do that."

Alice stiffened. What was it Tony had said about David buying the old formula of antifreeze to put in Marilyn's car?

"Why would someone shoot Marilyn if she was being poisoned?" Connie said.

Exactly.

"You have to call Detective Cabrera, or I will," Connie said as she handed Alice's cell phone to her. "You have to tell her about the antifreeze you saw in the garage. And you have to be careful how you tell her because—"

A knock at the front door made them both jump.

"That'll be Trish and her brother with more of her things," Alice said.

It wasn't Trish. It was Detective Cabrera.

"Oh, Detective, I was just going to call you," she said, holding the phone up for Cabrera to see.

"Is that right?"

"Yes. I think I have some information that may be relevant in both Marilyn's and David Rhodes's murders."

At once, Connie was at Alice's side, nudging her away from the door. "Come in, Detective," she said.

Watching Alice's face, Cabrera ignored Connie's invitation to sit. A uniformed officer stood by the door, legs apart, arms straight at his sides.

"Coffee? Hot chocolate?" Connie said.

The officer shook his head. Cabrera didn't respond. Her eyes were still riveted on Alice's face as she took out her notepad and yellow pencil.

"What is the information you have, Ms. Abbott?"

The few moments it took Connie to get everyone settled had given Alice a chance to ask herself why Cabrera was there. The detective hadn't given Alice the time of day before this. Now here she was, with a police officer, in her home.

"Ms. Abbott?"

"Oh, uh—I wanted to ask about David Rhodes. I had an appointment, and he—"

"You said you had information about his murder. Where did you hear that he'd been murdered?"

Connie sat on the arm of Alice's chair and rubbed her friend's back.

It hit her like a hammer: She'd promised Mark she wouldn't say anything until details were released to the press.

Heat crawled up her neck and onto her face. She folded one hand into the other and held them in her lap. The room had grown cold. She glanced at the fire, which had burned down to white coals.

Cabrera tapped the eraser end of the pencil against her bottom lip.

"I'm neither confirming nor denying that Mr.

Rhodes was murdered. I'm here to ask you about a container of antifreeze in Marilyn Quinn's garage. Did you know it was there, Ms. Abbott?"

Alice didn't answer.

"Ms. Abbott, we need you to come to headquarters with us."

Connie leaped to her feet. "What do you mean? Are you accusing Alice of something? What makes you think she knows anything about antifreeze in Marilyn Quinn's garage?"

Cabrera stood and put her notebook and pencil away. She glared at both women before she spoke. "Ms. Abbott's fingerprints are on the container."

SEVERAL HOURS LATER, Connie drove Alice home from the police station downtown. The women were cold, hungry, and tired. The sleet had let up earlier in the day and started up again while they were at the police department. Connie took her time driving, careful behind the wheel.

"How much trouble do you think Mark will be in?" Alice said.

"A lot. But it's done, Alice. Let it go. I'm more worried about the trouble you're in."

"I need to find a lawyer."

"What questions did she ask you, Alice?"

Alice's exhale was part-sigh, part-sob. "Too many to remember, frankly." She paused. "One question surprised me, though."

"Was it about the antifreeze?"

"No. It was about the Christmas lights at Marilyn's. She asked if I knew where the control panel was."

THE HOUSE INSIDE WAS colder. Trish had delivered more boxes, intensifying the precarious half-in/half-out ambience Alice had felt earlier. Even Arthur's presence seemed odd, like a ghost from some former life.

Connie settled Alice in the recliner and rushed to the thermostat. "I'll start a fire," she called.

"There's no wood," Alice murmured.

"No problem. I'll bring some from my house. Be right back."

Dazed, alone, Alice stared at cold ashes in the fireplace. Arthur cried for attention, but she didn't respond.

What in God's name had she done? She was a suspect in a murder investigation, she'd been fired from her job, she'd put both Mark and Lillo in precarious legal situations. And Haydn was implicated in Marilyn's murder and also in Caitlin's murder because his fingerprints were on a gun she had given to the police.

What was it she had whined about just before Detective Cabrera wandered into her garden on the day of Marilyn's murder? Had she complained about being bored?

How could she have been so stupid, so arrogant?

A bottle of sedatives that Connie must have left for her caught her eye. She settled her bag on her lap and took the bottle in her hand. *How many would it take?* she wondered, opening the cap.

Connie burst through the door, three heavy logs tucked under her arm.

"I'll get this started in a jiffy! How about a glass of wine?"

Alice shoved the cap back on the bottle and stuffed it in her bag. "Yes. Sounds good."

"Great. Just let me get this started, and then—"

Someone knocked at the door. Connie looked at Alice, quizzical as she frowned. "You expecting someone?"

Alice shook her head.

Connie brushed her hands on her pants and opened the door. She glanced at Alice, and then stepped outside.

A moment later she returned, followed by Detective Cabrera and several uniformed policemen. The policemen walked through the house without a word or a pause. Arthur watched each one of them pass, swiveling his head from right to left as if he were counting them.

Alice pushed herself up from the recliner. "What's going on?"

"I have a warrant, Ms. Abbott." She handed a sheet of paper to Alice.

"A—"

"An expensive pair of earrings is missing from Marilyn Quinn's estate. We have reason to believe they're somewhere in your house."

The three women—Alice, Connie, and Cabrera—stood motionless in the cold, cluttered room until one of the policemen returned from Alice's office with Marilyn's earrings in his hand.

CHAPTER 22

L ate in the afternoon the next day, Alice was released from jail after an entire night and day of waiting in a crowded central holding cell with about thirty other women. She suspected she had been kept for so long thanks to Ava's friends in high places. The cell reeked of unwashed bodies and the contents of one open toilet bolted to the floor in the middle of the cell. As the time passed, tempers that were already short when she arrived escalated into dramatic outbursts.

Despite the revolting and terrifying circumstances in the cell and more than twenty hours with no sleep or anything to eat, one emotion overrode all of her disgust and fear and discomfort. She boiled with rage.

The link between Geoffrey and Ava was clear to her now. Geoffrey had broken into Alice's home, not to steal anything, but to leave something—Marilyn's earrings. He was somehow involved with Ava, and Ava needed to have Alice out of her way.

The arrest was a declaration of war. Geoffrey had warned her to keep her nose out of Haydn's case, first by restricting access to Haydn, then by delivering the red-triggered gun with Haydn's fingerprints. Having her arrested for stealing Marilyn's earrings was the volley that Geoffrey expected would end Alice's involvement altogether.

When David died, Geoffrey had to hustle to focus attention on Alice. He instructed Ava to accuse Alice, not Trish, of stealing the earrings, and a friendly judge had signed a search warrant.

The gloves were off. Alice was ready for a bare-knuckle fight. No more I'm-too-old-for-this whining and no more reservations about Ava's murdering David and Marilyn. And as a high possibility, Caitlin, too.

Free on bail, Alice stomped down a windowless hallway, eager to get away from the jail compound. Connie sat in one of several metal chairs that lined one wall, while scores of other inmates' friends and family waited for loved ones in shabby clumps among the chairs. Dressed in hot-pink hospital scrubs, beautiful, red-headed Connie was a lone petunia in a patch of onions.

WHEN THEY GOT BACK to Alice's, Connie parked in her driveway. A dark SUV waited, its motor running, just a door or two down the street. Connie didn't seem to notice it, so Alice said nothing. She didn't think Geoffrey was finished with her.

As she and Connie walked through the front door, the house exploded with laughter.

"Hello?" Alice called.

"*In cucina!* In here!" Lillo bellowed from the kitchen. "*Venite!* Come! Come!"

They dropped their coats on the sofa and followed his voice. A thick, fragrant lasagna bubbled on the stovetop, waiting to be served. Connie's partner, Patsy, perched on a counter with a glass of wine in her hand, and Trish sat next to her brother Thomas, a construction contractor who looked so much like Trish that he could have been her twin. The three of them had helped Lillo empty a couple of bottles of Lillo's favorite Tuscan Chianti Classico. Arthur frolicked among his guests like an over-stuffed kitten.

Trish's loud, open-mouthed laughter and the rosy flush in her cheeks diminished the bags under her eyes and made her almost beautiful. She wore a dark fleece sweatshirt over jeans, at last having shed the uniform that had become part of her personality. What a difference in the woman. Was it the wine, or the relief that she was off the hook for the missing earrings?

Alice showered and changed her clothes, vowing to burn everything she owned that stank of jail, and then took a seat next to Lillo in the kitchen. A beautiful meal with friends old and new seemed a fitting way to erase the wretched hours she'd spent in custody.

The SUV parked down the street chewed at her thoughts, but only until someone refilled her glass and the magnificent lasagna was served. After that, more wine and a mountainous garden salad, followed by more wine and a panna cotta with hazelnut sauce that turned out to be Arthur's favorite dish of the evening. Then cups of frothy espresso poured into dainty cups from the machine Lillo had brought along for the occasion. And as a finale, slender, frosted glasses of Lillo's homemade limoncello.

At some point before Alice's second helping of lasagna, Lillo leaned over and whispered in her ear, "This is what makes *una famiglia, Carissima*—sharing food, wine, laughter, tears with people you love. You didn't miss out, Alice. You have it all right here."

After three hours of eating, drinking, laughing, Alice realized she hadn't felt so good in weeks. At the end of the meal, she begged everyone not to drive. The weather was bad, and they had had a lot to drink. She and Trish trudged across the frozen lawn to Connie's and Patsy's house, and the men slept at Alice's.

Fighting to keep her eyes open, Alice peered through the curtains in Connie's guest bedroom. The SUV was still parked where it had been when she and Connie had returned from jail. She sniffled and then collapsed onto the bed. She pulled the blanket up to her chin and gave only a fleeting thought to the horrors of the jail holding tank before she fell asleep.

CHAPTER 23

It was almost nine o'clock in the morning when Alice woke up. She'd slept long and well, and she was ready to face whatever came her way.

Ignoring the cold, she shoved her feet into her shoes and left the room.

Both Connie and Trish were already up, nursing large mugs of coffee in the living room. Connie had lent Trish one of her caftans. It was stretched tight over her chest and belly and reached only halfway down her calves, but the plum color complemented her hair and skin.

"Good morning," Connie whispered. She pointed to a closed bedroom door. Patsy must be sleeping in. "I have aspirin in the kitchen if you're suffering."

"No, thanks. I feel a lot better than I have any right to, after last night."

"Me, too," Trish added. "That must have been a step or two up from the wine I'm used to drinking."

"It is partly the wine, but mostly it's eating rich, healthy food, drinking lots of water, and laughing with good friends that makes the difference. If Lillo had prepared that meal in Italy, he probably would have served at least one more course," Connie said.

"Gotta love those Italians."

Alice pinched the draperies away from the front window and peered through the sleet. The SUV was gone. "Are the guys up yet?"

"Oh, heavens, yes," Connie said, handing Alice a mug of steaming coffee. "They left early. But sit a minute. It's miserable out there."

Alice shook her head. "I can't, Connie. I have some things I need to do. You stay, Trish. I'm glad you two are getting to know each other."

Connie looked worried but didn't press her. She understood that Alice wasn't sharing much with Trish.

Connie handed Alice a bright red umbrella and an orange raincoat and sent her across the lawn with a thermos of hot coffee.

THE HOUSE WAS WARM, and the aroma of last night's lasagna lingered. A pair of Trish's tennis shoes, one atop the other as if she'd peeled them off with her feet rather than bending to untie the laces, waited by the door. And Arthur howled his welcome while he wrapped his plump, hairy body around her ankles. For the first time in a long time, she felt like she had come home.

She took the thermos into the kitchen. Arthur leaped to the countertop and begged for her touch, so she held him close to her as she struggled to call Mark's number with one hand.

No answer. She left a brief message asking him to meet her.

The new latch on the back door caught her eye. She had told Cabrera about the break-in when she was questioned yesterday, but now wished she had told her as soon as it happened. Alice hoped that wouldn't turn out to be another mistake.

How she wanted to talk to Haydn, the old Haydn, the one before the love message he left on her flip phone. She had often drawn strength from his still-ness, his warmth. Now she would have to find her own strength.

She had no doubts about what she needed to do.

Her old desktop computer sputtered and complained over its reluctance to start the day and then flashed an oversized photo of Arthur sleeping on his back in a patch of sunlight in the garden, his huge tummy puddled at his sides. In the center of the photo, a request for a password.

She entered her password, opened her email account, and watched as the inbox downloaded more than a month's worth of messages, way beyond the few daily ads and other routine trash she usually received.

When the download was complete, she counted more than fifty messages. Only four of them were addressed to Alice. The rest had been forwarded from Marilyn's email account.

She took a deep breath and chose the first one to read, hoping to find something to help her crawl into

Marilyn's mind in the days and hours before she was killed.

Ava had backed up the feed by two days preceding Marilyn's death. A thread of a conversation between Marilyn and one of her best clients about some silk upholstery fabric was doubtless the conversation Ava had wanted her to monitor. It would yield an enormous commission.

But there were other conversations, too, including one between Marilyn and Javier Johnson and one between Marilyn and David.

Yes! These personal emails were exactly what she had hoped she'd find.

She opened the one from Javier first.

Marilyn: Your phone message has me quite upset. I've left several messages for you. Please let's talk. Your refusal to reimburse what is owed to me has me reeling. Ava paid far more for the Santa Fe house than it's worth. I have options, of course. Let's talk. Javier.

"Interesting," Alice muttered. This had to be the loan David mentioned when he showed Alice the gun with the red trigger. Ava had borrowed money to buy a house.

The date of the message was January 2, the day of the dinner party. The day Marilyn picked up the private investigator's report at Vivian Lombard's salon. The day Marilyn died.

Marilyn had replied to Javier's invitation within minutes.

Javier dont hammer me on this. its avas problem. she made the loan. she needs to pay it back. tell Geoffrey i want to see any paperwork that involves me or my estate asap
georgia wants you and wife for dinner tonight. dont bring this up. i don't want georgia to know about it
and don't bring your daughter
m

Marilyn's preferred email style, no caps and little punctuation, made some of her messages impossible to sort out. This one seemed clear.

Geoffrey. Of course. As general counsel of Javier's company, Geoffrey would have been the one to oversee contracts and loan agreements and do other assignments at their bidding. Assignments like breaking into someone's house and planting expensive diamond earrings.

And then it hit her. Could Ava have been so sure Marilyn would die from her heart attack that she used Marilyn's estate as collateral for the loan she got from Javier? Georgia would have been Marilyn's heir, but Georgia would give her aunt whatever she needed. Ava would be the only family Georgia had.

When Marilyn survived the heart attack, Javier must have asked Marilyn to pay Ava's debt. How

Marilyn must have hated her sister, realizing Ava had been picking her carcass even before she was dead. Ava was invited to spend Christmas in Austin only because Georgia had insisted, and Marilyn wouldn't have said no to Georgia.

It seemed reasonable to Alice that the loan would have been the topic of the argument at the dinner party the night Marilyn was killed. If so, was it also logical to expect the argument continued after the Johnsons left? That very day, Marilyn had picked up Jay Pierce's investigative report verifying David's affair. She would have been enraged.

But would the argument have gone on until midnight? Marilyn didn't have the stamina to sustain that kind of exhaustive back-and-forth. She must have slept and awakened later to see or hear something so shocking that her only option was to run.

Alice scrolled down to a message from Marilyn to David dated December 30.

david come home tonight or don't bother coming home at all

And an email response from David's cell phone about an hour later.

You're overreacting, Darling. My interview went well, but I'm absolutely exhausted. I'll see you tomorrow as early as I can. I love you. David

That would be the interview at the Lexus dealership. That's not all that had gone well for David in Houston.

Alice scrolled through the rest of the inbox contents. One message from David had no reply. Alice stiffened when she read it was addressed not to Marilyn, but to Ava.

Ava, I hope that by using Marilyn's email I can get your attention. You sure as hell won't answer my phone calls. I have done everything you asked, but you are screwing with me. You will be sorry. I'm done. David

There it was: the threat. The love affair was over. The date of the message was January 15, the day David died.

Alice walked to the kitchen and washed her glasses in the sink. Her view from the window told her that yesterday's ice storm had exhausted itself. The long, elegant blades of the monkey grass that meandered across the yard slumped low to the earth, but it would survive. It was going to be a perfectly gorgeous, but cold, January day.

ALICE AND MARK AGREED TO meet at Summer Moon, where she found him sitting at the window bar, his long body curled over his cell phone, two paper cups of hot coffee on the bar in front of him.

She hugged him tight from behind.

Laughing, he stood and returned the hug.

He straightened, placed his hands on her shoulders, and studied her face. "You're amazing. No evidence at all that you spent a night in a holding cell. No decent person should ever have to walk into that place."

"I'm good," she said. "Guess I'm tougher than I thought."

She climbed onto the tall stool next to him, pulling herself up with her elbows braced on the counter. "I wasn't sure you would ever talk to me again after that blunder with Detective Cabrera. I'm so, so sorry."

"Don't worry about it. I wouldn't have helped you if I hadn't wanted to."

"But will you lose your job?"

"Just did. I quit."

"No!"

"It's really okay, Alice," he said. "In fact, you did me a favor. I hated that job. If I hadn't quit now, I may have stayed forever."

"But still—"

"I've been thinking the last few months of trying something different. My parents left me a little money, so I'm good for a while." He paused. "You'll still let me help, won't you? I can at least do some leg work or research even without having access to police files." He was propped against his stool, facing her.

"No. You've helped enough. I came to apologize

and to ask what I can do for you."

"You know what?" he said, the Howdy Doody smile tugging at his lips. "I couldn't admit this to you while I was a cop, but the fact is I loved playing detective with you. It was the paper-pushing I hated in my job. Looking for evidence in a murder case is awesome."

As if on cue, the espresso machine behind the counter blurted a loud burst of steam like a rimshot after a punchline. Mark and Alice turned toward the machine and laughed.

Alice studied his face and then picked up the coffee he had bought for her. She blew into the steaming cup, looking at him over the rim, a question in her eyes. "Well, I *have* grown accustomed to your face."

He pointed a finger gun at her and laughed. "*My Fair Lady*, right? I remember you showed us that movie after we read the play."

"*Pygmalion*." She sipped her coffee. After a few moments, she placed her cup on the counter. "Thank you, Mark. In fact, if you're serious, I can use your help. What was the talk at the department just before you left?"

"Well," Mark said as he settled himself onto the stool, "your *blunder*, as you call it, has breathed new life into the Quinn murder investigation. The police are exhuming Ms. Quinn's body to test for antifreeze poisoning."

"Good. It needs to be investigated. But the big question is, if she was already dying, why was she shot?"

"Yeah, I've been thinking about that," Mark said between sips of coffee. He put his cup down and looked at her. "What if there are two murderers, one who was killing her slowly with poison and another who shot her out of rage?"

"I've been thinking along those same lines. But in my scenario, I see only one murderer, someone who needed her to die before the poison could kill her."

Mark had turned to say something when his attention was diverted to the entrance of the coffee shop. Looking over Alice's shoulder, he let his wide, toothy smile make its full appearance.

Alice turned to find Lillo standing behind her.

"Lillo!" she cried, embracing the big man. "You smell like a bakery." She laughed. "What are you doing here?" She looked from Lillo to Mark and back again. "You know each other?"

"Lillo contacted me when he heard you were in jail," Mark said. "I think if I hadn't stopped him, he would have broken in and forcibly removed you."

"I'm here to offer my services," Lillo said. "I want to help you. Mark and I have decided to be your, erm, uh…" He rubbed his head. "*Aggiunti.*" He threw up his hands in frustration. "Ah, what's the word, Mark?"

"Deputies? Sidekicks," Mark said, laughing. And then he added, his smile relaxing, "We know you're not going to stop helping your friend, so we're here for you."

"Yes. We need a plan, the three of us *insieme,* "

Lillo said. He glanced at the small tables scattered around the room. "*Purtroppo*, I can't talk here. The chairs are too small for me."

THEY SAT IN FRONT OF a bright fire in Alice's living room, Lillo and Mark on the sofa, Alice in her green recliner with Arthur splayed on her lap. She had told the men her suspicions about the loan and now rubbed the big cat's tummy, absentminded, focused on what might lie ahead.

"So you're convinced Ava is behind all of this?" Lillo said. "The murders? Your arrest?"

"Yes, absolutely. With considerable help from Javier Johnson. And David Rhodes. And Geoffrey James." Alice straightened her position, careful not to disturb the cat.

Both men leaned forward.

"Ava was poisoning her sister because Ava needed money to repay a loan to Javier," she said. "Geoffrey was involved in Ava's plans from the beginning because he was Javier's lawyer."

"But didn't Javier have legitimate cause to be repaid? Couldn't he have taken Ava to court?" Mark said.

"I seriously doubt there's any written contract between Ava and Javier. She used a living woman's will as collateral, remember? Besides, Javier doesn't need anything in writing when he has muscle." Alice shook her head. "I thought all along that it was Ava with the friends in high places. It was Javier instead."

"Are you sure about this, *Cara*?" Lillo said.

"I'm not sure how complicit Javier is in Marilyn's actual murder, but I'm sure he knew what was going on because of the loan. Mark is going to look into just how big the loan was—right, Mark?"

Mark nodded.

"I've been trying to find out if Ava was in her sister's will, but I don't think it would matter. Ava could manipulate Georgia into getting anything she wanted." Alice rubbed her temples as she recalled Charlotte Bauer talking about Ava's abominable treatment of Georgia when she was a child. It made no sense that Georgia was so close to her aunt as an adult. Was Ava holding something over the younger woman's head?

"You okay?" Mark said.

She continued. "So Ava and possibly David were adding tiny amounts of antifreeze to Marilyn's food and drink some time just before Christmas, when she started getting sick. That's what made every-thing taste so sweet to her, Lillo."

"*Lo sapevo!*" the big man cried, slapping his thigh. "I knew something was being changed to the food I prepared for her. *Troppo dolce*," he said with a sneer. "Italians don't eat sweet food."

Mark patted Lillo on the back.

"It was a brilliant idea, actually," Alice went on. "Antifreeze in tiny amounts can be a slow killer, but Marilyn's symptoms would be seen as reactions to the medications her doctor was prescribing. Without a specific test for antifreeze, her doctor—and certainly the coroner—wouldn't know she was being poisoned. It was going to be the perfect crime."

"I'm still confused about David," Mark said, rubbing his hands together. "He wasn't going to inherit anything. Why would he agree to Ava's plan to kill Marilyn?"

"I think David was involved based on something Marilyn saw upstairs that night that shattered her so deeply she couldn't process it. In spite of how sick she felt, she grabbed her car keys and her telephone and tried to run away. Ava knew what Marilyn saw, and she rushed downstairs to keep her from leaving the house."

"Why would Ava care if she left the house?" Mark said.

"For starters, she could put Georgia's inheritance into a trust that paid out only so much monthly, not enough to share with Ava. Marilyn may have mentioned that possibility during dinner with the Johnsons. Maybe she threatened to amend the will that night." She paused for a moment. "I don't think Ava would hesitate to shoot her sister dead. And then brutalize her dead body by kicking it."

Silence.

"And David, *Bella*?" Lillo murmured. "How is he connected?"

Alice sat forward in the recliner and pushed Arthur to the floor. "First, I think he bought the antifreeze my fingerprints are on. But more important, what Marilyn saw the night she was killed was David and Ava in bed together."

"What?" Mark yelped. "How screwed up are these people, anyway?"

"Marilyn suspected David was having an affair. She hired a private investigator to confirm her suspicions, and she got that confirmation the day of the dinner party, the day she was murdered." She explained how she'd gotten the information from Jay Pierce's office.

"When Marilyn woke up that night and realized David wasn't in bed with her," Alice went on, "she dragged herself to Ava's room and saw him there. Humiliated, abandoned, sick, her impulse was to run."

Both men sat with their elbows on their knees, their hands clasped under their chins.

Mark tented his fingers. He looked at Alice. "You're sure, Alice? You're sure it was Ava?"

"Well, I wasn't there, of course, but it makes sense to me. Both Haydn and the surveillance camera had a clear view of the lawn, and no one approached the house from the front or back for at least an hour before Marilyn was shot. So unless I'm missing something, the murderer must have been in the house, could have followed Marilyn down the stairs, gone outside while Marilyn was getting her coat. She was shot from a spot near the Christmas-light panel on the veranda. The murderer would have waited there for

Marilyn to open the door."

Lillo and Mark exchanged glances.

"Four people were in the house that night. One: David, who could have poisoned her, but I can't see him shooting her in the face. Two: Georgia, who loved her mother, didn't need money, and couldn't have gotten down the stairs. Three: Trish, who is terrified of her own shadow. Four: Ava."

The men looked at each other again and back at Alice.

"But, *Cara*," Lillo said, "I must remind you that Haydn could have been outside the door. His fingerprints were on the gun."

"The timing is too coincidental. How could Haydn place himself at the door at the precise moment Marilyn opened it? No one called him, because no calls were made on any of the phones. Someone in the house knew Marilyn was going downstairs. Someone heard her or saw her."

"*Sì. Lo capisco*. How well do you know Trish?"

"Well enough to know she couldn't commit murder," Alice scoffed. "Also, Ava's a crack shot with a gun, and the bullet that killed Marilyn was a clean shot from yards away into her left eye."

Like a flash of lightning, she recalled that Trish was a good shot, too. Could Trish—? No. She dismissed the thought right away.

The men sat silent, Lillo with his eyes closed, deep in thought, Mark rubbing his big hands together.

"You know," Mark said, raising his forefinger, "I

saw photos of both of the guns. The one used to kill Marilyn was small, a Glock 26, a Baby Glock. It's a popular conceal-carry gun for women because of its weight and size." He looked from Lillo to Alice. "The gun that killed Caitlin, the gun with the red trigger, had been modified for a really short trigger reach."

"For the hand of a woman?" Lillo said.

Mark nodded. "Both of the guns were designed more for women than men." He paused for a moment. "Man, you gotta really hate someone to shoot them in the face." He rubbed the back of his neck, his eyes closed. "And then to kick the dead body."

"*Che peccato.*"

The fire popped, as a log fell into the bright ashes of the burned log below it. Alice jumped, and they all turned, each of them mesmerized by the flames that darted upward toward the flue, each of them haunted by the betrayals and the cruelties Marilyn suffered in the last, unhappy days of her life.

"WHAT ABOUT DAVID," Lillo said, "and the girl?"

They needed a break, so all three bundled up and drove to Bouldin Creek Café for lunch. The place was packed, but the waitress pointed to the dining room beyond a painting of Bryan Cranston in his full *Breaking Bad* scowl. The actor wore a chef's cloche embroidered with the words "Let's Cook!" pulled tight on his head.

"Somethin' should open up in the back in fifteen,

twenty minutes," she said, playing with a silver nose ring. "You wanna wait?"

It was a Friday, so they would have to wait wherever they went. Mark gave the waitress his name, and they leaned against a wall covered in colorful music performance announcements, personal ads, and business cards.

When they were seated at last, the noise in the restaurant had escalated. By the end of the meal, their faces were inches apart as they struggled to hear each other.

"It's hard for me to see anyone kill a lover so brutally," Mark said above the din. He popped the last of his grilled cheese sandwich into his mouth and pushed the plate away.

Alice sighed. She toyed with a bowl of granola but hadn't eaten much. "I think the affair with David was only a dalliance for Ava, a way of hurting Marilyn. And David apparently had a thing for older women. He was crazy about Ava."

"Why do you say that, Alice?" Lillo had finished an omelet and used the tip of his napkin to dab sour cream from his mustache.

"His temperament," Alice said, giving up on the granola. "When Ava was in town, David was on top of the world; when he met Ava in Houston for their trysts, he came home happy; when he couldn't contact her, he was inconsolable. "

"Maybe David had become more than a nuisance," Mark said. "He told you he was going to blow the top off of something. That's a threat."

"Yes," Lillo chimed in. "And Ava was here in Austin when David died. But how did she make David take the antifreeze, *Cara*? Surely he would be *un po' sospettoso*? Erm…" He touched his forehead and closed his eyes, trying to pull up the right word.

"Suspicious?" Mark said.

Lillo looked to the ceiling and held both hands high, palms up. "Yes. Suspicious. Thank you, Mark."

"Good question," Alice said. "Unfortunately for David, he loved sweets, so I think adding antifreeze to an already-sweet drink would have been easy to pull off. And it must have been a pretty good amount because he died so soon after he took it. Marilyn, on the other hand, had been sick for a long time."

The men nodded at each other.

"David was terrified of being followed," she went on, "and of not being allowed to leave Austin."

Both men leaned in closer to hear.

"David blamed Ava for that and for not keeping in contact with him. In the end, he sent an email to Marilyn's account threatening Ava, and he died the same day."

"But Javier had a motive, too. He hated David because his daughter liked him so much. He probably thought David was encouraging her," Mark said. "What makes you think Javier didn't kill him?"

"I think Javier was in on David's murder, but I can't see David and Javier sitting down for a cup of coffee laced with antifreeze, can you?"

The men nodded again.

"What about the young girl?" Lillo said.

A tattooed arm slipped between Mark's and Alice's faces, and they all bolted upright.

"Y'all need this?" a turquoise-haired waitress said, her fingers curling around the neck of a quart bottle of Valentina Mexican hot sauce.

"We're good," Mark said.

The waitress took the bottle, spun around, and raced off to another group of diners. They resumed their former positions, leaning into one another over the table.

"What makes you think Ava killed Caitlin?" Lillo continued. "Your friend's fingerprints were on the gun that killed her."

Mark explained that Haydn had taken David's gun from Georgia and replaced it in David's car.

"Still, that murder was the hardest one for me to work out," Alice said. "That is, until Mark told me the body had been moved to Marilyn's front lawn. Caitlin followed David like a lovesick puppy, so I think she must have seen David and Ava in a compromising position and threatened to tell Georgia."

The men looked at each other and signaled their agreement.

"Ava could have killed Caitlin anywhere," Alice went on, "and then had David move the body to Marilyn's front lawn. A woman like Ava, a woman who would kill her sister, likely wouldn't think twice about doing away with a nobody like Caitlin."

"Killed her with the red-triggered gun and then brutalized her, smashed her face," Mark added. "Same MO."

They allowed the racket to invade their space for a moment.

"You are good at this, *Bella*," Lillo said. "You make a good *donna di polizia*." Lillo covered Alice's small hand with his own bear claw and gave her one of his rare smiles.

Alice blushed. She hoped her imagination wouldn't get them into even more trouble than they were already in. She had omitted two details from her interpretation of the events at Marilyn's, two details that she simply couldn't work out. Neither of her friends had mentioned them, though, so she chose to keep them to herself. At least for now.

"If you're right, Alice, Ava is a *psicopatico*."

"Right," Mark said. "A psychopath. And that means she's very dangerous. You have to be careful, Alice. We all have to be careful."

"So, how do we get this information to the right people, the people who can do something?" Lillo said, looking from Alice to Mark and back to Alice.

"We don't," Alice said, "not until we have all the loose ends tied up." She leaned close to the men and lowered her voice. "We push. We do it ourselves."

CHAPTER 24

A small mention of David's memorial appeared in the obituary section of the paper. Alice didn't expect a service to be arranged at all, but knowing what Ava was like, she dared not risk raising any questions if his death went unacknowledged.

So David's body was to be cremated. Friends and family were invited to pay their respects at three o'clock at a mortuary on North Lamar Boulevard. Alice left Lillo and Mark at Bouldin Creek just in time to attend.

She was alone when she entered the tiny chapel of the funeral home. A framed photograph of David had been propped on a table at the front of the room. Conspicuous by their absence were flower arrangements or any other expressions of condolence.

She took a seat at the back of the room and folded her hands in her lap. The room was warm and quiet. She closed her eyes and whispered goodbye to David.

Who was this man who had gotten involved in a cruel murder scheme with people far smarter, far more sophisticated in the art of lying and cheating than he could imagine? A man who could be gracious and considerate—she glanced at the handsome smile in the photograph and couldn't resist a smile in response—a man who married under false pretenses and helped to murder a woman whose only crime was having money. A lot of money. A man who left a woman in her sickbed to slide into another bed with the woman's sister.

Had he helped Ava serve the antifreeze to Marilyn in small doses over several weeks? Was he the one who added it to her tea or stirred it into her soup? Had he supported her head in his hand as she struggled to sip the brew? Had he felt no pity as she swallowed the sweet-tasting stuff, knowing what the effects would be?

What were David's thoughts when Ava shot Marilyn? Was he at Ava's side when she kicked the dead body?

David wasn't going to inherit anything when Marilyn died, so he must have felt that winning Ava's love was a worthwhile payback for selling his soul.

All at once, Alice realized that someone was standing in the chapel door, a small woman who held a spray of red roses, the tips of the petals edged in gold glitter. She exchanged a glance with Alice, walked to the front of the room, and laid the flowers next to David's photo. Then she took a seat in a chair on the aisle and pulled a tissue from her handbag. She bent her head and dabbed her eyes.

Alice watched her for several minutes before she slid into a chair near her.

"Hello," Alice whispered. "I'm Alice Ann Abbott. I

was a friend of David's. What a terrible way to lose him."

The woman wiped her eyes. She could have been much younger than she looked. Years of sucking at cigarettes had left deep lines along her lips, and something—bad diet? hard work? worry?—had caused her eyes and cheeks to sink, giving her face a pinched appearance.

"Yes, it's terrible," the woman said in a thick West Texas accent. "I'm his wife. Married to him for forty-two years." She held up her left hand, showing a thin metal band.

Alice swallowed. "Oh," she stuttered, "I'm so sorry for your loss, Mrs. Rhodes."

"Well, I thank you, but it's not like I was ever used to havin' him around. He was never really a part of the family. He didn't spend a lot of time with me and the kids over the years." She pressed the tissue into her eyes. Her shoulders heaved.

Alice moved closer to the woman. She put her arm around her thin shoulders and let her cry.

When the woman pulled away, she blew her nose and straightened her posture. "I brought flowers," she said, gesturing to the roses, "but there ain't even a casket to put 'em on." She dabbed at her eyes again.

They sat in silence.

"How'd you know David?" the woman said.

"I worked for his—the woman he was with."

"Was she young? Beautiful?"

"She was older."

"An' very rich. I heard." The woman blew her nose and groped for a clean tissue in her handbag.

"When did you see David last, Mrs. Rhodes?"

"I was tryin' to remember that on the bus. Two? Three years ago?"

"You never thought of divorce? Getting on with your life?"

"Nah. He got me pregnant my freshman year of high school. I dropped out and he married me. I knew even then I wouldn't keep him." She glanced at Alice and twisted the band on her left hand. "He was too pretty, had way too much potential to be somethin' better." She looked at Alice and smiled. "But I got two kids by him. Good kids."

"Who contacted you about his death, Mrs. Rhodes?"

"My brother called me last night," the woman said.

Last night? That meant David's wife didn't know about his death until after he was cremated. So, Javier had managed to order the cremation without permission from his next of kin. Alice recalled the warrant Geoffrey got to search Alice's home for Marilyn's earrings and the ridiculous amount of time she herself had spent in that awful holding cell. Javier Johnson had some powerful connections, indeed.

"My brother an' David worked together for a while at Top-of-the-Line Used Cars in Vegas," the woman said.

David sold cars for Javier in Las Vegas. Mark had

told her that.

"Sometime last month, my brother called to tell me David was gonna be rich, live someplace in Texas. Next thing I knew, my brother said David was back in Vegas, gettin' married. 'He can't do that,' I told him. 'He's married to me.' My brother said, 'I know. I'll take care of it.'"

She paused for a moment and then added, "My brother never liked David." She lowered her gaze to her hands and rubbed at a rough spot with her thumb. Her eyes were open, but Alice felt she might be praying.

"I guess it's all over now," the woman said after several moments, wiping her eyes with the palms of her bare hands. She stood and held her hand out to Alice. "Thank you, ma'am. I'm glad I didn't have to sit in here by myself."

"Of course," Alice said. "It's hard to grieve alone, Mrs. Rhodes."

"Call me Candy." The woman headed to the door.

Alice called after her. "Will your brother be here later, Candy? I'd like to meet him."

The woman turned and shrugged. "Maybe," she said. "Name is Billy. Bill Wilcox."

BILL WILCOX, THE CHEF WHO served that hideous meal the night Marilyn was murdered, was David Rhodes' brother-in-law? Trish had said David knew the chef.

Alice waited for as long as she could for Bill Wilcox

to show up, but Mark called and asked if they could meet at the Taco Shack just a few blocks from the funeral home.

The restaurant was almost empty. Mark was at the counter ordering. "Diet Coke?" he called to Alice.

She nodded and took a table at the front, near the windows. The moment he joined her, she told him about Bill Wilcox.

"Holy shit!" Mark enunciated each syllable, as if in a trance. "The bad chef?"

A muscle in Alice's jaw twitched. "We need to try to find the guy."

Mark shook his head, trying to process this new development.

"Why did you want to meet, Mark?"

He had much better news than she expected. "Do you know Haydn's housekeeper?"

"Gwen? Of course. I got Arthur from one of her cat's litters."

"That explains the pants," Mark said, looking at the floor.

"What pants?"

"When the housekeeper read that you'd been charged with stealing the earrings, she went straight to Cabrera with a pair of Geoffrey's pants. She said that on the day of the break-in at your house, she saw Geoffrey examining expensive-looking earrings in Haydn's study. She took a few days off to visit her daughter in San Antonio, and when she returned, she found all of Geoffrey's dirty clothes strewn on the bedroom floor. Among the clothes was a pair of pants that were covered from the knee down in cat hair. Arthur's hair, the housekeeper insisted."

"Did they confirm it was Arthur's hair? How did they—?"

"Get a sample of Arthur's hair?" Mark smiled. "Anyone who's ever visited you has samples of Arthur's hair, Alice. Guess that's not such a bad thing."

Alice rested her elbows on the table, slid her glasses down her nose, and rubbed her temples.

Mark patted her back. "You can expect the theft charges to be dropped any time now," he said.

"I'm so relieved," Alice said. She wiped her eyes and rearranged her glasses. "I didn't know how I was going to pay an attorney."

"There's more," Mark continued. "I discovered the sale of a house in Santa Fe. That is, if you can call a $6.5 million mansion 'a house'. Guess who the buyer was."

Alice's eyes grew wide. "Ava Lynn Sauvage?"

"Bingo! It seems there were a lot of people interested in buying the house around the time Marilyn was supposedly dying of a heart attack. The owner wanted to sell it immediately, and Ava saw an opportunity. Looks like you could be right about Ava taking a loan from her friend Javier Johnson, using Marilyn's estate as collateral."

"Yes," Alice said, grinning.

But the smile faded as Alice considered the

implications of the loan. "What a surprise for Ava when Marilyn survived. And how devastating for Marilyn to know what her sister had done." She sipped her drink. "It wasn't the heart attack that turned Marilyn's mood so sour. It was realizing how vulnerable she was, how alone."

Her eyes darted to Mark. "Do you think that's why she married so fast? To have someone to protect her?"

"Could be. Makes sense, doesn't it?"

"Ava would have to scramble to pay off the loan. That's why she sold her boutique."

"That's what I'm thinking."

"But," Alice continued, "apparently whatever she got wasn't enough. She would never pay off the loan without Marilyn's money."

"Yep," Mark said. "Looks like Ava had to have Marilyn's money, one way or another."

MARK LEFT ALICE AT THE coffee shop. She wanted to let Connie know the theft charges would be dropped, and she wanted to thank Gwen Newberry.

After she made both of those calls, she left the shop and started across the parking lot, which was almost empty. The day had turned very cold, so she pulled the collar of her coat over her ears.

Without warning, tires screeched behind her and then someone shoved Alice. She fell hard to the pavement. A dark sedan sped out of the parking lot into the street and raced away. Alice blinked and reached for a sharp pain on her forehead. Her fingers drew away blood.

Someone was murmuring in her ear. She turned her head to find the sound, her glasses dangling broken from her ear.

"Are you okay?" someone said.

"Who—?"

"Sorry I pushed you so hard, but that car almost rammed into you."

"I—I—" Alice tried to rise to an elbow.

"Don't move, please. I'm going to call an ambulance."

"Who—?"

"My name is Bill Wilcox. Please don't move."

And then everything blurred into black.

"ALICE? CAN YOU HEAR ME?"

It was Connie. Alice blinked, struggling to make out pieces of an image in front of her.

"Connie? What's—?"

"I'm here, Alice," Connie said. "You're in the hospital. You've been in an accident."

Alice watched scraps of color come together to reveal Connie's beautiful face. Her features were contorted into an expression of concern.

Alice's head ached. Yes, she'd fallen, she remembered. Someone shoved her. Someone important. Someone saved her from being hit by a car.

"You're going to rest here for a day or two," Connie continued. "You're fine. A bit banged up, but it turns out you're pretty resilient for a seventy-three-year-old woman. No bones broken. Only a few scrapes and a very mild concussion. You amaze me, Alice."

Connie stood and adjusted the drip valves on Alice's IV bag. In seconds, Alice was deep asleep.

CHAPTER 25

A t Alice's insistence, Mark made arrangements for her to meet with Bill Wilcox at Torchy's Tacos on Congress. They sat in a booth by a window, Alice and Mark facing Bill.

"So this beautiful millionairess met a used car salesman in New York City and fell in love with him?" Alice said, fingering the dressing on her forehead. It was Alice's first day out of the hospital, and the awkward bandage annoyed her.

The stocky man sitting in the booth across from her chuckled as he shoveled the last of a burrito into his mouth. Pale eyebrows danced on his rugged face with lines and scars that indicated a hard life. He wiped his lips. "Well, it seems so. I never saw her, but apparently he fell hard for her, and I know why. She was classy. Definitely his type."

"Not to mention she appeared to have a lot of money," Mark added.

Bill Wilcox shrugged. "Yeah. David wasn't a fan of hard work, but he sure loved money."

"I have to ask, Bill, how did you get that chef's gig at Marilyn"s?" Alice shook her head.

"Ha," he said, sipping the last of the coffee in a

mug close to his plate. "When I found David, he was pretty nervous. Said he was getting a big payoff for my sister Candy and the boys. 'Course, I knew that was a lie—he had no intention of sharing anything with my sister—but I went along with his little game."

Bill pursed his lips and ran his tongue across his top teeth. He dabbed at his mouth again with the napkin. "David told me about the dinner at Marilyn's," he continued, "and that no chef was available. Seemed like the perfect opportunity for me to get close to Javier without him knowing I was around." He smiled, full of pride. "Learned to cook in the army."

Alice stirred her coffee. "What's your interest in Javier Johnson?"

Bill sucked the remains of a Love Puppy brownie from his fingertips and finished his coffee through thin, colorless lips. He seemed muscular, but the bulges at his shirtsleeves and around his middle hinted at a tendency to gain weight. He didn't appear to be the kind of man who worried about carrying a few extra pounds.

"I'm a retired cop," he said. "Little town in Nevada. Javier Johnson is both a liar and a cheat—maybe more—and I've been trying to find hard evidence to prove that for years. With Javier in the mix, I figured David was into a lot more than a phony wedding."

"What do you mean?" Alice said.

"Javier was acquainted with Marilyn Quinn. They were neighbors. He knew she was attending a conference in New York. Javier paid David's plane fare and expenses, along with a good sum to court her. It seemed strange that David would return to Las Vegas for the wedding, so I dug around and found out that Javier took care of all the arrangements. He had that stuffed-shirt attorney, Geoffrey James, perform the ceremony, even though the guy isn't certified to do that. The whole marriage was a sham, a joke at the Quinn woman's expense."

Alice and Mark exchanged glances. Alice pushed away the bowl of ice cream Mark had brought her and drew her coffee nearer.

Bill went on. "They didn't want to use a preacher, or anyone else who would issue a legitimate marriage certificate or want proof of divorces and such."

"What do you know about Geoffrey James, Bill?" Mark said.

"He and Javier go way back. Somehow, Geoffrey's mother was connected to people Javier knew in Boston. Geoffrey contacted Javier before he started law school in Vegas, and Javier put him on the payroll. When Geoffrey graduated, Javier sent him to Houston to make contacts there." He shook his head. "They're thick as mud, those two."

"And you're pretty sure it was Geoffrey driving the stolen car that almost hit Alice in the parking lot?"

"Oh, yeah. The windows were dark, but one of the back windows was open. He didn't see me, but I saw him."

Alice liked Bill. "You've been following me for a long time, haven't you? I'm so grateful you were there in that parking lot."

Bill caught the waitress's eye and held up his coffee mug. "The cops turned their investigation over to the DA way too soon. I wouldn't be surprised if that was a favor from some high-ranking politician to a big donor," he said, "probably Javier. But you kept poking Geoffrey in the eye. I figured you could get yourself in a lot of trouble."

He inhaled for a moment, held it, then exhaled and sat back as the waitress filled his mug. He rested his arm on the back of the booth. "So, what do we do next?"

"Whatever it is, it needs to be soon," Mark said, elbows on the tabletop, his big hands rubbing together. "My contact at headquarters tells me that Haydn's in pretty bad shape. His attorney says he's refusing medical attention."

"What?" Alice said. "Why... why would he... he—"

"There's no telling what Geoffrey has told your friend," Bill said with a shrug. "Maybe he doesn't even know about Geoffrey breaking into your home. Or that I've accused Geoffrey of trying to run you down with his car."

"That's right," Mark added. "Even though Geoffrey has been questioned about the earrings and his possible assault on you with his car, no charges have been filed yet. He's still Haydn's lawyer, and he controls everything Haydn hears. Haydn's decision and Haydn's loss," Mark said.

Bill stroked his chin. "Pretty big loss."

Alice touched Mark's shoulder and looked at Bill. "Haydn's still trying to prove something," she murmured, "still trying to win a dead woman's forgiveness. We can help him by getting a confession from Ava as soon as possible. He has diabetes, and he's nervous and easily upset. He's… delicate. I don't know how long he can hold it together in jail."

"Well, we need to move fast. Cabrera has given Ava permission to return to Santa Fe tonight."

THE PLAN DEVELOPED FOR Alice to call Ava and tell her that she had found a small, locked lacquer box belonging to Marilyn. She wanted to return the box to Ava before Ava left town, insisting she didn't want to be accused again of stealing.

"Leave it with the realtor," Ava told her.

"Not after the earrings. I don't want to be responsible for anything valuable that belongs to your family." She was certain Ava would respond to the word *valuable*.

She was right.

Alice would meet Lillo, Mark, and Bill at a filling station close to Marilyn's neighborhood at 5:30 and then all of them would drive to Marilyn's together. They would be at Marilyn's front door by 5:45 to confront her with the evidence they'd collected.

It was still early. Alice's head ached. She needed

to rest.

"YOU SURE YOU'RE COMFY, Alice?" Trish said. "I can get another pillow."

The bruises on Alice's face had darkened. She looked a lot worse than she felt.

"I'm fine, Trish. I'll just rest for a few minutes."

Trish had settled her into a nest on the sofa, insisting lying straight would be better for her than dozing in the recliner.

"Okay, then. I'm leaving the front door open—it's such a pretty day—but I'll latch the screen. If you need me, call. I'll be in my room watching my story."

Thank God Trish had brought her own TV. Alice would go mad if she had to sit through the back-to-back episodes of the soap opera Trish recorded during the week.

Alice turned on her side and welcomed Arthur, who was a bit hesitant about napping on the sofa. Wasn't that why they had a recliner?

Doubtful, he curled up close to Alice's stomach. He looked into her eyes and then away. He scratched his ear with his back paw. Soon, his head drooped, and he slept.

Alice stroked the big cat until her eyes felt heavy. She was anxious about confronting Ava later in the day.

Just on the verge of falling asleep, she realized that the living room was darkening. Her eyes fluttered open. Something at the front door blocked the sunshine. It was Geoffrey James.

He looked through the screen and said, "Hello there, Ms. Abbott. Can we talk?"

Alice struggled to sit up, unsure what to say. Had he come for her help, or was he here to finish what he'd started in the parking lot a few days ago?

"Um—" she mumbled, "I don't know."

"Not to worry, Ms. Abbott. I'll only take a moment of your time." He opened the screen door and let himself in. Trish had forgotten to latch it.

Arthur jumped to the floor and rushed to welcome the guest, crying a greeting and winding himself around Geoffrey's legs.

Geoffrey bent to pet him. He wore long black gloves. "You bad kitty," he said, smiling. "You got me in trouble last time I came to see you, didn't you?"

Arthur cried again and offered his neck for a friendly scratch.

Geoffrey gathered the cat in his arms and held him close as he approached Alice. She sat frozen to the sofa.

Geoffrey stopped at the edge of the sofa, so close to her that she couldn't move. Arthur's eyes were level with her own.

"Ms. Abbott," he said in a slow and quiet voice, as he held Arthur with one hand and stroked him with the other, "I have had enough of you and your interference. You have cost me more than I ever expected to lose. My job, valuable contacts, and a bright future as a lawyer are gone. All gone because of you."

Silence. Alice caught a reflection of her own eyes in Arthur's. The cat rubbed his head against Geoffrey's sagging chest and purred.

"I will not give up my rightful inheritance. Do you understand me? I will have Haydn's estate."

Voices on the TV from Trish's room carried into the living room. A man declared his love; a woman called him a cheat.

"Put him down," she whispered.

"What?"

"Put the cat down. Please."

"Just give me a moment, Ms. Abbott. And then you can have him."

She watched in horror as one hand closed around Arthur's front paws and the other slipped a thin wire around Arthur's throat.

Alice gasped. "Stop!" she shouted. She lunged off the sofa and grabbed for the cat. Arthur scrambled out of the room, the loose wire dancing behind him.

In front of her, Geoffrey lay motionless on the floor with a large, bloody crater in the right side of his face. Behind him, her mouth open wide in surprise, Trish brandished a cast iron frying pan.

ALICE LEFT TRISH WITH GEOFFREY, who remained motionless on the floor in Alice's living room. He was breathing and he had a pulse, but Alice was pretty sure he wouldn't be running a marathon anytime soon.

310 - ☙ - SUSAN TOALSON

Detective Cabrera was on her way.

It was already 4:45, and Alice couldn't be late to her meeting with Ava. Cabrera would want to keep her for hours.

She arrived at the filling station at 5:25, grateful to have a few moments to clear her head before she met her friends. Her cell phone showed a text message from Mark saying they were caught in traffic caused by an eighteen-wheeler turnover on the expressway.

At 5:30, another message saying the traffic was moving again. *Please wait for us,* Mark wrote. *If we miss Ava, we'll go to Santa Fe and confront her.*

Alice didn't answer the text. "We can't do that, Mark," she said to herself. "By the time we get to Santa Fe, Ava could be out of the country, and Haydn could be dead. This has to be done now."

She crammed the phone in her bag and turned the key in the ignition.

ALICE DROVE INTO THE FAMILIAR circular drive and followed it to the front of Marilyn's home. As she got out of the car, she pulled herself to her full height and, bracing herself against the pain in her knee, she walked, keeping a slow and steady pace, toward the door. Ava would not see any weakness in her today. Not today.

She rang the bell and waited.

Ava answered the door, opening it just wide enough to step outside as she held her open palm out to Alice. She wore a cream-colored silk blouse tucked into wide-legged black trousers and black stiletto heels. A huge pearl pendant hung from a thick gold necklace and kissed a bit of cleavage. Alice recognized one of Marilyn's favorite knotted gold rings on Ava's finger. The contents of Marilyn's safe-deposit box had already been plundered and found a new home.

Ava gave no indication she noticed the bruises on Alice's face. "The lacquer box? I'll take it," Ava said, her tone cold, extending her hand. "As I told you on the phone, I'm in a hurry."

"I understand, Ava, but I need a few moments to explain something to you. It's important."

Ava waited with her hand outstretched. When Alice showed no sign of giving in, Ava pushed the door open wide and stood aside while Alice entered. A suitcase waited by the door.

"Well?" Ava said, closing the door behind her.

Facing the woman like this caused Alice to waver for a moment. Ava's face hardened into a hideous mask.

She's a monster, Charlotte Bauer had said.

"Well?" Ava's eyes flashed, but Alice refused to respond. Instead, she turned and walked into the sitting room as though she were an invited guest. Ava followed, her stiletto heels tap-tapping on the marble floor.

"Damn it, Alice. My taxi will be here any minute. I don't want to hear anything you have to say to me."

Late afternoon sunshine bathed the beautiful

room, spilling in through the twin French doors.

Alice took a place behind one of the wing-backed chairs that flanked the fireplace. It was the same chair, she realized, she had collapsed into the day Marilyn was murdered, the day Detective Cabrera ushered her past the yellow cookie-cutter pattern of Marilyn's body in the entrance hall.

Georgia was in the room, seated in a winged chair on the opposite side of the fireplace. The cumbersome cast on her right leg rested in front of her left ankle. Ava stood behind Georgia's chair so that Ava and Alice looked straight into each other's eyes.

"Your face," Georgia said with alarm. "What happened, Alice?"

Both aunt and niece wore their dark hair loose, and Alice was reminded again how much alike they looked.

How could Alice accuse Ava of Marilyn's murder with Georgia in the room? Surely the younger woman had been through enough tragedy to last a lifetime.

"It's nothing serious, Georgia," Alice said, touching the bruise. "I took a fall. How are you, dear?"

"This isn't a social visit," Ava said. "Just get to the point and then get out." She flounced onto the sofa and crossed her legs and her arms. "Say it, then. Say what you have to say."

Alice glanced toward the entrance of the room, half expecting Geoffrey or Javier to join them. She caught her reflection in one of the twin antique mirrors on the back wall and then returned her attention to the women.

"My friend, Haydn Lawrence, was arrested for murder," she started. Her voice was softer than she had intended. She cleared her throat. "But he didn't kill Marilyn. He didn't kill Caitlin Johnson. And he didn't kill David Rhodes."

Ava rolled her eyes. "And you, with all your experience and intelligence, know this how?"

"I know this because I know who the killer is," Alice said.

"Spit it out," Ava said. "Unburden yourself, you toad."

Toad? Alice hadn't expected name-calling.

Where were her friends?

Ava looked at her watch. "Can we get on with it, please?" she said, annoyed as she tapped her foot on the Oriental rug.

Alice swallowed, stole a quick look at the clock over Georgia's shoulder, and pushed her chin forward. "Yes." She cleared her throat. She would not back down from this bully. All she had to do was hold out until her friends arrived.

"I know Haydn is incapable of murder," she said, taking her time. "I thought I could talk to Detective Cabrera, but she made it clear that the police were off-limits to me, that the only way I could help my friend was to work with his attorney, who, I sincerely believe, wants to see Haydn convicted. He proved it to me each time I tried to share valuable information with him. After all, Haydn's attorney benefits if

Haydn is put away."

Alice paused. There was a slight possibility that Ava wasn't aware of Haydn's relationship with Geoffrey. With no questions, no indications of surprise, she went on.

"On the night of her murder," Alice said, "something made Marilyn climb out of her sickbed and go downstairs to the kitchen, where she took a coat out of the closet near the back door and made a telephone call. The telephone call was to me."

Ava's eyes widened. She caught herself, but in the next second relaxed her expression.

"From the kitchen, she made her way across the entry hall and to the front door. The moment she opened the door, someone shot her. Marilyn remained where she fell until the police arrived."

Silence. The clock ticked on.

"Marilyn was sick," Alice continued. "Someone was poisoning her."

"What? Poisoned?" Ava said. "She was shot."

Alice turned to Georgia. "I'm sorry, dear, but maybe it's best you hear this, too."

Georgia didn't move or even look away.

"With antifreeze," Alice said to Ava. "It's a slow, steady death that a general autopsy wouldn't have revealed. And her doctor was prescribing drugs that could have caused her misery, so he wouldn't know either. That would explain why poor Marilyn suffered such awful stomach trouble after her honeymoon, don't you think?"

Ava's eyes were fixed on Alice.

"She didn't have long to live, so it made no sense that someone would use a gun to kill her," Alice went on. "My first thought was that there were two murderers.

"Murderer 'A' was willing to wait for the antifreeze to work, knowing that it would likely be confused in a typical autopsy with the lithium she was taking and that poisoning would never be suspected."

Ava blinked.

"Murderer 'B,' probably acting out of rage, wouldn't have known she was dying, so he used a gun, a gun that was immediately tossed into the woods where Haydn waited to catch a glimpse of the girl he thought may have been his daughter." Alice looked at Georgia, whose eyes now focused on the hearth. The papers had mentioned the possible father/daughter relationship Haydn had suspected, so Alice wasn't surprised when Georgia didn't react.

Ava shook her head. "Get on with it, Alice," she blurted.

"Startled, Haydn grabbed the gun and dropped it as soon as he realized what it was. He ran to his car, was caught on the security cameras speeding away. He's guilty of poor judgment, of carelessness, but not of murder."

Ava turned to look at the clock and Alice followed her gaze. Not even five minutes. She felt like she'd been talking forever. The men were now almost fifteen minutes late.

"Caitlin was next. And, conveniently, the gun that killed her had Haydn's fingerprints on it, too, because he took it from you, Georgia, and returned it to David's car. I know the gun was David's because he showed it to me."

It was Georgia's turn to blink.

"Again, my friend made a stupid mistake by trying to help you, Georgia, but he didn't kill anyone."

The clock chimed six soft notes.

Alice looked at her hands; they were trembling. She dropped them to her sides and continued. "And then David died. Of antifreeze poisoning. And suddenly I realized that one person had murdered all three victims. Marilyn was being poisoned, but something she saw or heard the night of her death forced the killer to act quickly to silence her."

Ava moved to the side of Georgia's chair and perched on the armrest.

"Some time after Marilyn was killed, Caitlin saw the same thing Marilyn had seen, so Caitlin had to die, too. And then David threatened to go to the police, so he was killed."

"*Enough!*" Ava shouted, jumping to her feet. "What does all this have to do with us?"

Alice stepped around the chair and shoved the bridge of her glasses tight to her eyes. The heat rose in her neck.

"You said you found a lacquer box that belonged to Marilyn. Give it to my attorney. We're leaving," Ava said over her shoulder as she picked up her coat and gloves. "Let's go, Georgia."

"Wait, Aunt Ava. I'd like to hear the rest."

Georgia hadn't moved from the chair, hadn't changed her posture.

Alice figured this exposure of the truth would be a relief for her, a kind of closure. It would also mean she would lose the last of her family.

Georgia looked straight into Alice's eyes.

"We'll miss the—" Ava said.

"We'll get the next one," Georgia said, never taking her eyes off Alice. "Please sit, Auntie."

Ava flounced back onto the sofa. She crossed her legs and swung the top leg at a rapid tempo.

"Go on, Alice," Georgia murmured.

Alice moved to the front of the chair and sat on the edge of the cushion. She clasped her hands in her lap, interlacing her fingers to hold them still.

"When I understood that one person was responsible for all three murders, I knew the person had to have been in the house just before Marilyn was killed. The surveillance camera didn't pick up anyone approaching or leaving the house except Haydn."

"Please continue," said Georgia.

"I also learned Marilyn was having David followed by a private investigator."

Ava's foot froze, mid-swing. "A private investigator? Why? What—?" She stared at Alice, unable to formulate a question or a comment.

"Right," Alice went on. "Why in the world would Marilyn need a private investigator?"

Silence. The room absorbed the late afternoon sunshine like a sponge.

"The answer was a total shock to me," Alice said. "Marilyn suspected David was having an affair."

Ava gasped. "What?"

"I know," Alice said. "An affair. And even worse, she was right. He *was* having an affair."

At this point, Georgia spoke up. "Alice, I don't want to hear it all again. I told you David killed my mother. The police arrested someone else."

"Oh, Georgia, I'm so sorry. You are the one who has suffered the most in this ordeal. But you also suffered growing up, didn't you? I talked to Charlotte Bauer, who told me about your childhood."

"Charlotte?" Georgia said.

"Yes. She cared for you occasionally when you were young. Do you remember her?"

Georgia's eyes were blank. She shook her head in slow motion.

Ava, who had recovered from her earlier shock, spoke up. "Just please get on with it. Is there anything else you discovered about our personal lives that you want to share with us?"

"Well, yes, there is, Ava. I know, for example, that you took a loan to buy a house in Santa Fe, one you can't possibly afford, and that you've sold your business, probably to help make payments on the loan. With Marilyn gone, your money problems are over."

Ava shot a glance at Georgia, who still watched Alice.

"Some time ago," Alice continued, "David mentioned a loan you took out with Javier Johnson. It appears you borrowed the money, hoping to pay it back when Marilyn died of the heart attack she had last year? It must have been a horrible disappointment when she survived and discovered what you'd done. I'm guessing Javier approached her about paying your loan off at about the time her disposition changed, when she became such a bitch to work for. She must have felt she couldn't trust anyone."

The wall clock ticked as Alice paused.

"Marilyn and Javier had words at dinner that night," Alice went on. "He pressed her to pay off your loan, and she refused. My first thought was that Javier called Marilyn after the dinner party and asked her to meet him outside. But a friend in the police department confirmed that no such call was made to Marilyn's phone."

Alice's palms turned sweaty. She unclenched her fingers and laid them open on her lap, one atop the other. A glance at the clock told her it was ten minutes after six o'clock. She was close to accusing Ava of murder. How much longer could she stall? How much longer before the taxi arrived to take Ava and Georgia to the airport?

Ava strolled across the room toward Alice. "You stupid, stupid cow. You think I killed her, don't you? And that I shot that little slut from next door? And then fed poison to David? Because of a loan you think I can't pay?"

Alice pushed herself up from the chair and stood to face her.

Ava seethed. "Who do you think you are, accusing me of murdering for money?"

"Not only for money, Ava," Alice said, her tone even. "Also to protect yourself. You were the woman David was having an affair with, weren't you? It was you who persuaded Javier to find someone to marry Marilyn so he would be the most reasonable suspect when she died. Marilyn saw you in bed together that night. You followed her downstairs and waited for her outside with a gun in your hand. Later, Caitlin found out about you and David, so you had to kill her, too. Finally, when David threatened to expose you, you had to kill him."

Ava spun on her heel toward Georgia. "Georgia, please!"

"What shall I say, Auntie?" Georgia said.

Ava's eyes widened, the color drained from her face. She rushed to the sofa, grabbed her coat and gloves, and watched in horror as the doorframe filled with the imposing figure of Lillo Cambria.

Ava backed away. She stared in disbelief at the huge man, who stepped aside to make room for Mark to enter.

"Detective Cabrera is on her way, Alice," Mark said. "I phoned her while we were stuck in traffic. Seems she's been looking for you."

Right. She had almost forgotten the image of Geoffrey James's body sprawled on her living room floor.

Mark turned to Ava. "Please make yourself comfortable for a few moments."

No one moved. No one spoke.

And then a voice from the entry hall. "I'll take over here, Ms. Abbott."

Alice turned toward the speaker. Detective Cabrera marched into the room with Bill Willcox. Two uniformed policemen entered the room behind them and approached Ava with handcuffs.

ALICE STOOD BY GEORGIA'S CHAIR with her hand on Georgia's shoulder. They were alone in the house. Cabrera had taken Ava into custody. Georgia had changed her flight, and Alice had called another cab. Alice wanted to stay behind with Georgia until the cab arrived.

"It's like I lived through it all again, Alice. I can't even cry. I feel so alone."

"I know. Can't you stay for a few more days? I can help you get stronger before you go."

"No. My cab will be here soon. Would you mind getting my suitcase and my coat? They're upstairs."

Alice glanced at the suitcase near the front door.

"That one is Aunt Ava's. She won't be needing it, will she?"

A tiny ring from inside Alice's handbag interrupted them. Alice smiled at Georgia and shrugged. "Guess I'd better get that."

She fumbled in her bag and realized it was the flip phone ringing, not the one Ava had given her. She opened it and the number came from Jay Pierce's office in Houston.

"Hello?" Alice whispered, turning away from Georgia.

"Ms. Quinn, it's Marta Rodriguez again. I'm calling to make sure you received the text I sent with the photos Mr. Pierce intended to attach to his surveillance report. I was finally able to get into his computer. I warn you, they're pretty graphic."

"Oh, the, uh—" Alice stammered. "Yes, yes. One moment, Marta. I'll check." She opened the email account. Marta's name appeared with an indication she had sent attachments. She opened the mail and clicked on the first attachment. Her eyes grew wide, and she held her breath as she opened the other attachments. "Thank you, Marta. I have it all now."

She stared at the phone and then slipped it into her pocket.

"I'll just get your things, dear. I'll be right down," she said to Georgia.

She climbed the elegant staircase and found Georgia's suitcase and her coat in her bedroom. She folded the coat over her arm and took the handle of the suitcase.

She wasn't surprised to see Georgia standing at the top of the staircase waiting for her, a small gun in her hand.

"What was the phone call about?" Georgia said.

"It finally all makes sense," Alice said. "I was so careful about scrutinizing every bit of evidence I gathered, but I kept ignoring two questions because I couldn't answer them."

Georgia raised an eyebrow.

"The first was that the Christmas lights went out at exactly the same time your mother was shot," Alice continued. "But the control panel for the lights was hidden behind a bush on the veranda. Ava wouldn't have known where the panel was. But you did. You watched Owen working on the panel just before you fired him."

"Clever girl," Georgia scoffed.

"You're a good shot, aren't you? You and Marilyn and Ava loved to shoot. Marilyn had planned to build a shooting range. You could have easily hit Marilyn in the eye from across the veranda with one shot."

Georgia shrugged.

"The second question was actually a question. When Marilyn called me on the night she died, she asked, 'Why would she—?' Seeing Ava in bed with David would have been disappointing, but not upsetting enough to make her run away. Ava had slept with Marilyn's first husband, so it wouldn't have been shocking if she'd done it again."

A slow smile worked its way across Georgia's beautiful face.

"Seeing her *daughter* in bed with her husband would have been a totally different thing," Alice continued, placing the suitcase on the floor and folding the coat over it. "I'm thinking that would have shattered her. Broken her heart. Made her ask something like, 'Why would she do this to me?'"

Georgia giggled.

"Did you hate her, Georgia? For abandoning you? Did you hate her enough to kick her as she lay dying on the floor?"

Georgia looked at Alice, the smile still on her face.

"And now," Alice went on, walking closer to Georgia, closer to the gun, "I realize I chose to ignore the clues about your broken ankle—the time you were downstairs, but David hadn't carried you; Trish's complaint of how you'd left that supposedly permanent cast on the floor; the mention of someone who said she saw you dashing around a shopping mall in Houston."

Silence. Alice and Georgia locked eyes.

"Your ankle isn't broken."

Georgia raised the gun, but said nothing.

"You're penniless, too, aren't you? Charlotte Bauer mentioned she hadn't seen you in magazines in years. Were you as desperate for money as Ava, or were you going to give it all to her?"

Georgia stood motionless. "I hate Ava. She helped me figure out how to kill Mother. I don't owe her a thing."

"Dear, beautiful Georgia. You professed to love David and then convinced him to pretend to love your mother so you could accuse him of poisoning her."

Georgia laughed. "He was so easy."

"You promised him you'd run away with him and belong to him forever as soon as your mother was out of the way. He loved you. He wanted you all the time. He wasn't working in Houston. He wasn't *looking* for work in Houston. He was meeting you there. That's why David couldn't be allowed to leave Austin— he would go straight to you and ruin everything, wouldn't he?"

Georgia tucked a strand of hair behind her ear. She smiled.

"Did Caitlin also find you and David together? I'm thinking that's what happened. Poor thing was shot walking away from you. Was it David who moved her body to Marilyn's lawn so it would be found there when you asked Haydn for his help? Help in returning to David's car the gun that killed Caitlin. You knew poor Haydn well, it seems. You knew he would be too rattled to wipe the gun completely clean? "

Georgia shrugged. "I know his type."

"When David finally realized he would never have you, he threatened Ava, by telling her he was going to expose the whole scheme so he had to be killed, too. Was it an ultra-sweet cocktail you served him, promising him you would be his forever?"

"Yes, Alice. It was a champagne cocktail. The sweeter the better for dear old David." She pointed the gun at Alice's face just as the doorbell rang. The taxi had arrived.

As Georgia glanced over her shoulder, Alice reached out and pushed. Georgia dropped the gun and tumbled down the staircase, landing with a soft thud on the entryway floor.

The doorbell rang again. Alice would have to answer it before the driver left, but first she opened the flip phone again and stared at one of the photos Marta Rodriguez had sent. It was Georgia in a naked embrace with David, Marilyn's handsome husband.

Georgia's hair was a mess.

CHAPTER 26

A few months later, Alice stood in her kitchen, putting the finishing touches on two large bowls of green salad. She hoped they would be enough. It was the first time in at least a year she'd cooked for a crowd. Haydn, Lillo, Mark, Trish and her brother, Bill Wilcox, Haydn's maid Gwen, and Connie and Patsy were coming for dinner, and she wanted everything to be perfect.

She put both leaves in the dining room table, so it stretched over the wooden floors from the built-in credenza on one wall into the living room. When she crowded in enough chairs, almost every inch of floor space was taken. They'd be tight, but no one would mind.

What a joy to take out her best tablecloth and napkins, her favorite dishes and silverware, her water and wine glasses, and set the table for her friends.

Outside the open windows that lined the dining room wall, thick, lilac-colored wisteria clusters drooped from a vine on the fence. In front of them, bright fuchsia blossoms clung to the long, elegant limbs of a redbud tree. In a splash of sunshine in

Connie's yard next door, a few bluebonnets and primroses were stirring. Spring had come to Austin.

She picked Arthur up and carried him to the recliner. He pressed his heavy body against her, rubbing the top of his head under her chin as he waddled first left to right, then right to left across her lap. His chest vibrated with the low love song he murmured when he was thoroughly content.

She was a bit anxious about seeing Haydn for the first time since she turned down his proposal of marriage a few days earlier. She hoped they wouldn't feel uncomfortable with each other.

Their first meeting after Haydn was released from jail had been awkward. Although he was exonerated of all suspicion when a new attorney took his case, Haydn still bore the scars of the ordeal. He was shrunken. Not only physically—his thin body looked draped over his bones; the hollows in his cheeks carved dark holes in his face. His emotional expressiveness had changed, too. Haydn's happy, kooky personality had died. In realizing how Geoffrey had planned to hurt him, he lost his faith in life. Alice held hope that he would recover, but she feared the worst.

Dear Haydn. He had so wanted a family.

In contrast, Trish's life had taken a happy turn. She had met a man. He was small, a Mutt to her Jeff, but they suited each other to a tee. Alice expected their marriage before the end of the year.

Mark Upshaw was a new man. He had used the

inheritance his parents had left him to open a detective agency. His good reputation had already landed him several clients in need of his investigative skills. Alice served as his co-investigator and Jill-of-all-trades at a much better salary than Marilyn had paid her. Bill Wilcox—hammering hard on Javier Johnson's involvement in what a *Statesman* journalist called the Quinn Affair—would be joining Mark's team as soon as he relocated from Las Vegas to Austin. He would bring his sister, Candy, with him.

It was karma that made Georgia land at the bottom of the stairs as she did. The fake cast on her leg had caught between two of the balusters and snapped her ankle in two places. She would be in a real cast for some time to come, at least throughout her trial for murder.

A few weeks ago Alice had remembered the jet-black horse that someone had poisoned in its stall. That hadn't been Ava, Alice told herself. It was Georgia, a broken young girl furious because the horse had bitten her.

Ava's trial would start soon. From time to time Alice wondered how Ava was adjusting to her new lifestyle, doubtful that stilettos were an authorized accessory for prison jumpsuits.

"We're doing okay, huh, buddy?" she said to Arthur, ruffling the fur on his head.

She was now sure she could keep and maintain her home, so that burden was officially off her back.

Twyla, who had come home from Buenos Aires in a dark depression over her divorce, turned around in no time in the presence of her sister. The two were different enough that they never bored each other, but enough alike to share the same worldview.

They would become housemates in a few weeks. Alice had a home, a home that buzzed with activity and laughter and love.

And her health was good. She'd lost a few pounds in the last few months, and—thanks to Connie's insistence—a simple cortisone shot had dissolved all the pain in her knee.

Lillo would be leaving for Italy soon to prepare for his wedding to the lovely Sofia. Alice and Twyla were planning to attend, using Twyla's airline miles to cover the cost of the tickets. Connie and Patsy were in the process of adopting a child.

The oven timer chimed, telling her the lasagna was ready. Reluctant to push the cat off her lap, she scooped him up and took him with her to the kitchen.

Two large dishes of thick eggplant-and-ricotta lasagna, Lillo's recipe, bubbled and smelled divine. The dishes would rest on the top of the stove while everyone enjoyed a glass of wine before they sat down at her dining table to eat.

She dropped Arthur on the floor and took a bottle to the sink to open it, humming to herself. As the cork popped out of the bottle, she glanced out the window to the backyard.

There, following the monkey grass across the

garden, bobbed the happy, colorful heads of Connie's tulips that Alice had planted last winter. Forever ago. Alice laughed and rushed out to the garden to cut some for a centerpiece.

Arthur stayed behind with the lasagna.

THE END

ACKNOWLEDGMENTS

The completion of this, my first book, could not have been possible without the participation and assistance of so many individuals whose names may or may not be mentioned here. I would like to express my deep appreciation and indebtedness particularly to the following:

Ms. Pauline Priore, of Florence, Italy, who read and edited tirelessly and enthusiastically, and who helped me breathe life into Lillo, one of my favorite characters in the book.

Mr. Jim Young, an Austin attorney who guided me through the legal process.

A number of published authors in Ajijic, Mexico, including Judy King, Karen Blue, and Rachel McMillen, who shared their professional suggestions and personal support.

My baby boomer friends, whose issues with ageing mirrored my own and thus validated Alice's challenges in coming to terms with becoming an older woman.

My dear sister, Carolyn Purcell, and my lovely daughter, Suzy Shelor, not only for putting up with me as the book developed, but also for encouraging and supporting me until the very end.

My classy, talented publisher, Cynthia Stone, whose sharp eye and professional expertise turned more than 74,000 hard-written words into a beautiful book.

About the Author

As one of the first of the baby boomers, Susan Toalson is re-inventing what it means to age. She's in her 70's and still active, healthy, and curious about the world. Unlike women of her mother's generation, she expects to have another twenty good years ahead of her, and 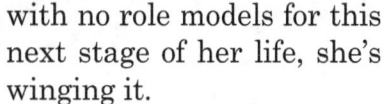 with no role models for this next stage of her life, she's winging it.

 Covid-19 has cramped her style a bit. Before the pandemic, she split her time between Florence, Italy, and Austin, Texas, where she shares a home with her sister, Carolyn, and their Labradoodle, J. Alfred Prufrock. During the lockdown, she's at home in Austin, working on her second novel. Her suitcase is packed and ready for the European borders to re-open.